Friday's Child

Clare Revell

Friday's Child

Contact Information: titleadmin@pelicanbookgroup.com

All scripture quotations, unless otherwise indicated, are taken from the Holy Bible, New International Version(R), NIV(R), Copyright 1973, 1978, 1984 by Biblica, Inc.™ Used by permission of Zondervan. All rights reserved worldwide. www.zondervan.com

Cover Art by Nicola Martinez

White Rose Publishing, a division of Pelican Ventures, LLC
www.pelicanbookgroup.com PO Box 1738 *Aztec, NM * 87410

White Rose Publishing Circle and Rosebud logo is a trademark of Pelican Ventures, LLC

Publishing History
First White Rose Edition, 2013
Paperback Edition ISBN 978-1-61116-279-0
Electronic Edition ISBN 978-1-61116-278-3
Published in the United States of America

Dedication

For Rhys.

With grateful thanks to Fiona.

Other titles by Clare Revell

Glossary

Pi - Patrick's nickname, pronounced Pie. Hence his other nickname of Agent 3.14 after the math term

Li - pronounced Lie - Liam's nickname

Ni - pronounced Nigh - Niamh's nickname

Niamh - pronounced Neeve

Spook - an MI5 agent

Siobhan - pronounced Cher-vaughn

Resus - This is the large critical care room in the ED in which all patients with life-threatening injuries are taken. It gives the doctors and nurses more room to stabilize and treat patients before transferring them to surgery or ICU.

ED - Emergency Department. Also known as A&E or casualty or the ER

CO19/ARU - the armed response unit. The only armed police officers in the UK

CPS - Crown Prosecution Service. The British equivalent of the DA.

Monday's Child must hide for protection,
Tuesday's Child tenders direction
Wednesday's Child grieves for his soul
Thursday's Child chases the whole
Friday's Child is a man obsessed
Saturday's Child might be possessed
And Sunday's Child on life's seas is tossed
Awaiting the Lifeboat that rescues the lost

1

Friday's child is a man obsessed…

If I speak in the tongues of men or of angels, but do not have love, I am only a resounding gong or a clanging cymbal. If I have the gift of prophecy and can fathom all mysteries and all knowledge, and if I have a faith that can move mountains, but do not have love, I am nothing. If I give all I possess to the poor and give over my body to hardship that I may boast, but do not have love, I gain nothing. ~ 1 Corinthians 13:1-3

"You really agreed to a drop here?" His partner asked.

Agent Patrick Page, MI5, nodded and looked up at the library, certain he was insane. Either that or he was going soft in his old age, letting informants insist on a dead drop location somewhere as public and quiet as this. Recently extended, the library was an interesting mixture of two modern A-frame wings of brown timber and huge panes of glass, with the original Tudor style wattle and daub central part sandwiched between. Colored posters lined the windows and an enticing display of books peeked between them.

It's not insanity, it's middle age, the small voice within him insisted.

Thirty-seven is not old, no matter what you *want to*

think.

Great, now he was arguing with himself.

Niamh, his sister, had summed it up last night over dinner. "You just work too hard. All work and no play have made Patrick a dull man. A man obsessed, with no time for anything, fun or otherwise." He'd tried brushing the comment off, but she hadn't let it drop. "You need to get out more, Pi. Do something other than work for once. Don't do what I did, because it ruins your life."

"Earth to Patrick?"

Patrick still stared at the library, through the pouring rain. He didn't have time for fun. Not with his heavy case load. And not with this twisted case he was currently embroiled in. The tip off had come from Scotland, from an American of all people. He still couldn't get his head around why an American cop would be working for the Scottish police, although he hadn't had time to exchange pleasantries with the Lieutenant.

Detective Inspector he corrected, as the guy had recently been promoted to an equivalent UK rank. Which was even more of a puzzle. One that could wait for a better time. Right now, he had work to do.

"Patrick, are you all right?" Shay Williams, his partner of five years, sounded concerned this time.

He shifted his gaze to her. "Yeah, I'm fine."

"Then how about answering me rather than staring into space. You're letting this case get to you, aren't you?"

"No more so than usual."

Why had his contact, known only by his street name of Skinhead, given the library as the location for the drop? More to the point, why had he agreed?

Accessibility? Hardly, given the library's odd opening hours. An urge to read? Again, not likely either for him or his contact. No, for Patrick, it was his desire to catch this guy and make the charges stick this time. And while odd, he could go in and out of a library frequently without arousing suspicion.

He checked his watch. It was time he actually did what he was paid for, rather than just sit here. Rain pounded against the car windshield. Even the wiper blades on super-fast made little impact on the downpour. Patrick pulled his collar up against the power of the elements and jumped out of the car. He opened the back door and leaned in to grab the pile of books.

Raising an eyebrow at his blonde partner in the driver's seat, he shot her a mock look of imposition across the top of the seats. "I should make you take these back yourself, Agent 7x3," he said, using her nickname. She hated it, but after insisting she was only twenty-one no matter how many birthdays she had, what did she expect? "After all, they're your library books."

Shay laughed at him. "But, it's raining, Agent 3.14, and I know you're too much of a gentleman to make a lady get out in the rain. Besides, it's your drop, right? Your contact, your drop, so by default, your turn to get wet."

Patrick scowled half-heartedly at her, teasing her back. "Pfft, woman. And there I was thinking we were partners. How wrong can I be? You can buy lunch for this."

Shay rolled her eyes. "You stop for lunch? That will be a first. And it'd explain the rain."

Not bothering to reply, he shut the door and

hurried inside the building.

Working for British Intelligence, Patrick's fast-paced life left him very little time for the niceties, like stopping for lunch, visiting the library, going out with family, getting to church or dating. He couldn't remember the last time he saw a woman socially that didn't involve undercover work either with Shay or an informant. Or the last time he made an entire church service without his pager going off.

He headed to the 'in desk' and stood in the queue. Glancing around, Patrick took in the huge windows, and walls lined with shelves of books. He hadn't been in a library in years, but the smell never changed.

The queue moved forwards and he placed the books on the counter, giving the librarian his best smile. "Hi. I'm returning these for a friend."

The librarian scanned them and nodded. "All done. Thank you."

"You're welcome." He paused, looking over the leaflets of things to do in the local area. He picked one up, taking his time over reading it, ignoring the queue behind him. Then he walked past the nondescript envelope on the edge of the desk and pocketed it in one swift action along with the leaflet, then stopped.

"Could you point me in the direction of the religious section, please?" While here, he might as well see if they had that book Liam recommended. Shay wouldn't begrudge him a few minutes. After all, he'd done her a favor.

She nodded. "Around that way, then to the right."

He smiled. "Thank you." He headed off in the direction she pointed. Liam had raved about this book for the past month. Either he found a copy here or he borrowed Liam's one. *H....h...there...* He ran his fingers along the books until he found the one he wanted. He pulled it off the shelf and turned around.

"Oh, I'm sorry." He looked at the woman he'd walked into and stopped short. *Elle?*

If it wasn't her, it was someone who looked just like her and was just as beautiful as she had been when he last saw her—even though the tweed suit she wore gave her a dowdy appearance with its long skirt and boxy style. With her brown hair pulled back into a severe bun and glasses perched on her nose, she was the epitome of a stereotypical librarian.

Warmth flooded him and a hard bolt traveled through his stomach leaving it in knots. He forced his voice to work past the huge lump in his throat, and held out a hand to her. "Elle? Eleanor Harrison?"

Her brown eyes widened with shock and recognition. "Patrick." Her fingers whitened against the pile of books in her hand, and she made no attempt to take his hand in return. "What are you doing here?"

"I'm borrowing a book." He dropped his hand and smiled, ignoring the shaft of disappointment. "What did you expect in a library?"

"No, I mean, here in Headley Cross."

"I live and work here. Always have." His phone beeped. "Excuse me. I should get this." He pulled the handset out of his pocket and checked the screen. *Bother. Just when I could do with a few minutes.* "I have to go. Can we meet up for coffee or something? Catch up on the past few years?"

Elle shook her head, backing away. "It's best to just leave the past alone. Bye." She hurried off.

Patrick stood still, the book loose in his hand. He and Elle had been at university at the same time. Two years above her, he'd been post grad and assigned as her mentor, but they had been inseparable none the less.

Until she'd vanished into thin air partway through the spring semester. He hadn't seen or heard from her since. Perhaps he had hurt her after all, though she had seemed pretty happy about their relationship, from what he remembered.

Shaking his head, he went to the desk and checked out the book. He glanced casually over his shoulder, always on alert, and saw her watching him.

Maybe he should go back over and speak to her. The more he thought about it, the more he was convinced he should. He might never have this chance again. He took a step towards her. A hand on his arm stopped him mid stride. He glanced around to see Shay. "What is it?"

"Sorry to bother you, sweetheart." She leaned into him, her hand squeezing him in an intimate gesture. Her voice was husky and low in his ear, as she played her part to perfection as always. "We've got to go. Suspect is on the move and we need to tail him. Did you get the intel?"

He nodded, pushing all thoughts of Elle from his mind. "I'll drive."

****

Eleanor watched as Patrick and the woman left. He'd filled out a little in the past few years, his shoulders were broader, his dark hair flecked with grey over his temples. She couldn't help but notice the snug fit of his shirt, how the cotton caressed his chest, and the way his long dark overcoat swirled around him. A shock of heat had flooded her traitorous body at their unexpected meeting.

He was the only person to have called her Elle. His Irish brogue was as strong as it had ever been and still thrilled her.

She clutched the books tighter in shaking arms, her breath fluttering and heart pounding.

This wouldn't do. She walked past the window, and glanced through the rain, in time to see Patrick climb into a smart black car. He smiled and joked with the woman accompanying him and her heart sank. Just as well she was steering clear of men. Apparently, the only one she'd ever been interested in was taken.

"So, who's the hunk?" Tina's sudden voice made her jump. "He seemed quite taken with you."

"Just an old friend," Eleanor whispered.

Tina's brows furrowed in thought. "Are you all right? You look like you've seen a ghost."

Eleanor sucked in a deep breath. For all intents and purposes she had. Patrick Page was from the past, her dark past, and that was where he had to stay. What occurred between them should never have happened and she was still living with the choices, consequences, and responsibilities of her actions.

She looked up from the books in her arms. "I'm fine. He's just the last person I expected to see here."

"When you say old friend, do you mean friend or boyfriend?"

The sixty-four thousand dollar question. "Yes, I dated him—for a while. Then I left university and never saw him again." *And tried not to think about him. Not that it worked.* She managed a smile. "But that was almost fourteen years ago."

Tina tilted her head and looked long and hard at her. "Is he the reason you swore off dating?"

Eleanor's cheeks burned as Tina hit the nail on the head. "One of the reasons, yeah. Granted there have been very few men in my life since, and those I was interested in wouldn't look at me twice. Sometimes I think I should be living in a convent."

Tina laughed softly. "First you'd have to become Catholic."

But they wouldn't want me either. What I did was unforgivable. Nothing will give me atonement for my sins. No matter how much I wish something could. The Ten Commandments weren't made to be broken, and even though her mother told her many times, "Break one and you break them all," she'd probably broken half. But two things haunted her day and night, things so terrible she'd rather forget them, but knew she never could.

"I guess so. I'd best get on." Eleanor headed back down the aisle, and slotted the books on the shelf with a little more force than necessary. She hadn't been able to get Patrick out of her mind since she left university years ago. He had been in the forefront of her thoughts, controlling her every word, deed and action since.

Had he really been here in this town the whole time? Where either of them were from had never really come up in conversation, although she knew from his accent he was Irish and born in Belfast. But she and her parents had moved constantly over the years, before finally arriving here in Headley Cross a few months ago. She doubted they were here to stay. Since her father died, her mother's itchy feet had increased. It made finding part time work hard.

She ran her hand over the shelf of books. How uncomplicated life had been back then when she was with Patrick. Walks in the park, studying together, dinners at the student union, soft drinks in the bar, weekends spent camping in the middle of nowhere simply because they could, house parties—

House parties. The first step on a slippery slope that had changed everything and send her life hurtling in a direction she'd never have chosen in a million years, but one that, despite everything, she wouldn't change parts of for anything.

Eleanor sighed and pushed her hands though her hair. *If only I could turn back time, and change what happened, but I can't. What I need is a way to change the present. Put right the wrong I have done, the wrong we've all done. I can't do that either. There is no way out of this mess. Fallen beyond hope of redemption into a hole and I'm digging myself deeper every moment. My life is just one lie after another and I hate it. I wish...I wish I could find salvation, but even that is prohibited.*

God had turned His back on her, and she deserved it.

2

Patrick waited at the door to the nightclub and looked at the text on the phone in his hand. Stood up at the last minute by his brother, Liam, who'd decided to stay in and watch football instead, he now had two choices. He could either call Shay, or sit in the club alone like the lonely bachelor he was and hope his cover wasn't blown.

Not that Liam knew he was going to be the cover story for being here tonight. If he had, he'd never have agreed to come in the first place. His brother had made it perfectly clear he was a teacher, not a spook and had no intentions of pretending to be one again. No matter what the reason.

What was this singer's name? Lisa something. Lisa Bellamy, that was it. According to Liam, who kept raving on about her, she was the best soul singer around.

He sighed. Normally when he frequented clubs and bars he was undercover and usually with Shay by his side. Tonight she had some social engagement, so he'd "planned" a guy's night out with his little brother, a rare occurrence since Liam had fallen in love with Jacqui, but as she'd given him his brother back, he'd forgiven her. Liam really wanted to hear this singer in person. And now he'd shied off at the last moment.

What should he do? Ring Shay and ask her to come, assuming she could just duck out of this other engagement? Or was he really that afraid of being alone and 'on the shelf' as Niamh put it, that he'd forgotten how to have fun by himself. He chuckled to himself at the thought. Time was he preferred to work alone and had fought tooth and nail about having Shay assigned to him. Now he preferred her being at his side, and not just on these assignments. Of course, there was a safety net there, too. Shay was a very happily married woman. And he was... alone.

Loud music poured from the open door, the thud of the bass vibrating in the still night air. A large purple and green neon sign proclaimed the name of the club, which was incidentally the same as its address: HC1. The letters reflected off the rain spattered windscreens of the cars and puddles on the ground.

Sliding the phone into his jacket pocket, he made a decision. He was here and wired and it would be a waste of resources otherwise. He moved over to the door and showed the bouncer his "driving license." Not that he looked under twenty-one, but rules were rules. He put it away, making sure it went in the opposite pocket to his actual ID. The last thing he wanted was to whip out the wrong one and break his cover.

Patrick winced as he entered the club. The noise level increased in volume threefold. He hadn't thought that possible. They weren't going to get anything over the background noise here. Guess it was old fashioned surveillance time. He crossed the heaving dance floor and reached the bar.

"What can I get you?" The bartender raised his voice above the level of the music.

"I'll have coke with ice and a slice, please." Even

off duty, he refused to drink. Not that being a Christian would prevent it. But he'd seen firsthand how alcohol had nearly destroyed his brother and had no intentions of going down that path. Patrick pulled money out of his pocket and exchanged it for the drink. "Thanks."

He turned his attention to the people gyrating on the dance floor. They were all so young, either that or he was showing his age. *Enough of the old. You already had this conversation with yourself once today.* He sipped his drink, the music reverberating within him. Glancing around, he spied a table to one side. Grabbing a handful of peanuts, he crossed over to it and sat down. Hopefully this Lisa would start singing soon, before the bass did serious damage to his ears.

He caught a glimpse of a woman making her way to the small stage. Her long white dress, split to mid-thigh, glowed in the blue lighting, her features and very feminine curves enhanced by it. Her brown hair hung almost to her waist. She looked older than the teens bopping to the latest dance hits on the floor. If he had to guess, he'd say around his age. *What is this fascination with age? Sooner I am out of here the better.*

The dance music stopped. As the woman sat on the stool near the center of the stage and picked up the guitar, Patrick's heart stopped. Lisa Bellamy was none other than Eleanor Harrison, his former girlfriend and the dowdy librarian from earlier. Was she really as good as Liam said she was?

In which case, why was she a librarian? Something didn't add up.

Wow, but she looks cute in that outfit. So much better than the librarian getup... Then he quickly caught himself. He was working and until proved otherwise, he had to assume that no one was above suspicion of

12

wrong doing.

This was the center of the operation.

It was this bar that the drugs were coming in and out of, as well as the money. On the surface, things looked fine. The place turned a tidy profit, and nothing had come to light during the routine police and health and safety checks. All the employee checks as far as he knew were fine.

But the intel he'd received from Scotland pointed to something far deeper. And if Elle worked here, she could be involved. Should he get someone else assigned? Ring Shay, ask her to come and take over? Catch Elle before he left, find out what she was doing here?

He slumped in his chair trying to make a decision, but as the lights came up he realized it was too late. He was caught in the edge of the spotlight and it would be blatantly obvious if he went anywhere. He nursed his drink, wishing fervently he could sneak out and leave, and glanced at her as she strummed the guitar and began singing.

Wow. The same word resonated in his mind as he sat up straight.

She was good. No, more than good, she was fantastic. For the next twenty minutes, Patrick sat entranced as Elle sang. Blood pounded in his ears in time to the music, his fingers tapped on his glass and his feet moved in perfect rhythm. He wanted to catch her attention as she glanced around the audience, but she didn't look his way. Did she know he was there and was avoiding eye contact?

The set finished and he applauded and whistled. His heart leapt as she finally looked straight at him.

He beckoned to her, and his pulse pounded in his

neck as Elle finally acknowledged him and came over. Before she could say anything, he stood and clasped her hand. Warmth shot down his arm, straight to his belly. No woman had affected him like that in years. Not since she left him. "That was incredible. Can I buy you a drink?"

"Just a water, please. I have another set to do in a bit."

"Be right back." Patrick pulled out a chair for her and helped her sit. He hurried to the bar, afraid she'd be gone by the time he got back. Silent prayers ascended heavenward. Even if it were only a few minutes, simply to talk with her again would be wonderful. Pleased she was still there, he slid back into his seat.

Cool fingers touched his as she took the glass. Her eyes sparkled in the lighting, but there was something else there that he didn't remember and recognized only too well. Sadness, something almost haunted. What had happened to cause the joy to go out of her? And how could she sing so well without it?

Patrick cradled his drink and sipped it, looking at Elle. Up close that dress was well—too revealing. *Lord, please, a little assistance here. I need to focus on my job right now, not on my past.*

"So what's a beautiful girl like you doing in a place like this, Elle?" He cringed as the cliché was out before he'd realized.

Elle took a long drink. "It's Eleanor, not Elle—"

"You'll always only be Elle to me," he said. "Although I should probably call you Lisa tonight if you're working."

She nodded slightly. "Lisa would be better here. And I'm not that beautiful, although you always did know how to flatter a woman." She managed a faint smile. "The lighting and the amount of make-up I'm wearing make me look years younger. What are you doing here?" The words tumbled from her and she glanced nervously over her shoulder. "Are you following me?"

"No, I'm just checking the place out. My brother's been raving about this soul singer I should hear. I never dreamed it would be you." He automatically followed her gaze. A tall, blue suited man stood just off stage, his eyes firmly fixed on the two of them. Patrick's senses went on full alert. "I thought you worked in the library. I assume you're not moonlighting?"

She shook her head. "No. I hold down two jobs. Neither seems to interfere with the other right now."

Patrick tilted his head a little. It wasn't his place to interrogate her, not here and not now, but he couldn't stop himself. "Two jobs?"

Elle nodded. "Times are hard and singing isn't what my mother calls a "proper job". She keeps on at me to quit, but with Dad gone, I need to bring in as much money as I can."

His hand closed over hers. "I'm sorry. When did he die?"

"He was shot in a hunting accident three years ago. He died instantly. So it's just me, Abbie and Mum now."

"Abbie?"

She stiffened, catching her breath. A light flickered in her eyes for a brief moment before it was extinguished. "What is it with all the questions? Are you some kind of cop?"

"Sorry. I ask a lot of questions at work so it's a

force of habit."

"Are you a cop?" she repeated. Again the nervous glance over her shoulder.

Mr. Blue Suit had moved closer. He looked familiar, but Patrick couldn't place him. He looked back at Elle. "It's not just cops that ask a lot of questions at work," he hedged. "Psychiatrists do. Private investigators do. The bouncer on the door did as well. Besides, it's been almost fourteen years since I've seen you. That's a lot of catching up to do."

"Yeah."

He smiled and winked, going back to his previous question. "So who's Abbie? Hamster, goldfish, tortoise, that dog you always said you wanted..." He hoped his teasing would put her at ease, but she stiffened even further.

"Abbie is my sister. She's thirteen and very precocious with it."

Patrick tilted his head, something clanging in the recesses of his mind. "That's a big age gap."

She jerked her head, something glistening in her eyes. "Yeah. You don't expect a baby sister when you reach twenty-two. Mum said they missed—" A hand dropped on her shoulder and she froze. Glancing up, she acknowledged Mr. Blue Suit who had managed to come up right behind her, without Patrick noticing.

That was more than a tad disconcerting. Had he got so focused on Elle that his training went right out of the window? Especially when he'd already identified him as a possible threat.

"Zeke, this is Patrick, an old friend. Patrick, this is Zeke."

Patrick offered the tall, thin chap a hand. "Pleased to meet you." The hand that took his was firm, the handshake brief, and the glint in his eyes warned him off as surely as the hand on Elle's shoulder did.

Dropping his hand, Zeke turned his attention to Elle. "Don't be long, Lisa. We need lots of orders for the CD tonight."

"OK."

Patrick narrowed his eyes as Zeke ran his eyes over Elle. He was glad when the man nodded and walked away. "He seems a little possessive. Is he your boyfriend?"

She shot him a scathing look, causing his cheeks to burn. "No, not that it's any concern of yours, but he's my manager. He doesn't like me resting."

"He pays you to work, not fraternize?"

Elle studied her glass, running a finger around the rim. "Something like that."

Patrick wanted to ask more, but her tone indicated it was a closed subject. There was a time to push things and a time to leave them, and right now was definitely the latter. His mind whirled, trying to assimilate all the information he'd gleaned. Not to mention work out where he'd seen Zeke before.

He nodded to her empty glass. "Want another one?"

She shook her head. "Thank you for the offer, but I won't. I didn't think clubs were your scene."

"I was coming with my brother Liam, who claims to be your biggest fan this side of the equator. However, he stood me up in favor of the game instead. His fiancée, Jacqui, likes football as much as he does. Either that or she's just humoring him. I wasn't going to play gooseberry despite it being a cup match."

"I prefer rugby."

"Really?"

Elle nodded. "Thirty fit men in tight shirts and shorts running up and down a field. At least, according to the girls I work with."

Patrick laughed. "Jacqui says the same thing."

"But going back to rugby, what I like is the fact the players don't fall down and act hurt like footballers do." She smiled properly for the first time since joining him. "They fall down, and they get right up again and carry on, bleeding all over the place. Footballers lie there and go, 'Ref, he tripped me up!'"

The laughter died down. Patrick studied his glass for a moment. He had to know why she left all those years ago. "What happened that weekend of the house party, Elle? Where did you go? When I woke, you were gone. No one saw you after that. You just vanished off the face of the planet."

Elle set the glass down on the table. "Stuff happened. I had to go home."

Patrick pressed his hands together, his stomach twisting. "Was it…?" He took a deep breath. "Was it something I did or said? Did I hurt you or push you away?"

She shook her head, shoving a hand through her hair. "No, no, it wasn't you." But her voice wobbled and experience told him she wasn't being entirely truthful. "I have to go." As Patrick reached over to grasp her hand, she pulled away, rising quickly. "Please don't. I have to go. Thanks for the drink."

Patrick's entire body chilled and numbed as she moved away from him. What had he done? One minute she was chatting and the next the portcullis came slamming down, the drawbridge went up and she was gone. Whether Elle was here or not, the guy he'd been watching for hadn't made an appearance. He listened to half of the second set, and then walked out to where he parked his car.

He wasn't at all happy with the fact she worked there. Was she involved? Or, if not, could he warn her and get her away before she did get caught up in it all? Why had she suddenly reappeared in his life now?

Lord, whatever is wrong with her, please, give me a chance to put it right.

****

Eleanor drove home, still unsettled. She had no idea how she made it through the second set. Patrick and his familiar presence had set her whole body on edge. How could he still cause a reaction like this after so long? What they had shared that year was magical. He made her feel wanted and loved.

But why had he left half way through the second half of her performance? He seemed to have enjoyed the first set. She'd perfected watching people unnoticed over the years. And he hadn't been able to keep his eyes off her.

It's not fair, Lord. Why bring him back into my life when I can't have him? Haven't I been punished enough?

She parked on the drive and let herself into the dark house. Blue light flickered from the open lounge door and she went in to find her mother sitting in front of the TV, waiting for her. Nothing changed, did it? "Hey, Mum. How's Abbie? Did she complain about her stomach today?"

"No."

"I really would like to take her to a doctor and have her checked out."

"And have you take time off work to do so? She's

fine. When you were her age, you always faked a stomach ache to get out of school, too. I'm wiser this time around."

Maybe Mum was right. Maybe it was nothing.

"I should check in on her, just to make sure."

"She's sleeping. How was your act tonight?" Mum stood and folded the blanket she was sitting under. Somehow, she still managed to make the word "act" sound dirty.

"The performance was OK. We got several pre-sale orders on the CDs—not enough to make Zeke happy, but then nothing's good enough for him these days. A man I was at university with, Patrick, was there."

Her mother's eyes darkened. "Patrick?"

"We were doing the same course. I haven't seen him in years."

"Is it *him*?" Mum's face hardened as she spat out the venom laced words.

"I'm not going to dignify that with a response as half the students on my course were men, Mum."

"Eleanor Jay, don't you talk to me like that. I always said Jay should have been Jezebel."

"I'm tired. I'm going to bed. Good night." She headed quickly up the stairs, biting her tongue. Why did her mother hate her so much? She peeked into Abbie's room.

Abbie lay curled up on the bed, her still figure illuminated by the shaft of light from the door. Her long fair hair spread out on the pillow behind her. Eleanor stood in the doorway, a lump in her throat. Years ago she'd tried all the options she could think of to get away, but they would never work out. She'd tried to take Abbie and move to the other side of the country, or even to Australia. But every single plan had failed. Now her mother was old, bitter, and ill-tempered.

One day it'll be different. I'll tell you the truth, and we'll leave here together. Just you and me.

Closing the door, Eleanor went back to her own room. She dropped to her knees and reached under the bed. Her fingertips grasped the edge of the shoe box and pulled it towards her. She sat on the bed and placed the lid beside her. A pile of photos gazed up at her. Rummaging through them, Eleanor found the one she wanted.

Patrick's broad grin and blue eyes sparkled up at the camera. His arms wrapped securely around a much younger her. A weeping willow hung over their heads, the lake behind them with a family of swans gliding across its calm surface. Her fingers ran over it.

I wish I could change the past and tell you the truth as to why I left, but I can't. And now I'm in too deep. I'm sorry.

3

Patrick sat in the office, the blinking cursor on the computer screen in front of him slowly driving him to insanity. He had typed up the report of the nightclub visit on Friday—not that it took long. Nothing had happened. The bloke had been a no show. The recording was useless. Mind you, that turned out to be a blessing in disguise as all it would have consisted of was him chatting up a nightclub singer.

And that would have gone down as well as a dose of the proverbial salts. He drummed his fingers on the desk. Nothing had gone right so far today. And that on top of the dead ends he kept running into, only served to darken his already foul mood.

Having spent the entire morning on a wild goose chase, Shay had gone to pick up lunch from the deli on the corner, leaving him sitting here. He pulled up Shay's half-written notes from the morning's escapade.

Received tip off from Tiny re FT seen at mall. Ten minutes later received call re shots fired and CO19 responding. Arrived to assist or apprehend FT. Mall open as normal. No FT. No CO19.

The phone in his pocket chirped. He pulled it free. "So help me, Shay, if this is you wanting to know if I want chips again—" He didn't recognize the number and immediately hit a button on his phone to secure the line. "Page."

"I need to see you."

"The lion and the unicorn were fighting for the crown." He waited. The response would tell him who it was.

"There I met an old man who wouldn't say his prayers."

Skinhead? He knew not to ring direct, and it wasn't contact day. He thought quickly. "Ten minutes. Mitre Square."

Patrick hung up and stood, pulling his coat on as he left the desk. Half way across the office, he met Shay coming the other way.

She held up the twin cardboard drinks carrier and paper bag. "I got you a cappuccino and chicken mayo on brown bread."

"No time."

She frowned. "Now what? You promised me you'd eat something."

"Meeting a snout in ten. If you're that bothered about the food, you eat it, and I'll go alone." He accelerated down the hall.

Running footsteps followed him. "Patrick, wait. I'll eat on the way. What's the rush?"

"Skinhead wants a face to face." He kept walking. "It has to be important for him to skip protocol."

"Maybe he just wants to see your happy smiling features," Shay commented. "In which case he's going to be disappointed. You have your grumpy head on."

"Oh, give it a rest, Shay."

"You need a caffeine fix."

"What I need is for things to stop hitting the fan and people to follow simple instructions." He unlocked the car.

She set the bag and coffees on the roof while she opened the door. "Chill."

Patrick scowled and got in the car, slamming the door. He started the engine as she got in beside him. "Don't have time to chill," he growled.

"Hey..." Shay grabbed the dash as he pulled quickly out of the space. "Watch it. I have hot coffee on my lap. You'll spill it."

"Chill," he tossed back at her. "Your skirt is coffee colored anyway. It won't show."

"It's dry clean only."

Patrick ignored her, instead focusing on the road ahead. He could come up with a dozen different reasons for this meet and none of them good. Hopefully Elle wouldn't be working today, as it was a Saturday. As much as he wanted to see her, he didn't want to have to explain he wasn't stalking her.

He parked and pulled the library book from the glove box. He hadn't read it, but he could borrow Liam's copy. "Watch the front."

There wasn't a queue inside, and he quickly made his way to the history section, the heels of his shoes tapping in the quiet building. They really should carpet libraries. It would do wonders for the noise level.

He studied the guide on the history shelving unit, and then slowly meandered down the aisle, hoping the book hadn't been checked out. A tall, skinny man in his twenties stood further down the aisle. His jeans had seen better days. Close cropped hair, leather jacket, chewing gum and plaid bovver boots completed the ensemble.

Patrick paused by the books on Jack the Ripper. Mitre Square was the place where Catherine Eddowes met her death on thirtieth September 1888. He pulled out the relevant book and started to flick through it.

The man moved closer, running his finger along the books until he pulled out the one on Catherine Eddowes. He glanced sideways at Patrick. "Post grad."

"Research for a script," Patrick responded. The name Skinhead fitted. He kept his gaze on the book. "Have you read this one?"

"Yes, there's a lot on Mitre Square in chapter seven."

Patrick nodded. "You were told no contact."

"This can't wait. There's something happening tonight at the club. Something big."

"What time tonight?"

"Late. You need to be there. Just keep my name out of it." He replaced the book and left.

Patrick stood still, continuing to flick through the book until he reached chapter seven. He slid the folded piece of paper into his sleeve. His mind whirled. Something big. But that could be anything. Another shipment in or out. Was it really connected to the Scottish case? He'd found no evidence to support that, despite DI Nemec's insistence.

Either way, it was going to be a long night.

****

Eleanor squeezed through the gap in the tables and made her way over to the bar. She looked at Zeke. "It's busy tonight."

"Yes. Don't leave after your set. There's someone important coming to meet you. He should be here in the next half hour."

"Who?" Immediately all her nerves went on edge. The last time Zeke had introduced her to 'someone important' it hadn't gone so well.

"The owner of the club."

"I thought Jake—"

Zeke shook his head. "This is the Big Boss. Owns every club you've sung in up and down the country. How do you think I find you work so easily? He's followed your career with interest and wants to help you."

She looked at him.

He leaned in and whispered. "You be nice to him, you hear me?"

Elle nodded, a knot of fear building in her stomach. She began her set, keeping an eye on the crowd. She spotted Patrick at the bar. Her heart began its familiar rhythm at the mere sight of him, but she ignored it. It was safer for both of them, if he stayed in her past.

Midway through *Ballad of Misty River*, a cold shudder ran through her. She was being watched. She knew there were dozens doing that in the audience, but this was different. She glanced to her left.

A tall man, dark curly hair, intense blue eyes leaned against the door marked private, his arms folded against his chest. White shirt glowed neon in the light, dark jacket undone, tie perfectly straight. A long jagged scar zigzagged down his cheek. Did she know him? His gaze indicated familiarity, but...

She finished the set and Zeke beckoned. She made her way over to the two men. Hopefully this wouldn't take long. She was tired, and just wanted to go home and sleep.

Zeke, unusually for him, was on edge, his fingers trembling as they gripped her arm. "Eleanor, this is PJ. PJ, meet Eleanor Harrison or Lisa Bellamy."

PJ's hand was cold and the handshake too long.

His frosty gaze ran over her. "Well, well. You really have grown into a beautiful woman, Eleanor."

"I'm sorry. Do I know you?" She tried to pull her hand away, but he didn't let go.

"You were very young, but I remember you. Come through to the office and we can talk about your new album, your career and how I can help you more than I have been already."

What? Alarm bells rang in the far recesses of her mind. "I'd rather talk here."

"I said in the office." Ice glinted in his eyes. "Jake said you'd object and said to remind you just who pays your wages."

"The office it is." She glanced at the clock. "I have thirty minutes before I need to be home."

"A little old for a curfew, aren't you?"

"It's something that can't wait."

"Thirty minutes is more than enough time." He held out a hand, a tattoo of some kind peeking out from his shirt sleeve.

She walked with him, feeling Patrick's eyes on her as they headed through the door into the back of the club.

****

Patrick glanced down at the image on his phone. Similar but not the same, the hair color was different for a start. He shook his head as the phone rang. He left now and he might miss this chap leaving or something might happen to Elle. On the other hand, it was DI Nemec so he couldn't just ignore it. As much as he hated people who reacted like this when he rang them, he only had one choice. He took the call. "Page. I can't talk right now. I'll call back later if that's OK."

He kept an eye on the doorway and waved over the bartender. "Another lime twist with ice, please." He slid a tenner over the counter. "And one for yourself. So who's the good looking dude that just went out back with Lisa?"

The bartender looked at him. "Someone from high up, out of town. He's just come down to check up on a few things. He'll be here for a while, then off again. Has a finger in many pies, if you get my drift. But he can't keep away from this place. He seems to be the center of things."

Patrick added a twenty to the ten already on the counter. "How so?"

The barman pocketed the money. "Looks can be deceiving. Helps he knows when the police are coming so the joint is clean if you get my drift."

That turn of phrase was getting annoying. He slid another ten over. "I thought those things were meant to be unannounced."

"The boss has contacts."

"How often is he here?"

"The boss is always here. Jake never leaves."

"No, this guy."

"Depends how often Lisa sings, but he's here a lot. At least once a week. He's a law unto himself. Has more money than I'd make in a lifetime." He leaned over as he pushed the drink across, picking up the money. "Rumor has it, he's more than slightly interested in Lisa. I reckon that's the last we've seen of her tonight."

"Does this boss have a name?"

"Mr. F is all I know."

Patrick took the drink. "Thank you."

He sat nursing his drink until the club closed, but Elle didn't come back out. Nor did Mr. F. He yawned. It was too late now to call DI Nemec, but he'd do so first thing in the morning. Time to go home and hit the hay, before the sun came up. He might just make it—once he'd written up his report.

****

"Come on, Eleanor, we'll be late. Especially if you're driving." Her mother's voice echoed up the stairs.

Eleanor finished brushing her hair and rose, pulling it into a tight ponytail. "I'm coming." She grabbed her bag and keys and left the sanctity of her bedroom. Going to church had to be one of her least favorite activities. This was funny considering how much she used to love going. At one point, the weekend couldn't come quick enough. Even at university. She and Patrick would go twice every week.

She shook her head. There was nothing in church for her now, despite her automatic prayers. Her mother insisted she attend for two reasons. Firstly, 'if you live under my roof you abide by my rules'. Secondly, to ram home what she was no longer entitled to. Forgiveness. Salvation. Love.

Abbie smiled at her as she reached the hallway. "Mum says I can sit in the front with you today."

Eleanor took in Abbie's newly cut hair in dismay. It looked so much better longer. Why couldn't her mother just leave things alone for once? "So long as you do up your seatbelt."

"Of course." She skipped outside and stood by the

car.

Eleanor looked at her mother, taking in the scowl at her black trousers and close fitting shirt. "I don't have time to change. Unless you want to be late."

The scowl deepened and her mother sighed before heading to the car. Eleanor closed her eyes for a moment, then followed them, locking the door. If only she hadn't fallen from grace, but then she'd be without Abbie.

****

Patrick slid into his normal pew just as the service started. He hadn't expected to get here at all, as he hadn't even left the office until four in the morning. He'd gone straight there from the club to write up his notes. He'd say he was conscientious, rather than anything else. His family on the other hand, would tell him to go get a life.

DI Nemec's phone had gone straight to voicemail. So deciding the bloke must be in church, Patrick decided to do the same thing.

His soon to be sister-in-law, Jacqui, shot him a sly grin and moved slightly before he sat on her coat.

"You're late," she whispered.

"You're lucky I'm here at all." He grinned as he whispered a reply, kissing her cheek. He reached over her to shake his brother's firm hand. "Hey, Liam."

Liam smiled and grabbed his hymn book as the first song was announced. Patrick followed suit, then decided to follow on the overhead screen instead. He stood as the music started, and slid his hands into his pockets. He started singing, then his eyes spun right, his soul captivated by a very familiar voice.

Elle stood in the pew in front, three people along. Having not seen her in fourteen years, he was suddenly finding her all over the place. *Why haven't I noticed her here before?*

Because I'm never here. He answered his own question and kept singing, forcing his eyes back to the screen, half wishing now he'd picked up the hymn book so he didn't have her in his field of vision.

As the children left, he caught her eye and shot her a smile. A stab of disappointment filled him as a weak smile met him in return. He looked away and reached for his Bible to follow the reading. *There's your answer, Patrick. She wants nothing to do with you. So ignore her and concentrate on the Lord. That is why you're here.*

His mind refused to co-operate. It rehashed that last weekend over and over. Patrick took a deep breath. *Fine,* he told himself firmly. *Then pray for her. That way you're not leaving God out of this. And Satan is not winning this battle. He's putting thoughts of Elle in my head to distract me from the service and my reason for being here, so I'll turn them back to the Lord in prayer.*

After the service finished, he sat for a moment. What did he do? Leave or say hello? Deciding it'd be rude just to ignore her, he slid into the pew next to them. "Hello again," he said, holding out a hand.

Elle looked at him and took his hand. Her skin was cold against his and she shook his hand lightly. Her smile was forced and she looked uncomfortable. "Hello. How are you?"

Patrick smiled, hoping the warmth of his greeting would help ease her. "I'm good. How are you?"

"Fine." Elle shifted slightly at the ragged cough from the severe, grey-haired lady. "This is my mother, Jeanette Harrison. This is Patrick Page. We were at

31

university together for a while."

Patrick extended his hand. "Pleased to meet you, Mrs. Harrison." He took in the hostile stare and the limp grip which was dropped as soon as possible.

"Were you in the same year?" Mrs. Harrison's voice was just as cold.

"No, I was two years ahead, doing my post graduate course. I was Elle's mentor."

"Ellie, look what I got. Charlotte gave it to me for my birthday."

Patrick turned to see a girl, possibly in her early teens run over, holding out a book. A beaming smile lit her face, making her blue eyes sparkle. This must be the little sister.

Elle took the book. "Wow, very nice. How'd you swing that one, squirt? It's not your birthday for a while yet."

The child grinned, tossing her short blonde curls from her face. "Did I say birthday? I meant my unbirthday."

Elle laughed. "You are terrible. Patrick, this is my sister, Abbie. Abbie, this is Patrick."

"Hello. I've seen you here before." Abbie, unlike the other two women in her family, gave him a wide grin.

Patrick smiled. "I'm here most weeks when I don't have to work."

"Ellie works a lot too. Mum, Charlotte's asked me to her house for dinner. Can I go?"

Mrs. Harrison nodded. "As long as it's all right with her parents."

"Cool. Bye, love you." Abbie ran off, beaming.

Elle watched her go and shot her mother a look that Patrick couldn't make sense of. Before he could say anything more, Jeanette stood.

"Eleanor, we should go." She nodded to Patrick. "Goodbye, Mr. Page."

Elle nodded and stood. "Bye."

"Goodbye." Patrick stood to let them pass. He sat down again, suddenly bereft. He didn't understand what just happened. The conversation had been as icy as it was brief. He glanced up as a hand fell on his shoulder. "Hey, bro."

Liam was staring him down. "Mum says to come for lunch. Don't think it's an option."

"Lunch sounds good, Li." He got to his feet.

"Who was that woman? She looks familiar."

"She works in the library." He wasn't about to give away her other identity.

Liam held his gaze. "Are you sure you're OK? You seem really distracted. You have been ever since you got here."

"I'm fine."

"Liar. And in church, too. Sit down and talk to me. We've got a couple of minutes."

Patrick took a deep breath, sitting heavily. "Her name's Elle. She's someone from my past. From way back in my uni days, that's all."

Liam sat next to him. "Sounds intriguing. Old girlfriend?"

"Way more than that, Li." Patrick spoke quietly, aware of the fact he and Liam were in church. Back then, he'd been a different person and acted in ways he wouldn't dream of today. His faith was nowhere near as strong then as it was now. "Elle and I, we, uh, we were close." Irritation rose at Liam's scrutiny, and he cringed, annoyed for letting his emotions control him.

"How close?"

"Let's just say I *knew* her. But then she vanished, and I haven't seen her since." He glanced up into his brother's stunned face. "Shocked you, haven't I?"

Liam struggled to find the words. Being an English teacher he always had a plethora of them at his disposal, most of which Patrick had had thrown back at him over the years. "I just never imagined you of all people—"

"Yeah, well. No one's perfect. And I'm sure you've done stuff you're not proud of, too." Patrick cleared his throat. "It's in the past."

"Uh huh. Your reaction says otherwise."

"Trust me, it's over. She's as cold as ice toward me now."

"And how do you feel?" His firm gaze gave Patrick nowhere to hide.

"That's irrelevant." Yet his mind drifted back to the cramped student library and the table crammed with textbooks.

Patrick finished explaining the passage that'd had Elle stumped for weeks. He grinned as the figurative light bulb suddenly flashed on over her head and the joy of understanding shone in her eyes. "You got it?"

Elle grinned back. "Yes, finally. Thank you so, so much."

His grin widened. "You're very welcome. I think we should celebrate. How about going to see a movie?"

She almost froze in her seat. "As in the cinema?"

"Yes. They're showing the new Hiram Davies film at the campus playhouse."

"Who's Hiram Davies?"

Surprise filled him. "You've never heard of Hiram Davies?" As she shook her head, he winked. "Wow. He's the current heartthrob of every female on campus."

"Except me."

He nodded. "Except you. Anyway, he's starring in the new historical film, An Arrow Through Time."

"Ohhh," she breathed, her eyes lighting. "I read that last year when it came out. It's good. Written by Tels Merrick. I always thought it would make a good film."

"Then come and see it with me." He tilted his head. "Or are you scared of dates?"

"Not at all. I'm not scared of apples or grapes either." She grinned at him. "I've never been to the cinema. Never been on a date, either."

"Seriously?" His amazement grew and his brows shot up into his hair before he could stop them. "You're kidding, right? You're in your third year at university and you've never been to see a film or gone on a date?"

"Nope."

"Are you a nun in disguise or something, Elle?"

A shy smile crossed her face. "No, I'm not Catholic. It's just complicated. So, sure, why not? If you still want to take me, that is?"

Patrick's heart leapt. "Brilliant. Of course I do. Two firsts in one night. Let's drop the books off at my place on the way over."

"Your place?"

"It's on the way. Or we leave them in my car and then I'll drive you home afterwards." He noticed the hesitation and a glimpse of what could be fear or trepidation in her eyes and carried on rapidly. "Look, I'm not going to jump you, all right? It's dark and it'll be even darker when we come out and it's not safe for a girl to be out there alone and I don't want anything to happen to you because if it did then I'd feel responsible and—"

Her fingers folded over his mouth, cutting him off. Brown eyes sparkled at him. "Breathe, before you pass out on

35

me. *That has to be the longest sentence I've ever heard. Yes, a lift home afterwards would be good. Thank you."*

He lifted her fingers away and kissed them, noticing the tips of her ears going pink. "Good. Want to know a secret?"

"Go on."

"This will be my first date, too. First date with you."

Her smile lit her face as she grabbed her books. "A night full of firsts then. First date, first movie...and first lift in that pile of junk you drive."

He rolled his eyes. "Just because my car's old..." He laughed. "It goes, what more do you want?"

4

Leaving Shay in the car, Patrick charged into the library, book in hand, and over to the desk in order to retrieve the new envelope placed there that morning. He smiled at the head librarian and handed her the book he'd borrowed as she slipped him the intel. "Hi. Is Elle, uh, Eleanor working today?"

"She's over in the children's section, doing story time."

"OK, thanks." He headed across the quiet building and leaned against the wall, watching her read the story of the three bears to a group of primary school children. When she finished, he waved to get her attention. As she came over, he whispered, "I need to talk to you."

She wrung her hands then wiped them on her skirt, bouncing slightly from one foot to the other. "I really can't do this. I can't see you. I'm sorry."

"I can see you're busy. All I want is coffee and a chance to talk, please, Elle."

Whether it was his pleading whisper or his insistence, he wasn't sure, but she nodded. "All right. I have my lunch break in an hour. I could meet you then."

He smiled. "Sure. How about we go to the Three-Sixteen café on the High Street?"

She hesitated. "No, maybe the precinct coffee shop would be better. It's just around the corner."

"OK. I'll see you then."

Patrick returned to the car. He handed the envelope over and looked at Shay. "She agreed to coffee at least."

"Good. Now can we possibly get some work done here?" Shay's tone was curt.

"Work?" he teased, trying to lighten the moment.

"You know, the stuff that pays the mortgage, keeps the country safe, and stops Nahum tearing strips off us at the end of every day."

"Ah, yes, work. Sure. I have an hour. Then I'm taking a lunch break." He raised an eyebrow at the comical expression that crossed her face. "Yes, me, taking a break. It happens."

"Pfft. We've been partners for five years now, Patrick. You never take a break, unless Nahum forces you to. You work twenty-four seven. I have never met a man more dedicated to the job than you are."

"Someone has to keep the streets safe."

Shay winked at him. "Not the way you do it. The rest of us, one way or another, manage to fit a personal life in somewhere along the lines."

He shrugged. "Let's just go check out this lead and then reconvene after lunch, as I also need to return a phone call. Again."

"Oh?"

"DI Nemec. The bloke is either never in the office or his mobile is switched off."

"See. He has a life."

"Point taken. You drive and I'll call him." He dialed the number, praying this time the call would go through.

"Nemec." The American voice still jolted him, even though this time he was expecting it.

He almost sighed with relief. "DI Nemec, this is Agent Patrick Page. Nice to finally talk to you rather than your voice mail."

"And you. Did you get the photo I sent?"

"I did. And I checked out the club on Saturday night."

"And? Is it him?"

"He looks similar, but this chap has a long scar on his left cheek and dark hair."

"Did he have a tattoo?"

"The lighting in the club is dark, but I didn't see one. Where would it be?"

"Left wrist. It's a dragon—very detailed one."

"The guy had long sleeves. The barman told me his name is Mr. F. He is in and out fairly regularly and seems to be the "center of things" and from "up high" to quote his exact words. He also apparently has a thing for the current singer, Lisa Bellamy. As far as the barman knows, his main interest in the club is the singer. Although he did say they get advanced warning of police raids."

"Interesting. That would imply someone on the inside again."

"Again?"

"Fits his M.O. That's what he did before. What did you say the singer's name was?"

"Lisa Bellamy."

"My wife likes her music."

"So does my brother. But going back to this Mr. F, no, I didn't see a tattoo."

"Maybe try talking to this Ms. Bellamy. See what she knows."

Patrick shifted uncomfortably in his seat. "She wouldn't be involved in this."

"Don't bank on it." Nemec's voice turned harsh. "This guy has a record. He sucks people in. He appears charming, but he's a psycho. Manipulating is what he does best."

"If this Mr. F is who you think he is."

"Can you send me a picture of him?"

"I'll do my best." He suddenly broke off and pointed. "There, red car. The plates match the APB the police put out this morning. Sorry, I'm going to have to go. I'll fax what I have later." He shut off the phone and hung on as Shay did a handbrake turn. "Going to have to arrest you for that, lady," he told her.

"Fine, once we catch him."

He barely concentrated on anything for the next twenty minutes. Not even the thrill of the chase and finally making the arrest. That at least took one bad guy off the streets and tied up a case the police had been working on for ages. That should please them at any rate. They handed him over to Manor Road Station and then headed back on the road.

His lack of concentration worried him. Despite her teasing tone, Shay was right. He didn't have time for anyone or anything, except his family and even that was limited. The one thing he did make time for was his relationship with God. Even if church consisted of downloading the sermon and listening to it as he fell asleep.

Aside from his job, his faith was the most important thing in his life, and that was the way it should be.

But now, instead of his latest assignment filling his mind, Elle was. He didn't care right now who thought she might be involved. She was the one person he'd loved and lost so long ago. She'd vanished after their one night stand. *Some things were best left for marriage only.* Now she acted as if he'd hurt her. Either way, he needed to apologize, and put right what he'd done.

The coffee shop was busy, but Elle sat just inside the door, nursing a coffee and sandwich. He smiled and went to order, half expecting her to flee before he returned. He slid into the seat opposite her. "Hi."

"Hello."

He picked up his cup, taking a long sip. "I needed that. How are you?"

"Fine, and you?"

"Busy. I kind of shocked my partner by stopping for lunch. Normally she has to eat while we keep working." He picked up his sandwich, inspecting the filling. "Which is kind of weird. You were the one who used to skip meals."

Elle nodded, looking down at her cup.

"Anyway, I was wondering if we could talk."

"About?"

"About what happened."

"What happened when?" Her eyes widened, but her smile never reached them. "Yesterday? Last week? Saturday night when you were at the club again?"

He held her gaze. "You saw me?"

"Yeah, I saw you. I avoid eye contact with everyone while I'm working, but I know who's there and who isn't."

He hesitated. That could be an opening, but he didn't want to discuss work right now. He wanted to talk about something else. For the moment, he wanted to keep the illusion that Elle wasn't involved in the operation at the club. "That last day at the house party."

"There is nothing to talk about. I'm sorry I left

without saying goodbye, but I had to be somewhere and left midafternoon. I'm sorry I left you stranded."

"Garth gave me a lift to the station, and I got a train. But we still need to talk."

She shook her head. "I really can't do this right now."

"I'm not going to drop this."

"Why? Why can't you just let it go? I have."

"Have you?" He glanced up as someone blocked the light.

Mrs. Harrison stood there, glowering at her daughter. "What are you doing?"

Elle jumped. "Mum. I'm having lunch. Patrick just stopped to say hi…"

"Really?" She placed her palms on the table and leaned down, forcing herself into Elle's personal space. Patrick watched as Elle visibly flinched and pulled back into her seat. "Just make sure you're home to be with Abbie tonight."

"I can't. I'm working tonight."

"Tough," Mrs. Harrison snapped. "I'm going out. Abbie can't be left alone. You sort it." She turned on her heel and left the shop.

Patrick glanced from her retreating back to Elle. She'd lost all the color from her face and her hands shook. "Are you all right?" He'd been trained to pick up on subtle gestures, facial expressions, postures, and all of that told him Elle was in some kind of trouble, and in deep.

"I'm fine. I have to go." She pushed to her feet.

Should he go after her? He rose, to follow her and make sure she was all right, but his phone rang. "Page…yeah, OK. Coming." So much for lunch and making amends with Elle. He'd go home tonight via the club and check on her then.

****

Eleanor spent the rest of the day in a complete state. The one man she'd never expected to see again had waltzed back into her life and seemed intent on turning it upside down.

One look from Patrick's steely blue eyes and her legs turned to jelly. One word made her heart race. She longed for his touch. She wanted...

No. I'm over him. I have to be over him...

She shoved the books back onto the shelf. Some choice. Her daughter or the man she loved. Not a fair choice. Not a choice at all. And she dreaded the conversation with her mother when she got home.

She eased her shoulders, taking another pile of books from the trolley.

"Ellie?"

She turned, and smiled at Abbie. "Hey, squirt. What are you doing here?"

"Mum's not in. She left a note on the door."

Eleanor's heart sank. She'd hoped her mother hadn't meant it. "Did you bring the note with you?"

Abbie held it out. Short, sweet, and to the point.

Gone out. Not sure when I'll be back. Go and meet Eleanor after school. She's in charge tonight.

"Oh."

"Aren't you singing in the club tonight?"

"I am. I guess you'll have to come too."

By the time she'd gone home, picked up her outfit, and cooked Abbie's tea, she was running late. She was even later by the time she finally found a parking space. She and Abbie went in the back entrance.

Abbie wrinkled her nose. "It smells in here."

Eleanor took a deep breath. "I guess it does. I'm used to it. It's all the alcohol."

"Ewww. You don't drink, do you?"

She ruffled Abbie's hair. "Of course not. It dulls your reflexes and makes you do stupid things."

"I don't need drink to do that," Abbie winked. "I can do stupid things without thinking about it. Where do you change?"

"I'll show you." She headed down the corridor to the small room designated her changing room. The title itself was laughable as it was little more than a cupboard.

Abbie sat on the stool in front of the dresser and mirror, while Eleanor put on her dress. "It's pretty. Wish I had one like that."

Eleanor studied her daughter in the mirror. Personally she hoped Abbie would never have to dress like this and do what she did for a living. "Maybe one day. Come on, we need to get out front. Bring your book and you can sit where I can see you, but no one else can."

As soon as Eleanor appeared, Zeke marched over to them from the bar. "You're late, Lisa."

"I'm sorry. Things just piled up and time got away from me. But I'm here, surely that's what counts."

"What's she doing here?"

"It's just for tonight."

He shook his head, his brows and eyes narrowing as he scowled. "She's underage. She can't be here. You know that."

"I have no choice. There's no one else to take her. Mum's gone out. She'll sit backstage and keep out of the way, I promise. She won't move."

"And am I supposed to give her coloring pens?"

"She's not a baby."

He shook his head firmly. "No way. Jake will lose his license if they find her in here, close us down, and you won't have a job. Can't her father take her?"

Abbie drew in a breath. "I... don't have a dad anymore."

Eleanor squeezed her hand. "Zeke knows very well Dad's dead."

Zeke peered at Abbie and Eleanor cringed at his leering assessment. "You look very much like your sister. Apart from your hair and your eyes."

Abbie shot him a small smile. "Ellie used to be blonde when she was younger as well. I want to be a singer like her, too, when I grow up."

"Very nice." His dark frown pierced Eleanor. "But it doesn't change the fact she can't stay here."

She swallowed, her stomach churning. "Then I can't sing. Come on Abbie, we're going home."

"You walk out and you're fired."

Abbie caught his arm. "Please. Don't fire Ellie, we need the money."

Zeke shook her off. "Get rid of the child, or no job."

"You'd really fire me?" Eleanor managed, past the lump in her throat.

Zeke walked closer and stood before her almost nose to nose. "No CD, no contract, no nothing."

"You can't."

"I think you'll find I can."

Eleanor turned away, angry tears stinging her eyes. She didn't have a choice. She had to sing, but she had to look after Abbie. If she recorded the CD, there was a good chance she'd get a recording contract with one of the major record labels and then Abbie wouldn't have to beg vile men like Zeke for mercy. Somehow, she had to dig her own way out of the mess she'd created.

Abbie tugged her arm. "I'll just go home."

"You can't. There's no one there to look after you."

Abbie put her hands on her hips. "I'm not a baby, I'm nearly fourteen. That's almost old enough to babysit someone else now."

Eleanor shook her head. The neighborhood wasn't the best. She couldn't leave Abbie alone.

One of the waiters crossed over to them. "I'm sorry to interrupt. There's a man at bar asking for Lisa."

Zeke scowled. "Tell him she's busy."

Eleanor glared at Zeke not caring whether she got fired or not, and took Abbie's hand. "You'll tell him no such thing. Come on, Abbie. Let's go see who it is."

The tall dark haired man leaning against the bar was the last person she expected to see. Relief flooded her. Concern filled Patrick's eyes as she reached him. He set his glass of water down and took three steps to meet them.

"What's wrong?" His low voice tinged with alarm.

"That man was horrid to Ellie. He won't let me stay here. Says he's going to fire her if I do, but Mum's out and Ellie has to work and I'm 'too young' to be left alone. I don't want her to get fired because of me." Abbie huffed the words and rolled her eyes. Normally Eleanor would attempt to staunch the blatant show of disrespect for any elder...but Zeke wasn't really respectable. Now with her anger cooling, Abbie began to sniff as silent tears began to fall.

Patrick reached into his pocket and pulled out a

tissue, giving it to Abbie. He looked at Eleanor. "He said what?"

She tried to control the tremble in her own voice. "He said Abbie couldn't be here because Jake would lose his license, but he's done it for other people in the past as a one off. Just not me."

"Jake?"

"Jake Reid. He's the manager."

"He owns this place?"

"No idea, but he's bent the rules for others. Just won't do it for me."

"I'll take her." His tone was firm and decisive.

"I can't ask you to do that." Even if it would solve the problem for now.

"You didn't ask. I offered." He smiled at her then looked at Abbie. "Are you too old for Disney films?"

"No," she sniffled. "Some of them are pretty neat. Ellie likes them. So you're never too old."

"Have you seen the new one?"

"No. I'm the only one in my class who hasn't."

"In that case, would you like to come see it with me? If Elle doesn't mind, that is?"

Abbie looked at Eleanor then back at Patrick. "I'm not supposed to go anywhere with strange men."

"And that's very sensible. But I'm not a stranger. You know me from church, and I'm a longtime friend of your sister."

Abbie looked at him long and hard before she turned to her. "We don't have to tell Mum I've gone to the cinema, and then you don't get fired because of me."

Eleanor hesitated. Was this really the best option? It was the only one she had that much was certain. She glanced over her shoulder and saw Zeke glowering.

She sucked in a deep breath, and then nodded. "OK. Just this one time. Just don't let Mum find out. She'll have my guts for garters."

Abbie flung her arms around her tightly. "Thank you, thank you, thank you, thank you, thank you. I really don't like this place anyway."

Eleanor hugged her back. "Enough of the thank yous," she whispered. "Go, have fun."

Patrick wrote his address on a serviette and handed it to her. "Come pick her up when you finish here."

"Thank you." She took the paper and slid it inside her dress. "It'll be about half ten or so. Later if Mr. F comes in and wants entertaining again."

He raised an eyebrow. "Mr. F?"

She shook her head. She didn't mean what he probably thought, but either way she wasn't going to explain in front of Abbie.

Patrick nodded curtly, something akin to irritation flickering in his eyes before he masked it. "No problem. Come on then, Abbie."

Eleanor watched them go and sighed. Being around a male figure would do Abbie the world of good. Something within her glowed at the thought of the two of them together. If only...

"Now the kid's gone, how about doing some work?" Zeke's harsh voice jerked her back to reality.

****

Patrick sat watching TV quietly. He and Abbie had had a great time. It was incredible how much like Elle she was. The same turn of phrase, even the way she flicked her hair to one side. He wondered if their dad had blue eyes, as that was the one main difference between the two sisters and he knew her mother didn't.

A light tap at the front door had him on his feet. He went to open it. Elle stood there, shivering slightly in her light jacket.

"Hey, come in."

"Thank you."

He shut the door behind her. "How did it go after we left?"

"It went all right, same as any other night. Sorry I'm late. How's Abbie?" She glanced around as if expecting her to appear, despite the hour.

"She's fast asleep on the couch. I think I wore her out. Can I get you some coffee?"

"I should really get her home, but since it's not a school night, coffee would be good, thank you. Just a quick one."

He smiled. "Come on through to the kitchen."

"I just want to check on Abbie first."

He nodded to the lounge. "She's in there."

By the time Elle appeared again, he'd made the coffee. He held out a cup. "Here you go. It's instant, but tastes just as good. Did you keep your job?

She shrugged. "I don't know. He didn't say another word to me after you left, apart from summoning me to a meeting tomorrow at nine thirty with Jake."

"That doesn't sound good."

"No." She took a deep breath, and sipped the hot liquid. "I sing for Abbie..." She broke off.

Surprise filled him. "For your sister?"

A cute red blush spread over her cheeks, tinting the tips of her ears. "Yeah. So we have enough money for clothes and books for her. Mum never worked outside the house. Since dad died, there's not much money coming in, and Abbie rarely gets treats."

"Ah. That explains her enthusiasm for the movie. She loved the film. I bought her popcorn and soda. I hope that's all right with you." He gave a little grimace as an afterthought.

She smiled wryly. "It's a bit late to ask."

Patrick sipped his coffee. "True."

"But yeah, it's fine."

"She said it'd be all right with you. When I asked what her mother would say, she shrugged and said you'd say yes and wished you were her mother, not her sister."

"Oh." She studied the coffee intently, her voice cracking. "What did you say?"

His senses triggered a full alert. There was more going on here than she was letting on. The only problem was, he couldn't see the wood for the trees right now. She so filled his senses, that it made thinking almost impossible. "I told her that she may not always get along with her mum, but she'd always love her."

Elle nodded. "Yeah, she will. Unconditionally."

He smiled. "It's actually amazing how much she looks like you. She even flicks her hair the same way that you do."

She ran her finger around the rim of the cup. "Does she?"

"She's a lot like you, apart from the eyes. Yours are brown and hers are blue."

She chewed on her bottom lip, fingers tightening on the cup. "It happens. Something to do with genes. I'm not going to pretend I understand."

"Yeah, me neither." He studied her over the top of his coffee. "Look, I know going out with you was a long time ago, and a lot of time has passed, but my feelings towards you haven't changed." He had to say it before he found himself too distracted.

She put the cup down. "I can't."

"Can't what?"

"Go out with you. Be seen with you. Talk about this."

"Why not? Elle, I need to know what I did to hurt you so I can put it right."

As he watched, the shutters came down again.

"Thank you for having Abbie, but I have to go. I need to get her home before Mum wonders where we are."

Patrick stood dumbfounded as Elle woke Abbie and left. Something was very wrong there, but what? And more to the point, what could he do to help? She could run as much as she wanted, but he had too many unanswered questions that needed an answer before he could do what she apparently wanted, and leave her alone.

5

Eleanor tapped nervously on the office door. Nine thirty on the dot.

"Come in."

She wiped her hand on her jeans and opened the door. Shooting the three men in the room her best smile, she entered. Zeke and Jake she'd been expecting, but what was PJ doing there?

"Shut the door. Sit down."

Zeke glowered at her from where he sat, and she hesitantly did as she was told. Her gaze went from him to the other man. PJ seemed different from the last time she'd seen him. Ice glittered in his eyes, his body was stiff and his hands clenched on the desk, fingers of one hand drumming.

Jake looked at her. "Eleanor, I believe you know PJ. He owns HC1. He heard about the incident last night."

"Oh...."

PJ scowled. "Explain last night. You brought a child into my club."

"That child was my sister. As I tried to explain, I had no one to leave her with, and I couldn't just fail to turn up here last night. I need the money, and I didn't want to let anyone down by not singing."

He drummed his fingers on the desk, the incessant noise grating on her nerves. "You know the rules?"

"I do. No one is allowed in the club under the age

of eighteen."

"Why is that?"

She squirmed under his glower. "Because the legal drinking age in the UK is eighteen, and you could lose your license if the police found someone underage here, or someone reported you."

PJ leaned across the desk. "Yet you assumed that rule didn't apply to you."

"I'm sorry. Some of the others had done it in the past, and I thought—"

He jumped to his feet, the chair flying into the wall behind him making Eleanor jump in fright. "I don't pay you to think! Nor do I pay you to do what the others do." He looked at Jake. "Find out who they were and get them in here. Now! And both of you get out and leave us."

Zeke and Jake both scrambled from the room, the door slamming behind him.

PJ moved over to Eleanor. He put an arm either side of her chair preventing her from moving and shoved his face into hers. "Now what do I do with you?"

"I'm...I'm sorry..." She could almost taste the fear flooding her. Her heart raced, her stomach churned. She flinched as he moved closer.

"Sorry. Doesn't. Cut. It." He spat each word individually. Fire replaced the ice in his narrowed eyes, his brow furrowed, and rage poured from every sinew. "I should sack you right here and right now."

"Please, don't..." She looked at him, hypnotized by his gaze, despite her fear. "I need the money."

His hand ran up her arm. "What would you be prepared to do?" he asked.

"Depends on what you want..." Her voice shook.

"I know things about you, Eleanor. Things you'd rather keep hidden. You do something for me and not only do you keep your job, but those things stay hidden. And your little sister stays safe and warm at home with her mum."

Her heart stopped. How could he know? Was he lying? How could she be sure, but she couldn't take the chance. Especially if Abbie would be safe if she did this. "What..." Her tongue nervously flicked over her lips. "What do you want me to do?"

He returned to the other side of his desk. He righted his chair and sat, smiling at her. "You know where the Moat House Hotel is?"

She nodded. "Yes."

He withdrew a large envelope from the desk drawer. "Take this. I want you to deliver it, in person, to the gentleman in room 624 at two o'clock this afternoon. Wait while he checks it, then return here with the package he gives you."

She took the envelope. What was the catch? "That's it? A simple mail drop?"

"For now. If it goes well, there may be others. You could earn a little bonus, as well. Go, run along. See you later."

****

The next three days, Patrick spent immersed in a case that drained him both emotionally and physically. A terrorist threat to the UK left him barely enough time to eat or sleep, never mind anything else. Everyone in the unit had gone home at least once to sleep apart from him. He'd lived at his desk, even dozed there. The pile of spare clothes from his locker had been depleted, and the only time he left his desk was to chase a lead or make use of the work showers.

This was precisely why he didn't have a life outside of work. Never had and never would.

Finally, just after ten o'clock on Thursday morning, he got the lead they needed.

"Are you sure about this?" Shay yelled dashing after him.

"My source places him in the Hyacinth Street Mall and says that is the intended target. If we don't move now it's going to be too late."

More running footsteps joined him as the rest of the unit pounded down the stairs. He unlocked the car from halfway across the garage and, in the same fluid movement, caught the Kevlar jacket someone tossed him. "Thanks. I'm driving."

"You drive like a maniac," Shay told him bluntly.

"If you drive, we'll either get there tomorrow or once half the town's been blown to kingdom come."

"Fine, you drive. But I'm not paying your speeding fine."

Patrick jumped in the car, starting it almost at the same time. "Not going to get one. And even if I did, Nahum would sort it."

He shoved the car into reverse and swung out of the parking space and away, leaving rubber on the concrete. He was dimly aware of Shay hanging on tightly as he wove his way in and out of the traffic, praying the whole time that the lights would stay in his favor, the police wouldn't pull him over, and, most of all, that they would arrive in time.

Screeching into the loading bay outside the mall, he jumped from the car, and ran inside. A security guard approached him and he pulled out his ID. "MI5.

I need you to start an organized evacuation of the entire building. Now. Preferably without causing a panic."

Not waiting for an answer, he moved inside the building. The place was a maze of shops, corridors, and staircases.

If someone was going to blow this up, it would have to be some place central to get as many people as possible, or somewhere strategic to maximize the damage.

He turned slowly, scanning the crowd of shoppers.

The tannoy crackled into life.

"Your attention, please. The mall is now closing due to an electrical fault in one of the shops. Please make your way to the nearest exit. Thank you."

A flash of light caught his eye and he spun around. "Up there." He pointed to the second of five floors and dashed to the stairs. Moving against the tide was almost impossible. The stairs were jammed with people trying to leave.

A gunshot echoed, causing panic. The orderly evacuation turned into a screaming mass of humanity heading to the exits, not caring who they trampled on in the process.

Patrick reached the upper level, and pulled his gun from its holster. He held it ready to fire as he approached the man on the edge of the gallery.

The man's coat stood open, explosives strapped to his body. One arm snaked tightly around a terrified shopper's neck, holding her against his side. In that hand he held the detonator, in the other he had a gun pointed at a security guard. His hands shook, sweat beaded his brow and he appeared to be muttering something under his breath.

Aware of everyone around him and the number of civilians still milling around and panicking, Patrick wasn't going to wait for the order to come. The guy was a threat and he had hostages.

"Put the gun down," Patrick ordered, taking charge. "We have you surrounded."

The man looked at him with cold, dark eyes.

He'd seen intent like that once before and spent the next week in hospital recovering.

Patrick sucked in a deep breath. "Put the gun and the detonator down. You don't want to do this."

The man raised an eyebrow. "Are you willing to take the risk?"

From the corner of his eye, Patrick could see two other agents taking aim. "Are you? I can guarantee you I'm a better shot than you are and I'm faster. Your finger so much as twitches on that detonator and you'll die. Is that what you want?"

"I'm ready to die."

"What about all these people?" Patrick kept his aim straight. "And the rest of the town?"

The gunman laughed. "You think I care what happens to this town? The whole point of this bomb is that there will be no more town."

Patrick held his gaze. "Shouldn't they get a choice? What about the woman there? What's her name?"

Nice one the voice crackled in his ear piece. *Try to keep him talking.*

"Stacey," the woman whispered.

"Will you ask Stacey if she's OK?"

The gunman looked at her. "Are you OK?"

The security guard moved towards him. The gunman swiftly turned and fired, sending him to the floor.

In the same moment, Patrick fired, his bullet neutralizing the gunman who landed on his back, the detonator falling from his hand. He knew the order, had he waited, would have been to kill, but he preferred to shoot to wound. Besides, this way they stood a chance of finding out why and who else he was working with.

Keeping the gun on him, Patrick moved swiftly, kicking the gun and detonator to one side. "Get the bomb squad up here, now. Next shot kills, so I'd keep very, very still if I were you."

The woman knelt where she had fallen, shaking and crying. One of the other agents gently helped her to her feet and led her away.

Shay appeared by his side, her gun also aimed at the terrorist. "You're an idiot to take a chance like that, Patrick. What if he had detonated the bomb? Or killed the hostage?"

He sucked in a deep breath, keeping his gaze on the man on the floor. "He didn't. He's down, and everything is secure. That's what matters."

"So the town is safe for another day. Agent 3.14 strikes again, winning another battle in the epic war against terror on our doorstep."

"Yep, with his trusty sidekick Agent 7x3 at his side."

Noah, their section leader glared their way. "Don't you two ever give it a rest?"

"No," they chodused.

"No," they chorused.

The bomb squad and paramedics arrived. Patrick kept his gaze to the man on the floor, not dropping his aim until he was sure all danger was passed.

****

Later that afternoon, Patrick sat at his desk, his fingers hovering over the computer keyboard. He'd filed his report. Now he had a spare five minutes, thoughts of Elle and the problems with her manager filled his mind. Not to mention the niggling seed of doubt planted by DI Nemec. Could he afford to get involved with her again if she were caught up in all of this? Should he declare his interest in her? Tell Nahum he had a past relationship with a potential suspect? He had to be sure before he did anything. He typed Elle's name into the database.

Shay leaned over his shoulder, putting a mug of coffee on his desk. "Here you go, just the way you like it."

He picked it up and took a deep breath, filling his senses with the dark aroma. "Thank you."

"What are you doing? Who's Eleanor Harrison?"

"She's a friend."

"You search all your friends on the national criminal database?"

He took a large drink. "No."

"Good. Because if you do, I am so glad I'm not your 'friend.'"

"I know it's an abuse of power, but there's something not quite right." He frowned at the smile on her face. "Don't you laugh at me."

"I'm not. It's kind of cute. Anyway, it's about time you got yourself a girlfriend."

"Ex-girlfriend, actually."

"Oh, that just makes your actions seriously creepy. It's like stalking her on one of these social media sites just so you can see what she's posting or who she's going out with instead of you." Shay plunked herself down on the chair next to his. "I want all the details."

Patrick laughed. "Does that make you a voyeur, too?"

"Nope, I'm merely looking out for my partner. And an interested party."

Nahum stuck his head around the edge of his glass office. "Patrick, Shay, get in here now."

Patrick grinned. "Sprung. I swear that guy is omnipresent and knows what I plan to do before I actually do it."

"He probably just wants to moan because you shot to wound rather than killed the guy in the mall. Of course, if you'd taken the kill shot without permission, he'd still be moaning." Shay winked.

"Maybe, but at least we can get intel from the bloke now. Assuming he talks." He got to his feet and grabbed his coffee. "But I'm taking this with me. Right now, I need the caffeine to stay awake. I've lived on adrenaline for too long. Come on." He crossed the room, noticing Nahum shut the door behind them. "What's up, boss?"

"Have either of you heard of the soul singer Lisa Bellamy? Real name Eleanor Harrison."

Shay shook her head. "Nope."

Patrick drew in a sharp breath. Elle was on the MI5 radar? Why?

Nahum looked at him. "Patrick?"

"Yeah, I have. I heard her sing the other night. What about her? She in some kind of trouble?"

Nahum nodded and held out identical sheets of paper to them both. "Knowing her will help. Read this, tell me what you think."

Patrick took the paper, his heart pounding and his

mind reeling, fearing the worst. He read the copied letter slowly. *Eleanor is being sent threatening letters and for this they contact us? That makes no sense.* Setting his coffee down, he read the letter again.

"You're kidding. Why us? Surely the police can handle this. They have a protection program, don't they?" Shay commented. "They don't need us for that."

"Keep reading."

Patrick carried on reading. He sat heavily in the chair by the desk, the wind knocked from him. His stomach cramped and his tie threatened to choke him. Reaching up to his collar, he undid the top button and loosened his tie a little. He'd hoped Elle only sang at the club. No, this indicated her ties ran much deeper. "This is tied into the info from DI Nemec, right?"

How did she get mixed up with this?

Nahum studied him, inclining his head slowly. "That is why we've been asked to protect her, as we're running this op anyway. And also why you and Shay are being assigned this case. So far we have no idea how she got involved with Foster, but Noah and Frank are checking that out as we speak. Thoughts?"

He shuffled through the papers, trying to control his thudding heart and prevent it from breaking free from the confines of his chest. "I'm still not convinced this bloke I saw at the club is Foster. Nemec knows that. I'm keeping him in the loop. As far as Elle...Miss Harrison goes? I know her, knew her years ago. There is no way she'd be involved in anything illegal."

Nahum's eyebrows shot up into his receding hair line. "First name terms? Knew her in the past? How?"

"I was her mentor at university. We haven't seen each other in years. Well, not until we bumped into each other last week at the library when I collected the drop from one of my snouts. I want the lead on this one. First thing we need to do is pull her out."

"She's our contact. We work with her, keep her on the inside."

"I'm not sure that is the right way to do things. Get any information she has, sure." Patrick blurted. "But if she's being threatened, we get her out now."

"Perhaps someone more impartial would be better suited for this investigation."

Patrick set the file down. He'd almost slipped up then—he needed to be more careful. "I am perfectly capable of being impartial. Like I already said, I want this one. She might be more willing to work with us if it's someone she knows."

Nahum held his gaze, his brows furrowing. "You mess up, even a tad, and you're off the case, is that understood?"

Patrick didn't flinch. The slightest movement of his eyes and Nahum would pounce on it. "Perfectly. My thinking is, get her into protective custody. Escort her to and from the club, at least for now. That way we can keep tabs on what she's doing, get info from her and keep this Mr. F from getting suspicious."

"Then fine. Move in with her. Do what you have to do. Just keep her alive and safe. Find out what she knows."

"I'll move her into my place."

"Not a good idea, especially if you know her. I can't have you compromised in any way. Use the safe house on Brook Street. And use your head. We have no idea how involved she is in this. It could be a ruse to take the heat off of her."

"And it might not be." Shay voiced what he wanted to say.

He shot her a grateful glance. She always seemed to know what he was thinking. The art of a good partner.

"This is exactly why we're taking her into safe custody. Go home both of you. Pack for a few days, then pick her up."

Patrick drained his coffee and exchanged a long glance with Shay. "Fine. Where is she?"

"Manor Street police station. They're expecting you."

****

Eleanor sat in the police station, biting her index fingernail down to the quick. Her stomach churned, the butterflies and nausea making her head pound. With every passing moment, the need to throw up grew. Her skin alternated between hot and cold and clammy. The officer she had spoken to had put her in a small office and, once he'd taken her details several times, left her alone.

Strictly speaking, the building itself was busy and there were plenty of officers around, and the office probably had a CCTV camera hidden somewhere, but she was alone none the less.

Why were they treating her like the criminal here? She didn't know who'd sent her the letters. She wished she did. There had to be a better option than being dead. Although being dead wasn't an option. It would leave Abbie with *her*—

Abbie...she had to get to her, protect her. Maybe if she just left, no one would stop her. She could come back later, with Abbie.

She stood, heading to the door.

The door creaked as it opened. She jumped, seeing a man in the doorway. Her heart pounded, blood raced in her ears and everything finally became too much and she fell into the all-consuming darkness...

A voice echoed through the black tendrils claiming her. It called her name, beckoning her back towards the light. A voice from the past.

Strong arms held her, soft fingers stroking her cheek. "Elle?"

Her eyes flickered open, focusing on the face above hers. She hadn't imagined him. "Patrick?"

"Yeah, in the flesh." He gently held a glass to lips. "Drink this. It's water."

She took a couple of sips. "What are you doing here?"

"Working."

Her face creased. She didn't understand. "Working?"

"I've been assigned your case. Drink a little more for me."

She obediently swallowed a couple more times, then sat up, pushing out of his grip. A girl could get too comfortable there, like she had before. "I'm confused. What do you mean they 'gave you my case'? When you said you were security I thought you meant private investigator or something. If you're a police officer, why didn't you just say so?"

Patrick's smile had its usual effect of her. Her heart thudded and her knees weakened. It was a good job she was sitting down or she'd have fallen again.

"That's because I'm in national security." He tilted his head. "I'm a spook." His voice was low and guarded.

"Why did they send you?" she whispered.

"The reasons are twofold. First of all, I know you professionally and personally. My boss figured it'd be easier on you if you knew at least one of the agents assigned to protect you. Secondly, Foster is on our radar. He has been for a while, which makes it our case and not the police's. So I'm taking you from here to a safe house."

She did a double take, not knowing who this Foster was, but not going to look stupid by asking. "What? What about my things and Abbie, Mum, and work?"

"We can pick up a few of your things on the way. Abbie and your mum have not been threatened. It would put them in greater danger if they remain with you. Abbie stays with her mum and work is off the agenda, at least for a day or so. Until I have chance to debrief you."

"You don't understand. I have to work, I have no choice." She barely kept them going as it was. And if she stopped both the singing and delivering the packages, then PJ would carry out his threat. Her secrets would be made public. Patrick would find out about Abbie and she couldn't let that happen.

"We can talk about this later. Let's go." He helped her to her feet.

6

Rushed through her packing, and then driven way too fast to the safe house, Eleanor didn't feel as if her feet had touched the ground. She slowly walked around the bare apartment. It was sparse, to put it mildly. There were none of the comforts of home. And it was filthy. She wouldn't even keep a cat here.

And Patrick being assigned to protect her? What was his role in all this? She had to bear in mind that he was a spook who worked for the government and not her friend and mentor any longer. Had he really found her accidentally? Or had he been watching her, tracking her all along?

The mere idea that he been spying on her all the time made her shiver. The 'innocent' meet at the library? The way he kept turning up at the club? The 'oh my brother really wanted to meet you, but then he dumped me for a football match' line. The fact he came back several times, she'd thought to hear her sing. She'd even asked him if he were a cop—twice— and he had brushed her off. Had all of it been a lie? So much for the 'catch up over coffee chat for old time's sake.' He was just after one thing.

Was he here to give her a false sense of security, in the hope she'd tell him everything she knew because he knew her? She didn't know anyone called Foster and that was the name he'd used a couple of times on the way here, never mind in the police station. But that didn't alter the fact she wasn't happy with this turn of events. Being separated from Abbie wasn't part of her plan when she went to the police.

She dumped her bag on a single bed in a tiny room and went to find Patrick. He deserved a piece of her mind, and boy, was he going to get it.

He stood silent in the kitchen, filling the kettle. "Find everything all right?"

"This place is a dump. There's no pictures, no windows that open, the sofa is stained by goodness only knows what, the fireplace is filthy, the bathroom doesn't look as if it's ever been cleaned..."

Patrick sighed. "Will you listen to yourself? This isn't a holiday home. We are trying to keep you safe, but if you don't want it, then fine. There's the door. No one is going to make you stay here. But *you* came to *us*, remember?" He held out a hand. "That reminds me. I need your phone."

"My what?"

"Phone—you know the thing you make calls and texts on."

"Why?"

He sighed. "Just give me the phone," he said slowly.

Eleanor reached into her shirt pocket and slowly handed it over, watching as Patrick swiftly removed the battery and sim card.

The doorbell rang. Patrick pulled the gun from his holster and motioned her to stay still before moving into the hall.

She stood there in shock. He had never spoken to her like that before. Ever. Even when she messed up on tests and forgot everything he'd taught her. In fact even when she'd had the car accident that was her fault, he hadn't yelled at her.

But then this was Patrick now, not the Patrick she'd known and walked out on fourteen years ago. Oh, if only he knew the truth, but she couldn't tell him. He'd changed, and if she didn't think he'd have believed her back then, there was no way he'd believe her now.

She leaned against the kitchen counter, staring into the garden. A cat sat in the middle of the lawn staring back at her. A cat...

****

The car skidded, the sickening thud still reverberating in her ears when another crunch brought them to a shuddering halt. Her hands shook. "I hit it."

"Stay there." Patrick jumped out of the car and disappeared into the darkness behind them.

She couldn't stop shaking. She'd seen a brief glimpse in the headlights, of a cat, wide eyes shining, fixated on the oncoming car. She'd tried to brake and swerve, but she hadn't been quick enough.

Patrick moved around the front of the car and motioned to her to back up slowly.

She wound down the window. "I can't."

He moved around to the window. "Don't give me that. Just put the car in reverse and go slowly."

"But the cat?"

"Elle, forget the cat. Back slowly off this log or we're not going anywhere."

"OK," she whispered. The car jerked as she reversed slowly.

"Great, now stop and put the hand brake on, so I can

check underneath."

The light of the torch vanished under the car. She closed her eyes tightly. This was meant to be a simple trip to the cliff top house owned by Garth's parents. His parents were away, so he'd invited twelve of them from university up for the weekend before Easter break. Studying for finals and partying was on the agenda for all of them.

The door opened and Patrick climbed back in. "No damage that I can see. A tiny scrape on the paintwork, but clear nail varnish will fix that up and stop it rusting." He smiled. "You all right to drive or want me to?"

"I'll do it. You don't want to go home?"

He shook his head, kissing her cheek. "Of course I don't. I get to spend the whole weekend with you. Why would I want to go home?"

****

Eleanor shook her head, pushing that day and those images far from her mind. If he knew what she'd done, he'd have nothing but contempt for her. She deserved every harsh word, angry look and irate tone he gave her.

The door opened and Patrick came back in. With him was the blonde haired woman that had been with him in the library, who close up, was even prettier than she remembered. She carried a bag of what looked like takeaway. Patrick carried another one. He grinned at his companion, seeming at ease in her presence, laughing at something she'd obviously said in the hallway.

Patrick put the bag on the counter. "Elle, this is my partner, Shay Williams. Shay, this is Eleanor Harrison, or Lisa Bellamy."

An unexpected surge of jealously at the word *partner* flooded her. "Hi." She shoved her hands in her pockets, not meaning to appear so openly hostile, but unable to stop it.

"Hello. I hope you still like Chinese. Patrick said it was a fairly safe thing to get for lunch."

"Yeah." She glanced at Patrick, hating the way he grinned at the other woman. Things had just got too much for her to deal with. Once the letter came she knew she needed help. She asked for, needed protection of some sort, but she didn't expect to be whisked away from everything and everyone and hidden. She'd thought maybe a cop would follow her around, like in a movie. She hadn't, even in her wildest dreams, expected that her protector would be Patrick, nor had she imagined he'd be an MI5 agent.

What had she gotten herself mixed up with if the top security agency in the country were protecting her? Didn't they deal with terrorists? There was no way she was a terrorist. She was simply a nightclub singer, trying to find a break. More to the point, she was irritated, no, way more than irritated, that he hadn't been truthful with her.

As if you've been truthful with him.

She ignored her nagging conscience. There was a huge difference between what she'd done and this.

And that partner of his. Did she have to be so pretty? And they were as close as she and Patrick once had been. Was he so fickle with his relationships? Did he treat all women alike until he got his way with them? Were they more than just work colleagues?

She knew she was being irrational, but it still hurt to think about the relationship she had thrown away. She bowed her head.

God, I know I don't have the right to ask You for anything, but help me not to be angry, when I have no right to be. And help me not to feel so jealous. After all, I left Patrick, not the other way around.

****

Patrick chatted with Shay as they ate, trying to compensate for Elle's sullen demeanor. He didn't know why she was suddenly sulking like a three year old and acting as if her life had been ripped from her. It wasn't as if the protection was being foisted on her against her will.

As soon as she'd finished eating, Elle rose and left the room without a word. Patrick sighed and pushed his hand through his hair.

"So she's your old flame from university, then?" Shay sounded more bored than curious.

"Yeah. But I honestly don't know what's gotten into her. It must be me. She's been a bit frosty the past few times I've seen her."

"Oh, this is beyond frosty, Patrick. It's more like icy or even beyond icy. I thought she wanted our help?"

"Maybe it's just *my* help she doesn't want. I'll talk to her."

Shay stood. "You do that while I go grocery shopping. Think I have the better deal actually."

Patrick winked at her. "I think you could be right." He went to find where Elle was sulking. If she was running true to form, she'd be in her room or by the fireplace. Not that she'd admit she was sulking, because she was far too mature for that, but it was as close to sulking as a person could get.

71

He tapped on her bedroom door and pushed it open not waiting for an answer. She lay on her stomach, reading. She didn't look up, so he stood between her and the window, blocking her light. "Elle, can we talk?"

"Why?"

"I need the truth, Elle. All of it."

"My name is Eleanor, not Elle. And talking won't change anything."

Not bothering to hide his irritation, he flopped down on the bed beside her. "Look, *Eleanor*, if you don't play ball, we can't protect you. We need to know anything you've seen or heard that might have gotten you noticed."

"You're MI5. You figure it out." Again she spoke over the book, not even looking at him.

He caught his breath, his hands curled into fists, and his jaw tightened. This was a mistake. He should never have taken this assignment. And he wasn't going to start calling her Eleanor either. Reaching out, he snatched the book, closed it, and tossed it to the side in a swift single movement.

"Hey, I was reading that," came the immediate indignant protest.

"What happened to you, Elle?"

She sat up and glared at him. "Me? What you mean, what happened to me? University was a long time ago. Maybe I grew up. Just like we all did. Grew up and changed. None of us are the same people we were back then. For instance, why didn't you tell me you were a spy?"

"Need to know," he snapped back.

"You've changed."

"You too, way more than I expected. You used to

be—"

"I used to be what? Innocent?" She tossed her head, sending her hair shimmering over her shoulder. "In answer to your question, you happened to me, Patrick. You made me who I am now."

He caught his breath, doing a double take. *He* got her involved in drugs, if indeed she was? "Excuse me?"

She stabbed a finger at him, emphasizing every word. "That last weekend at the house party changed who I was forever."

He flung his hands up in defense. "Now, wait a minute. That wasn't all me. You agreed. You didn't say no or stop or…"

"I should have."

Patrick stood and stomped across room, shoving his hands through his hair. "So what *are* you saying? That I forced you to do something you didn't want to do? Because you know very well that's not true."

He grunted in annoyance as his pocketed phone vibrated and rang. "Don't you dare move. This isn't finished."

"I'll move if I want to." She scowled at him, and marched over to the window, keeping her back to him. "Answer your phone before they ring off. There's probably a major terrorist threat you need to save the country from."

He snatched his phone free and glared at the screen before answering. "Page."

"It's Nahum. Abbie Harrison never made it home from school."

His anger dissipated faster than if someone had thrown a bucket of cold water over him. He fixed his gaze on Elle's stiff back. His free hand twisted through the hair on the back of his neck. *"What?* Say that again."

7

Patrick stood stock still, hardly daring to breathe, waiting for his boss to confirm or deny what he'd just said.

"Abbie is missing," Nahum repeated. "She left school on time, but never made it home. Is she with you?"

"No, of course she isn't. No one knows we're here except you and Shay, and she is out doing the grocery shopping."

"The police are searching the area between the school and the house. Mrs. Harrison is frantic. For some reason she's convinced this is Eleanor's fault. I need you to ask her if she has any idea where Abbie is or where she would go. A friend's house or somewhere like that."

"Hold on." Patrick turned away from the phone. "Abbie didn't come home from school."

"What? No...I thought she'd be safe if I did what he..." Elle broke off and spun around. Tears trickled down her cheeks, her skin pale. "You have to let me go and find her. Please..."

"Safe if you did what?" He studied her. Was that guilt? Again, something didn't ring true.

"Nothing, I meant nothing. Let me go and find her, please."

He let it drop for now. "The police are searching for her. Where would she go? Does she have a friend she'd go home with?"

She shook her head. "No, she doesn't have any school friends. At least not like that. She comes to the library to sit with me or the recording studio or she just goes home. No, wait, it's Thursday." She took a deep breath and sank on the bed rubbing a hand over the back of her neck. Was that relief in her eyes? "She has flute lessons on Grosvenor Square. I pick her up at five o'clock and then we go home together."

"Does your mother know?"

"About the lessons?" She shook her head, pushing upright again. "No, if she did she'd put a stop to them. It counts as enjoying yourself and therefore isn't allowed." She crossed over to him. "You have to let me go and find her. What if something's happened to her?"

He held up a hand needing to silence her for a minute. "What number Grosvenor Square?"

"One two four."

He turned back to the phone. "Did you get that?"

"One two four Grosvenor Square. We'll send someone over. Don't let Eleanor out of your sight."

"Oh, don't worry. She's not going anywhere. Let me know when you find Abbie." He hung up and put the phone back in his pocket.

Elle crossed over to the door. "I have to find her."

He grabbed her arm. "No, you don't. The police will find her."

"Will they bring her here?"

"No, she'll be taken home. Your mum is worried about her."

"Yeah, right."

"And I want to know what you meant by 'I thought she'd be safe if I did what he'?"

"I told you, I meant nothing. I say stupid things all the time. What matters is Abbie. Have you any idea how scared she's going to be when a uniformed police officer picks her up? She's going to assume someone's hurt." She paused as if something occurred to her. "Look, let me use your phone for one minute. Please."

"No."

"Patrick, please. Just one call."

"Whatever for?"

"Because you took mine away and I need to use it. Abbie has a phone. I bought her one, but Mum doesn't know. Let me just text her, warn her. You don't understand."

His face scrunched and his mind whirled. "You're right. I don't understand. She has a phone, but your mum doesn't know? Along with flute lessons she doesn't know about either? Why not?"

"It's complicated. Can I try to contact Abbie or not?"

"One text. I check it before you send it." He handed over the phone.

Elle snatched the handset from him and glanced at the screen. Her face fell. "I can't work touch screen."

He sighed and took the phone back. He tapped rapidly, bringing up the text screen. "Number?"

She hesitated slightly and then gave him what he wanted. "Start the message by saying it's Ellie. Otherwise, she won't open it. Then say, Mum freaked out because I forgot to tell her you'd be late. Police coming to get you. My fault. Sorry."

Patrick hit send. A minute later his phone beeped. He opened the message. "It says *great, so she knows. Bye bye flute lessons. Cops just turned up. Blue lights and all. Whose phone you using?*" He scowled. "That's just brilliant."

"Tell her Patrick from church. She'll be fine with that. Say I'm staying at yours for a couple of days for work purposes."

He raised an eyebrow. "You want me to lie to her?"

"It's not a lie. I'm staying with you. You're working. Please."

"Fine."

"Can they bring her here?"

He shook his head, typing rapidly and then hitting send. How many times did he have to answer the same question? "She stays with her mum."

"That's idiotic."

Shoving the phone back in his pocket, he stuck his hands on his hips and eyed her in exasperation. "She's a child. She needs to stay where she is right now and that's with her mother."

Elle straightened, and thrust one hand into her pocket, her left index finger pointing at him. "As I said, you've changed."

He shook his head. How could she flit from one topic to the other so seamlessly? "I have?"

"You never used to be this bossy."

"You never saw me working," he retorted. "Shay can tell you how bossy I am when the safety of the nation or a single person is at stake. I have been instructed to keep you safe. Having anyone know where you are, or someone else staying here as well is one more way for this creep to track you."

She seemingly ignored his last comment. "Are you married?"

"What's that got to do with anything? No, I'm not."

"Girlfriend?"

His scowl deepened. "I don't see how my personal life is any of your business, or at all relevant."

"Yet mine is?"

"*You're* the one in danger here. *You* came to *us* for protection, not the other way around." He took a deep breath as she sat back on the window ledge, almost deflated. His phone vibrated with an incoming text. "Abbie is safe now. The cops will take her home and everything will be fine."

"Fine, yeah, right." Elle rubbed her temples. "I'm sorry. I'm acting like a right moody cow. It's not your fault and I'm taking it out on you as if it is. It's just I feel like I've lost what little control of my life I have. Thank you for finding Abbie."

He took a deep breath and perched on the edge of the window sill next to her. "Tell me about Foster."

"Who is this Foster you keep mentioning? I don't know anyone by that name."

"The bloke I saw you with the other night in the club."

"Oh, him—we only know him as Mr. F, but that could stand for anything. Not much to tell, really. He's been in the club a few times. Seen him talking to Zeke, I've spoken to him twice maybe. But Jake Reid manages the club."

"Zeke is your manager?"

"Yeah. He also manages the club when Jake isn't around."

"Explain something to me." He braced his hands either side of his hips as he leaned against the sill. "How does a Christian end up singing secular stuff in a dive like HC1 every night?"

She shrugged. "I need the money."

"Do you write your own songs?"

"I used to. My first album was all my stuff. Now Zeke does the writing and I just sing what he wants." She sucked in a deep breath. "I haven't written anything in a long time."

"Maybe you should. I'm sure, with a voice like yours, you could get a major record deal without having to lower your standards." He rolled his shoulders. "In fact I'm surprised you do."

"Zeke's been trying to get a recording deal, but no one has been interested. The last album was all him. The new one too—assuming we get it made. Zeke managed to get it bankrolled."

"Who's doing it?"

She shrugged. "Some rich bloke. I don't know. I don't ask."

Patrick frowned. "You don't know who's funding your career?"

"No," she said looking down at her hands.

"But, Elle, you said one time you would only sing for God's glory."

"I'm not asking you to like what I sing or even join in." She shifted uncomfortably. "I don't want to talk about this."

"I do."

"Fine," she whispered. "Maybe I'm not a Christian anymore, all right?"

He hadn't been expecting that and straightened in surprise. "Why not?"

"That is none of your business." She swallowed hard, tossing his own words back at him. "Besides, you're a fine one to talk about morals and standards unbecoming a Christian. And I don't just mean in the past."

"What do you mean, then?"

"I know you own a gun, I've seen it."

He nodded. "Yes. I carry one all the time I'm on duty. I'm an armed officer. It goes with my badge and MI5 ID."

"And you shoot people? Kill them?"

"I prefer to shoot to wound given the choice, but if I have to, then, yes, I would kill. As a matter of fact, I used my gun this morning, in order to stop a man with explosives strapped to his chest from blowing up a shopping center, and half of Headley Cross along with it."

"Isn't there some law against killing people, Patrick? Some commandment or other—the sixth from what I remember. Thou shalt not kill."

"That is between me and God. I don't enjoy shooting people, but as it is part of my job if it needs doing then I do it."

"Same goes for frequenting nightclubs then?"

"Liam wanted me to hear you sing. Not that I knew it was you at the time." Patrick didn't elaborate that he was there working. Again, need to know. And until he had all the pieces put together, she *didn't* need to know. He didn't want to believe the girl he fell in love with all those years ago, was still in love with if he were honest, was capable of the allegations laid against her.

"I meant before, must be a few weeks ago. You came into the nightclub. I wasn't singing that night so you wouldn't have seen me, but I saw you. I assumed the woman you were with was your wife the way you were all over each other. She was definitely tarty."

"*Excuse me?*" He scowled. How dare she talk to him like that? The sweet innocent girl who wouldn't say boo to a goose he'd fallen in love with, had changed beyond recognition over the years. "I beg your pardon?"

"You couldn't even begin to call what she was wearing a dress. More like a belt. It barely covered everything."

His eyes narrowed and he felt his hackles rise. He wanted nothing better than to wipe that smirk off her face.

Help me keep my temper here. Don't let her get under my skin the way she is.

"Are you implying I'd only go out with a tart? What does that make you?" He laughed bitterly. "People who live in glass houses shouldn't throw stones. That outfit you wear on stage leaves very little to the imagination. Not that I need to imagine—"

He broke off as her mouth opened in a horrified, hurt expression. He shouldn't have said that. Biting his tongue before he said any more and regretted it, he calmly left the room, and closed the door behind him. He leaned against door, arms tightly folded against his heaving chest, his breathing heavy and labored.

The phone rang. He pulled it out in exasperation. He growled at it, and then slid it open. "Page."

"It's Nahum. Is everything all right?"

"Everything's fine. Why shouldn't it be?"

"You sound stressed."

"Nothing I can't deal with. Is Abbie home safely?"

"She is. Mrs. Harrison also asked me to pass on the message that her phone has been confiscated."

"Thanks for letting me know."

"We need you to take Miss Harrison to the club tonight as normal. In fact we need her to simply carry on as usual, so long as you escort her everywhere. Shay will need to go with you as much as possible. Don't bring the subject up. Wait for it to come from her, then play hard to get. We don't want her to think we want her there, if that makes any sense at all. The last thing we need is her to think we're suspicious."

"I understand. I'll speak to you tomorrow. Good night." He hung up and slid his phone back into his jeans. *Think we're suspicious?* Bit late for that. Red flags weren't just going up, they were flying loudly in a force ten gale.

What was wrong with Elle? She was acting like— he stopped and shook his head.

She was jealous.

****

Eleanor sat on the bed, head buried in her hands. Tears ran unchecked down her face. She was just a disappointment to everyone. Her mother, Abbie, God, and now Patrick. His words ran rampant through her mind and her answer seemed feeble even to her.

She couldn't tell Patrick about PJ owning the club. She knew something was going on behind the scenes. The rumors of drugs were rife—why else would the club be raided so many times. But she was on the verge of breaking free. A few more deliveries and she'd have enough money to go far away from this place and never have to sing in clubs again. Or the cops would give her a new name, a new life...her and Abbie. She wasn't going to go anywhere or do anything without her. And she was too valuable as a singer for PJ to mix her up in anything illegal, right?

Anyway, Patrick was looking for some bloke named Foster. And she didn't know anyone by that name.

Her conscience berated her, making her feel ten times worse. She shouldn't have sniped back at him. She stood and crossed to the doorway, intending to apologize, again. She opened the door.

A grunt of surprise greeted her as Patrick tumbled backwards through the opening, landing rather unceremoniously on the floor at her feet. His cheeks burned as he looked up at her. He must have been leaning against it.

She gazed down at him. "I'm sorry. Are you all right?"

"I think so." He scrambled to his feet, dusting himself off. "No harm done."

"Good. I wanted to apologize for the way I spoke to you. It was uncalled for. I'm not used to people inquiring after my lack of relationship with God."

He nodded. "But it's important, Elle. Just as important as your health is. If not more so."

She shook her head. "Let's just say I'm past saving and leave it at that."

"No one is past redemption, Elle. God is bigger than that."

She shrugged, really not wanting to have her sins hauled over the coals. Especially this one. Especially not with Patrick, her co-conspirator in the sin, if there even was such a way of phrasing it, standing right in front of her, looking every bit as handsome as he had done years ago. And even if God did somehow forgive her, Patrick wouldn't. She'd had his child and never even attempted to find him to tell him. All she had were excuses. Mum hadn't wanted her to, but she could have defied her, like she had with naming the baby.

She sucked in a deep breath and changed the subject. "I have a favor to ask. I have to go to the club and as my car is at home, I was wondering if you'd be able to take me in. Please."

"I don't think so."

"I have to. If I don't go in, he'll sack me and then Mum will..." she floundered. She had to go in. P.J. expected her and probably had another job for her to do. She just couldn't tell Patrick because he wouldn't understand.

"Your mother will do what? You make her out to be some kind of an ogre."

"Please, Patrick. Let me go in tonight. Don't you think it would tip them off if I don't show? I'll work something out with Zeke. Take some leave perhaps."

Patrick sighed heavily. "I'll check with my boss and make the arrangements. But I tell you for nothing, if he says no, you stay here. And you don't tell anyone you're living anywhere other than at home. Understood?" He pulled out his phone, and turned his back on her.

She turned and went back into the bedroom. Not that she had anything much with her. She had a toothbrush, which was something, and a week's worth of clothes. She hadn't picked up anything to sing in.

"People who live in glass houses shouldn't throw stones. That outfit you wear on stage leaves very little to the imagination."

His words echoed again, drumming home what she'd always thought of her work attire. She hated the slinky dresses. They made her feel cheap and dirty. But that was all she deserved.

She was tormented by images and feelings that, despite her wishes, wouldn't go away. She'd carried

this sin for the last fourteen years, unable to forget—
not that her mother would let her—even if she wanted
to. And after she discovered she was pregnant and
learned Garth died, there was no way out. It was all
linked, every inch her fault and there was no going
back.

Patrick's words floated through the doorway. It
sounded like a heated discussion, but if she weren't
mistaken he was arguing for her rather than against.
Why was that? She'd just angered him, made him fall
on the floor, and yet he was doing his utmost to do
what she wanted.

He turned back towards her, his smile stilted, but
a smile none the less. "You go on the condition Shay
and I come, too."

"Zeke won't like that."

"That is too bad." Patrick slid his phone back into
his pocket. "Soon as Shay gets back, we'll leave."

"Thank you."

"Welcome. See, it just needs a little give and take
on both parts."

"I give and you take?"

He tilted his head, a slight twinkle in his eyes.
"Something like that."

"I'll go change. Not that I have anything "tarty" to
wear."

"So wear something plain and simple. Go for the
understated look."

She glanced down at her jeans and shirt. "In that
case I'll sing as I am."

This time a real smile crossed his lips. "Looks
pretty good to me."

8

Eleanor nodded to Patrick and then headed through the back entrance of the club, while Shay went in through the front as a normal punter. She glanced behind to see him head around the front to join Shay. He'd tried to insist on coming in the back with her, but that would have been wrong. She'd have gotten into trouble for that.

The office door was shut and she heard PJ shouting at Jake as she passed. She glanced into Zeke's office, which was empty, then headed into the bar itself. She shivered as Zeke's gaze ran over her. He didn't approve, and she knew that before he even opened his mouth.

He reached her in several large strides. "You can't sing in jeans and a shirt. Where's your evening dress?"

"I can sing perfectly well like this, and my dress is at home. What I wear isn't going to affect my voice." She pushed past him, to find him grab her arm, his fingers digging in painfully.

"Just remember who you're talking to," he hissed. "I hold the purse strings and the record deal. That can vanish as quickly as you can blink."

"I know that." She kept her voice low, not wanting to worry Patrick. He stood by the bar, keeping his steel gaze on her. Shay had seated herself near the door. "But it still needs cleaning after you spilled that drink down it, therefore I don't have anything to wear. I can't get it to the cleaners for a couple of days yet."

"Then I'll give you an advance and you can go and buy one for tomorrow night." He opened the cash register and pulled out a wad of twenties. He folded them, and leaning forwards, tucked the notes inside her shirt. Her skin crawled and she shuddered. "PJ has given special instructions concerning you, babe. But if you think that makes you invincible, think again."

Her cheeks burned and she turned her face to one side, not wanting to see Patrick's reaction. She slapped Zeke's hand away, then her head jerked as his hand connected sharply with her cheek.

Suddenly Patrick was there. "Elle, are you all right?"

"I'm fine." Her face stung, but she wasn't going to give Zeke the satisfaction of knowing that.

"Do you want to press charges?"

"No, I need to go and get ready."

"OK." He looked at Zeke and lowered his voice. "You raise your hand to her again and I'll have you arrested for assault. No matter what the lady wants."

"I think you need to leave."

Patrick drew himself up to his full height. "If I leave, so does Elle."

Zeke stared at him, smirked, then raked his eyes over her. "Is that so? Is he your boyfriend or something? Are you really going to jump because he says to?"

She swallowed hard. She'd never stood up to him. She'd always been afraid of what he'd do. But now he'd actually hit her? She wasn't so scared. At least, not with Patrick at her side protecting her. "Yeah..." Her voice wavered. She cleared her throat. "Yes."

Zeke's face creased in shock. "I'm sorry?"

"I said yes. I asked Patrick here tonight. If he can't stay, nor can I." She held his gaze. "So, do I sing or do I walk?"

"Sing. Then we discuss this. You, me and the boss. Your boyfriend can wait here for you."

Patrick opened his mouth to argue but Zeke cut him off.

"It's non-negotiable. She won't be more than half an hour."

"Elle…"

"I'll be fine, Patrick." She turned to Zeke. "The meeting sounds thrilling. I can't wait." She pulled the money from inside her shirt and dropped it onto the bar. "I don't need this. As I said, what I wear doesn't affect how I sing. I'm sure the punters won't care either."

She walked over to the microphone to begin the first set. As she sang, she watched Patrick. He sat at the bar, sipping his iced water keeping his eyes alternately on her and everyone else. Shay sat near him but not with him, watching the crowds coming and going.

They made a good pair. Almost as good as she and Patrick once had — with him she'd felt invincible. She'd thought, hoped, prayed that they'd be together forever. But things had turned sour after one night in April and she had been left with no alternative but to run.

Before she realized, the music ended and the audience clapped. Was the first set over already?

She got up and walked across to Patrick, gratefully taking the glass of water he held out to her. "I don't remember any of that." Her hands were shaking

"Well, you knocked their socks off," he said, toasting her.

She chinked her glass against his. "Glad to hear it."

"You honestly don't remember singing?" He leaned forward, concerned.

"No. I assume I didn't fluff the words at all."

He shook his head. "Nope. At least not the ones I knew." He took a long sip. "Do they have the music for any that you wrote?"

"I don't know. Probably not here. Why?"

"I'd like to hear something that you came up with."

She tilted her head, studying him. Was he just playing with her now? Was she just a case to him? Or was he trying to reopen old wounds and continue the conversation from before despite her wishes? She had to keep him at arm's length because if she didn't he'd be back in her heart before she knew it. "Really?"

He nodded. "I expect it'd rock this place. Even if it were a secular one."

"I told you, God and I parted terms…"

He tipped his glass at her. "One thing you need to remember about the Lord, Elle. You may let go of Him, but He *never* lets go of you."

"It's too late," she whispered, grief filling her heart.

"Why?" he asked. "No one is beyond redemption, no matter what they think."

"I am. I can't explain here, but I am."

"You'll have to explain later."

She finished her water. "Maybe not tonight. I'm tired."

"Fair enough, it's been a long day for all of us. But at some point you're going to have to come clean."

She looked down at her empty glass, hesitating.

She didn't want to talk about it at all. Perhaps if she agreed, he'd drop it and then forget about it.

"OK." She touched his hand for a moment, jerking back. She hadn't expected the jolt of electricity to pass between them.

His gaze held hers and then he took her hand. "You felt it too."

"I did, but I can't act on it."

"Why not? We're both adults here. There is nothing stopping us from going out with each other once this is over. Start again, see where we end up."

She sighed. "Patrick, I made a promise to someone and I have to honor it."

He dropped her hand like a lead balloon. "Were you engaged? Are you now?"

"No. Nothing like that. I would have told you if there was someone else when we were together."

"A promise to do what, then? Stay single?"

Sucking in a long deep breath, she stood. "As it happens, yeah."

"A promise? Who to?"

"It doesn't matter," she whispered. "The promise stands. It has to."

She headed back to the stage. But it did matter, because she now knew without a doubt that Patrick had stolen back into her heart where he belonged.

****

Eleanor followed Zeke back to the office. Patrick had made his objections again, but Zeke had over ruled him. She glanced behind as the door shut, seeing Patrick sat at the edge of the bar, eyes trained on her and the door.

"You are treading a fine line here," Zeke told her. "Just because the boss fancies you, doesn't mean—"

"I'm sorry?" She looked at him in amazement. "The boss *what*? I am not involved with Jake."

"I mean PJ. He owns the club. Jake just manages it. Besides, everyone can see it. The cozy chats you have in his office. The huge pay rise he just gave you. Tell me, are you sleeping with him?"

Her hand shot out and slapped him before she realized what she was doing. "How dare you? No, I'm not, and even if I was it'd be none of your business." She stormed ahead, barging into the office without knocking.

PJ jumped at the sudden intrusion and turned, sliding something into his pocket. "Can't you knock...Eleanor, babe." He crossed the room and kissed her cheek. He glanced at the two men in the room and nodded to the man slumped between them. "Get him out of here."

The men nodded, dragging the unconscious man from the room.

Eleanor swallowed hard. Was that Jake? Was that blood on his shirt? Was he dead?

PJ dragged her attention back to him, by kissing her cheek again. "You were great tonight, watched you from here. Your outfit though leaves a lot to be desired. I thought I made it clear you had to sing in a dress. Not dressed like a tramp."

She snorted. "I look more like a tramp in those slinky silver things than I do in this."

Zeke scowled as he shut the door. "I told her she should change. She came up with a pitiful excuse why she couldn't. Her boyfriend even threatened to have me arrested."

"Only after you hit me," Eleanor snapped. She looked at PJ. "What's this about a pay rise?"

"I was going to talk to you about that. And something else. Have a seat. Zeke, leave us. I'll deal with this."

She perched on the edge of the seat, suddenly aware that she was alone with PJ and he was well and truly in her personal space. "I haven't got long tonight."

"Hot date? I assume it's the bloke who's been hanging around."

"Something like that."

He trailed his hand across her shoulders. "Known him long? Is Zeke right about him being your boyfriend?"

"I've known him a while. Years actually, we're old friends. Look, what is this? There is nothing in my contract that says I can't have a boyfriend, is there?"

"No. I'm just looking out for you." PJ sat opposite her. He slid another package over the table. "Keep this for now. I can't have it here."

"What is it?"

"Doesn't matter what it is. Look after it. It's sealed and I want it sealed when I get it back."

She slid it into her bag. "OK. Where do I take it?"

"You don't. Someone will come and pick it up. It's a one off doing it this way. It's perfectly safe, so don't worry." He smiled at her. "While you're here, I wanted to talk to you about your father."

She looked at him. "He's dead. He was killed in a hunting accident several years ago."

"Yes. Tragic, but if you play with fire, then you get burned."

"Huh? You've lost me."

PJ opened a file on his desk. "I thought I might have. I also thought it was time that someone told you the truth about him. Did you know he worked for me?"

She frowned. "That can't be right. Dad was an accountant, nothing to do with the music industry...or bars."

"I haven't always worked in music and nightclubs. I made my money elsewhere. Your father was my accountant when I first started out, a working relationship that lasted until his death. He was a pretty good one too; he'd worked for my father for a few years. That is, until he got greedy and started skimming the books." His eyes hardened and he shut the file with a resounding thud. "Then he decided to run something on the side, and got a little too arrogant. It didn't work."

She shook her head. "I don't understand."

"It was *my* money that put you through college. He worked for me for years. You kept moving because I told him to, to go where I needed him most."

"*What?*" Bile rose in her throat and she twisted her hands. "I thought..." Had her parents lied to her? They'd said it was the embarrassment of her illegitimate child and the shame of her being a nightclub singer. And she'd believed them...

PJ smirked. "Yes, Eleanor. Your father was as corrupt as they come. But a bent accountant has their uses. Hence, he kept working for me, and you kept moving when I needed him elsewhere. And with you singing in my clubs, I could keep tabs on you as well."

"Oh..."

"You can go far if you do what I tell you." His hand reached over the desk and ran up her arm.

"Record deals are just the tip of the iceberg."

She pulled her arm back, not wanting to talk about her father any longer. She needed to assimilate what she'd been told and she couldn't do that here.

"I need some time off." She took a deep breath. She hated lying but didn't have much of a choice. Patrick would never go for her coming here every night, not matter how much she begged. Once had been pushing it. "Looks like I need to babysit the next few nights and as I can't bring my sister here, then I need to stay at home with her."

"No can do. You'll need to find a babysitter. Hey…" he winked at her. "Maybe the boyfriend could do it. Zeke said he took her the other night. I'm sure he'd oblige."

"I can't ask him."

PJ looked thoughtful for a moment, then smirked at her. "If he loves you as much as it appears he does, he'll do anything for you. Ask him. I'll see you tomorrow."

****

Driving back to the safe house, Patrick glanced in the driving mirror at the two women in the back of the car. Shay was ever vigilant. Elle, on the other hand, had her eyes closed, exhausted, no doubt, by the twists and turns the day had taken. Totally understandable. He'd been pushed to the limit the last few days, without the emotional strain of Elle being thrust back into his life again.

Should he have tried harder to find her? What had happened to cause such a change in her? She only ever seemed to come to life when she sang.

He shot Shay a barely perceptible nod before he turned his attention back to the road.

Just as Nahum expected, Elle had pushed to go to the club. Just as planned, he objected then relented. He refused to believe Elle was involved in this drug ring, and the best way to clear her was to keep appearances as normal as possible and keep her singing. Not that he liked the way she dressed or the lyrics she chose. But it was her choice and she wasn't prepared to discuss her faith, or lack of it, with him right now. He wasn't going to let it drop, however. The fate of her soul hung in the balance.

Lord, Elle needs my help. Not just to keep her safe from Foster if that's who this Mr. F turns out to be, but to guide her back to You. I don't know what she thinks she did that was so terrible, but the very fact she says she's beyond redemption, indicates to me at least, that she hasn't done anything that unforgivable.

He glanced at her again. His feelings for her hadn't changed, yet he knew deep down there wasn't a chance of anything developing between them. And it wasn't just the fact he didn't have time.

She didn't want him anymore. Her attitude towards him made that perfectly clear. Well, that wasn't going to stop him from loving her, looking out for her, and protecting her to the best of his ability.

Whether she liked the idea or not.

And as for the fight with her manager? Someone in the club had threatened Elle, and he had a good idea now who it was. Whether he was involved in the drug ring or not, Zeke had just put himself on the MI5 radar. If Patrick had tipped his hand, it would have exposed Elle and that wasn't going to happen—at least not yet. He had a role to play here, and it *wasn't* to look threatening. Thus he'd sat back down at the bar and waited. He'd bide his time, then this Zeke bloke would pay for hitting Elle.

He parked outside the safe house and secured the area before nodding to Shay. She woke Eleanor and together they escorted her inside the house as quickly as possible.

Shay looked at Patrick. "I don't know about you, but I'm shattered. You all right if I go to bed?"

Patrick nodded. "Sure. I need to unwind for a bit first anyway."

"OK, good night." She headed up the stairs.

Eleanor looked at him. "Bit early to go to bed, isn't it?"

"We've worked pretty much every hour there is since Monday," he explained. "The case culminated in a raid and shootout this morning. The last time I actually saw a bed was Sunday night."

"But it's Thursday. How did you manage?"

"Cat napped at the desk. It's just the way it goes sometimes."

"If you want to sleep…"

He stifled a yawn. "In a bit. Once Nigel gets here."

Her face creased. "Who's Nigel? I thought you and Shay were my guard dogs."

He grimaced at her derogatory tone. He'd have preferred sheep dog given the choice. "He's doing the nightshift. He'll sit in the lounge and watch TV."

"OK. Silly question, but why can't you sleep now?"

"Because if I'm asleep, I can't protect you." He broke off as his phone rang. "Shame I don't get paid extra to answer this," he quipped. "Page." He listened for a moment. "What's wrong? Oh, no, is she all right?

I see. OK, no, no, you stay home and make sure she rests up. We'll manage. Yes—Give Laura a hug from me and tell her to go to bed and stay there. OK. Good night."

"What's up?" Her hand touched his arm, sending rivers of warmth pouring through him and straight to his stomach.

"That was Nigel. He's been at the hospital with his wife most of the afternoon."

"That's not good. Is she all right?"

Patrick nodded his head. Nigel and Laura had been trying for a baby for years. And a scare like this was the last thing either of them needed. "As long as she rests, she'll be fine. So I'll go take a cold shower to wake up some and then make a pot of coffee."

"There's no need. You don't need to watch me. I'm tired. If I go to bed, you can lock up and sleep, too. This is a *safe* house, right? No one knows where we are?"

"Yeah..." What was she getting at? Maybe he was more tired than he thought. Or she just didn't understand. Surely she wasn't that naïve?

"So we'll be fine. Lock up. Go to bed and sleep. You look exhausted. I trust you not to let anything happen. Good night."

He stood in the hall, completely dumbfounded, as she crossed the small space to the stairs and vanished up them. Locking the front door, he then pulled the heavy curtain across it and flicked off the light.

This Elle was a paradox. Just when he though he'd figured her out, she blindsided him with something else. Maybe the old Elle was still there. The Elle he'd fallen in love with, and still was in love with. But she'd made it clear she didn't feel the same way. He could live with that. Couldn't he?

He went upstairs, showered and returned to the sofa fully dressed. At least this way he'd be on guard, albeit asleep.

Lord God, keep watch over us tonight.

9

Eleanor woke as the sun peered over the horizon. She got out of bed and crossed to the window. There was something about the sunrise that drew her to it. A new dawn with the promise of a clean slate awaited everyone. Except her. She was doomed to keep repeating the mistakes of the past. Like Patrick.

She leaned her forehead against the cold glass. There was an apple tree in the garden. Memories of another apple tree from long ago came to mind.

Patrick grinned down at her. "It's not that hard, see. If I can climb up here, then anyone can."

She looked up at him. "That's easy for you to say now you're up there. What if I fall?"

"You won't."

"What if I get stuck?"

"You won't."

"Can you say anything other than you won't?"

There was a long pause. "Nope."

"Fine, but if I get stuck I'm blaming you."

"You won't."

She reached up, pulling herself onto the first branch. "That response is getting a little tiresome. I'm going to fall."

"Then the sooner you get up here, the better. These apples are delicious."

"I thought it was the woman who tempted the man with the apple," she said, breathing hard as she climbed laboriously upwards.

"It was. And I'm not tempting you. I'm enticing you. That's a totally different kettle of fish all together."

She glanced up into the leafy boughs, finally seeing his feet swinging above her. "Fish, too? Is there anything you don't have up there?"

"That would be you." He laughed.

Her whole body now shaking with effort, she reached the branch he was sitting on and lowered herself down beside him. She closed her eyes tightly, her breath coming in gasps.

"Was it that hard to climb up here?"

She shook her head, holding on tightly. "No…"

"Then what is it?"

His hand touched her face making her jump. She cried out, only her tight grip stopping her from falling.

"Elle?"

"Don't like heights…"

His strong arms folded around her, his scent and warm breath covering her. "Why didn't you say something, you silly goose?"

"You were already here, and I didn't want you to call me a scaredy-cat."

"Elle, I would never call you a scaredy-cat."

A thud made her jump. "What was that?"

"I tossed the pack down so I can help you. We'll do this one step at a time."

"I can't."

"You can because I'm helping you." He slid down on to the next branch. "Now do exactly what I say and we'll be down before you know it."

She smiled, turning away from the window. True to his word, he had guided her down, step by step, never letting her fall. Everything had been so simple then. He promised he'd keep her safe, she trusted him, she loved him, and she'd hoped he'd be the one man she'd spend the rest of her life with.

So much for that idea.

She left the bedroom and headed down to the kitchen. Today was a new day. Once again her life was in Patrick's hands, and she knew she was safe. And he was right, if she had a target on her back, Abbie was safest with Mum. She had to let him do his job. And she'd start by making up to him for being horrible yesterday.

The kitchen was warm and smelled of freshly-brewed coffee. Someone was already up judging by the scent.

She opened the fridge. *Good, there are eggs. Now all I need is flour.* Finding some in the cupboard, she began to make batter. She had no idea if Shay liked pancakes, but Patrick did. So did Abbie.

Abbie—

She'd never been apart from her for this long before and it felt like she was drowning. *I need to see her, somehow. This separation is tearing me up inside. Please, God...*

Eleanor broke off. She had no right to ask anything.

"Morning." Patrick stumbled into the room, looking dreadful. Pale and gaunt, with stubble over his cheeks, he still wore the same clothes as yesterday.

"You look awful."

"Thanks." He moved to the coffee pot and filled a cup. Draining it quickly, he refilled it.

"Did you sleep at all?"

"After Shay woke, a little, not much." He smiled faintly over the top of the cup. "Honestly I spent most of the night thinking about you."

"Me?"

"Yeah." He took a deep breath. "Praying for you."

"That's very kind, but I'm really not worthy of your prayers. They won't do much good. I'm unforgivable."

"You keep saying that." He finished the coffee and poured more. "You do know what the unforgivable sin is, right?"

"Of course I do." She flipped the pancakes, not wanting them to burn. "I wish…"

"Wish what?"

How did she phrase this? It really made no sense. She'd thrown away her salvation, but she wanted it back? "I envy you your faith," she said quietly.

"It does make life bearable. Knowing that whatever happens, God is in control and I can take everything to Him in prayer. Knowing He has my back at work and off duty as well."

She poured more batter onto the griddle. "How dangerous is your job?"

Shay laughed from the doorway. "The way Patrick does it? It's very dangerous." She came in and helped herself to coffee. "He almost got us all blown up yesterday. Along with the Hyacinth Street Mall and half of Headley Cross."

"I did not." Patrick protested, refilling his coffee mug.

"You did."

"Didn't."

Eleanor laughed as she carried the plate of pancakes over to the table. "That's the Patrick I remember. Come eat while they're hot." She looked at Shay. "I need to apologize to you both for my behavior yesterday. I wasn't very nice to you. It was a bad day and…" She broke off. "No, I'm not making excuses. I was horrid and I'm sorry."

Shay smiled. "Apology accepted."

"Apologies in pancakes are gratefully received." Patrick sat, not needing to be told twice. "I haven't had pancakes since you last made them for me."

Eleanor sat next to him. "Seriously? What about Pancake Day?"

He shook his head, taking three and covering them with lemon juice and sugar. "Nope. I could never make them the way you do."

"It's not that hard, really." She watched the look of pleasure on his face as he ate. "Think someone died and went to heaven," she teased.

He grinned. "Oh, I think you'll find heaven beats your pancakes by a long chalk."

"Really? And what is a long chalk when it's at home?" She laughed as Patrick spread his arms as wide as he could.

"About this big."

As the laughter died down, she ate slowly. Being with Patrick was so easy. Could she put the past behind her? Could they become friends at least? She'd like that. Maybe over the next couple of days that would happen—but could she ever tell him the truth? And not just about Abbie...All of it.

Clearing her plate, she studied him. With his sleep tousled hair and blue eyes shadowed with worry, he looked so much like Abbie. Had he guessed the truth? What would he do if he knew? Demand custody? Want access? Weekends and Christmas, four weeks in the summer?

How would a man who, by his own admission worked every hour God gave him, fit a teenager into his life? No, he had no time for Abbie or her. It wasn't going to happen.

"Penny for them," he said setting down his fork.

"I was thinking about Abbie. Is there any chance I could see her?"

"We talked about this yesterday."

"Please, Patrick…"

"She's safer with her mother."

She looked down at her hands, picking at her index finger. *But I am her mother.*

The phone rang. "Excuse me." Patrick stood and pulled his phone from his pocket, answering it as he headed from the room.

Eleanor pushed her chair back and started taking the plates over to the sink. She ran the hot water, watching the washing up liquid turn into bubbles.

Shay brought over the rest of the dishes. "You have a special relationship with your sister, despite the age gap."

She smiled. "Yeah. We've always been really close. She's a great kid."

"I'm like that with my sister. We can talk about anything. Some days it's us against the world."

"Exactly. If I'm not there she has no one to talk to. She needs me. And I need her."

"Elle—" Patrick's voice came from behind her.

Did she keep fighting the battle over her name? Her mother insisted on Eleanor and nothing else now, but the way he called her Elle sent perfumed flowers spinning into the air. It reminded her of a time when she was young and carefree.

She turned around and smiled. The smile died on her lips as she took in the look of devastation on his face. Maybe something had happened to his brother. She reached his side in a few seconds. "What is it?

What's happened?"

"There's been an accident. Your mum and Abbie have been taken by air ambulance to Headley General."

Her knees buckled. Her skin turned cold and clammy and a rock dropped her stomach into her feet. The air ambulance was funded solely by voluntary donations, and thus was only used in the most serious life-threatening cases.

"Whoa…" Patrick's hands caught her and guided her to a chair.

"I'm all right," she whispered. "What happened?"

"Your mum's car left the road and went down the embankment."

"I have to go to them."

"I know." His hand pushed the hair from her face, his eyes—Abbie's eyes—staring into hers. "Give me five minutes to shower, shave and change."

"Patrick, please…" Her voice was almost a whine, tears in her eyes.

"Five minutes." He glanced over her head at Shay. "I'll need you to drive. Then I can sit in the back with Elle."

"That's fine. Go change."

Patrick hurried from the room and Eleanor buried her face in her hands. *Please don't let them die. I may not like her but she's my mum…and I love her.*

10

Headley General Emergency Department was busy. Eleanor stood in the queue at the reception desk, her fear rising all the time. Every minute she stood here, was a minute Abbie was without her. If she lost Abbie, she didn't know what she'd do. She looked at Patrick. "I'm scared."

"Why?" he asked gently.

"I don't want to be alone."

"You're not alone, Elle. I'm here and God's here, too. Neither of us are going anywhere."

"All right." She nodded ever so slightly, but didn't sound convinced.

More minutes passed and still they hadn't moved. Eleanor looked at the clock. "How much longer...?" she whispered.

"This is ridiculous," Patrick said. "Come with me." He pulled his ID from his pocket and, taking her hand, queue jumped. "Excuse me." He flashed his MI5 card at the receptionist and gave her a charming smile. "Agent Page, MI5."

Eleanor cringed inside, feeling the disapproval of the others waiting in line.

"Can I help you?" the receptionist asked.

"We're looking for a Mrs. Harrison. I had a phone call saying she and her daughter Abbie had been admitted."

The receptionist nodded. "I'll get someone to come and see you."

Patrick lowered his voice. "We don't have time to wait. I need to see her now."

"Just give me a moment please, sir. Take a seat."

He sighed in exasperation and lowered his voice even more. "Do the words 'national security' mean anything to you?"

Eleanor would have laughed had the situation been different as the receptionist's attitude changed completely. Her mother and sister had nothing to do with national security and Patrick hadn't even implied they did, but merely mentioning the two words was as effective as saying open sesame.

"Would you like to come to the door? I'll get a nurse to take you through."

"Thank you."

Eleanor gripped his hand tightly. "Come with me, Patrick."

"That goes without saying, Elle." He glanced at Shay. "Are you coming with us or staying here?"

"I'll come. Guard one while you take Eleanor to see the other."

"Assuming they aren't in adjoining cubicles or both in Resus."

Eleanor walked numbly to the door. Each scenario in her head was worse than the previous one. They were fine and just needed a lift home. Or both had cuts and bruises. Or whiplash. Or concussion. Or numerous broken bones. Or amnesia. Maybe amputations. Or they were dead.

The door opened. "Agent Page?"

Patrick nodded. "Yes. This is Eleanor Harrison, daughter and sister. And Agent Williams."

"Sister Anderson. I'm the chief nurse here. Come on through."

"How are they?" Eleanor asked.

"Your mother is in Resus," Sister Anderson said as they walked down the short hallway. "We're waiting to take her up to surgery. She's bleeding internally and has a ruptured spleen. Her legs were pretty badly broken."

"And Abbie?"

"Cuts and bruises, mainly. She's broken her arm, some pain in her stomach."

"Can I see Abbie first?"

"It might be better if you spoke to your mum first." Sister Anderson lowered her voice, her tone concerned.

"How did the accident happen, do you know?"

"The police wanted to know when you arrived. They need to talk to you about that."

"Oh, right."

Sister Anderson pushed open the huge door into the busy resuscitation room. She led them over to one of the beds. An IV hung over the top, machines whirred. A doctor in scrubs, with a stethoscope slung around the back of his neck, examined the open fracture on one leg.

Eleanor swallowed hard, bile rising in her throat.

"Tony, this is Eleanor Harrison, her daughter."

The doctor looked up. "Tony Peterson, ED consultant."

Eleanor nodded. "How is she?"

"Pretty seriously injured. She's in and out of consciousness. Once there's an operating room free, we'll take her up."

She glanced down at the figure on the gurney.

"Mum…"

The eyes flickered open in the cut and swollen face. "Eleanor…"

"I'm here." She would have taken her hand, but her mother had always resisted physical contact.

Patrick let go of her hand. "You talk to her. I'm not going anywhere."

She moved closer to the bed. "You're going to be fine."

Her mother shook her head. "No…"

"Don't say that."

"I wronged Abbie and you. I'm sorry."

She tried to respond, but didn't know what to say. She'd never heard her mother apologize for anything before. "I don't…"

"Let me, finish. It was the only way to deal with it. Make him pay for what he did. But I was wrong to take it out on you all those years. Two wrongs don't make a right. History repeating itself."

"What do you mean? I don't understand. You're not making any sense. Make who pay?"

"Your dad… There's a letter in the firebox. It explains what he did."

Dr. Peterson came back over. "We need to take her to surgery now."

Eleanor nodded. "OK. See you later, mum. Love you."

Her mother suddenly reached out and grabbed her hand. "Look after Abbie. She's yours… I'm sorry."

She stood there for a moment as they wheeled her mother away. Taking a deep breath, she tried to shake off the feeling of foreboding and unease the strange conversation had left her with.

Her mother didn't apologize for anything, never

mind bringing up Abbie.

What could her father done that was so terrible? Could what PJ have said been correct? Had her father been a criminal and on the run?

Turning to the nurse, she was pleased to see Patrick still there. Although she hoped he hadn't overheard the conversation with her mother. "Can we go see Abbie now?"

Down the hall, Shay stood on guard outside a cubicle. Abbie sat on the bed, a bandage wrapped around her head and her left arm in plaster. Her face streaked with tears. "Ellie…"

Eleanor sat on the bed and hugged her tightly. "Hey, squirt. I came as soon as I could. Are you doing all right?"

"Do I look all right?"

"I've seen worse. There's a man out there with both legs in plaster."

"Where's mum? They won't tell me how she is."

"They've taken her to surgery. She's badly hurt. Do you remember what happened?"

"We crashed." She rolled her eyes in a typical teen fashion.

"I know, sweetie, but how did you crash? Did Mum lose control, go too fast?"

Abbie didn't answer. "They want me to stay in overnight. I don't want to. I want to go home."

Surprised by the sudden change of topic, Eleanor looked at Patrick. "Then I'll stay too, we both will. We can sleep in the chairs next to your bed."

Abbie glanced up at Patrick and rubbed a hand over her face. "What's he doing here?"

"I thought you liked Patrick? He brought me in to see you."

"Well, Mum said you're living with him now and not us anymore." She cut her eyes over to Patrick.

Eleanor could feel Patrick's eyes burning into the back of her head without looking at him. She hadn't told anyone where she was. Not that he would believe her if she said as much. Question was, how did her mother know? "I'm not living with him, Abbie. At least not like that."

"Then what is it like?"

"First let me ask you something. How did Mum find out about Patrick?"

"You sent a text from his phone yesterday. Said you were staying at his for work."

Eleanor exchanged a horrified look with Patrick. "Yeah, but you always read and delete your messages, don't you? Like I told you too?"

"Yeah...'cept this time as I was about to, Mum came into the bedroom and found the phone."

She closed her eyes for a moment and sucked in a deep breath. "It's too complicated to explain and I'm not supposed to talk about it anyway, but I'm staying in a safe house with him and his partner for a few days. Patrick's a government agent."

Abbie's eyes grew round. "Like the FBI? Cool."

She smiled as Patrick chuckled. "Pretty similar. He works for MI5 as an agent, but you cannot tell a soul. Only you and I know. And you can't tell anyone I'm not at home either."

Abbie kept looking at Patrick. "Does that make you like James Bond?"

"Only better looking." Patrick winked at her. "My brother and sister, have always called me 3.14. And now they and my partner call me Agent 3.14, so I'm way cooler than 007."

"Why did they pick that number?"

"It's because my nickname is Pi."

"Oh, the math thing."

"Exactly. Pi being 3.141592 and so on. I play dumb. They don't think I ever worked it out, but I did."

"How do you know pi to so many decimal places?"

Patrick grinned. "How I wish I could calculate pi. Each word is the next number in the sequence—you count the letters to get the number. How, three, I, one, wish, four and so on."

Abbie counted quietly then beamed. "That is so cool." She tilted her head. "Why didn't you tell your brother and sister you knew why they called you that?"

"It's far more fun this way, but I suspect they know."

Eleanor's soul twinged watching the easy way Patrick spoke to Abbie and put her at her ease. He'd make a great father. But he'd never forgive her either.

"But why's Ellie staying with you and not at home?"

Eleanor took a deep breath. "He's my bodyguard for a few days."

"Why?"

"I already told you it's kind of complicated."

Abbie frowned. "More secrets?"

"Sorry?"

"You. Mum. Too many secrets in our house. I hate it. Does it have anything to do with those men?"

"What men?" Patrick sat on the bed next to her. "Can you tell me about them?"

"They came to the house last night, looking for Ellie. I didn't like the man who did the talking. He shouted a lot. I'd never seen him before, but Mum called him Rick. She told him Ellie had moved in with her boyfriend. They didn't go away like she wanted them to. They sat outside the house in their car all night."

Eleanor caught her breath. Oh...the package. Was that what they wanted? She'd forgotten all about it. "Did you tell anyone?"

"No. Mum was mad at you, didn't want her to get crosser. Then this morning there was a weird phone call before we left for school."

"Oh..." she whispered.

Patrick silenced her with a glance. "Tell me about the phone call."

"I answered in case it was you, Ellie. This man wanted to speak to you, he sounded like the guy from the club. You know the one that wouldn't let me stay. I told him you weren't there. He shouted at me and demanded to speak to mum. I gave her the phone, but after she spoke to him, she got all funny and insisted we had to leave. She knew him, Ellie. Then the car from outside the house followed us."

Abbie stopped. She took a deep breath. "It drove us off the road. Hit us several times like in a film. We rolled over and over across the carriageway and then down the hill."

Tears filled her eyes and Eleanor wrapped her arms tightly around her. "It's all right now. You're safe." She glanced at Patrick. "We need to get her out of here."

Patrick nodded. "Let me go and speak to her doctor and make a phone call. Shay is right outside the curtain."

"OK."

Eleanor sat quietly with Abbie, holding her as she cried. "You did very well talking to him. He might need to get you to describe the men, can you do that?"

"Yeah. Photographic memory."

"I know."

"Is mum going to be all right?"

"I don't know."

The curtain moved and Patrick came back in. "Right, that's everything sorted. You're both coming back with me. Abbie, your doctor says that long as you rest you don't need to stay in overnight. But if you get a headache or stomachache you need to tell me or Elle immediately."

"I will. Thank you."

"Welcome." He held up a white paper bag. "He's also given me some pills for you and said he'd ring when your mum comes out of surgery."

****

Patrick sat in the car beside his partner with the mirror angled so he could watch Elle and Abbie as Shay drove them back to Elle's place. Abbie would need her stuff if she was going to move in as well. Nahum was sending a team in to dust for prints and do a fingertip search of the entire house, once they had picked up a few things for Abbie. He wanted to get in and out first as it would be best if Elle and Abbie didn't see that.

Shay parked and turned to look at the others. "I'll sit out here. You've got five minutes to pack what you need."

Abbie continued to complain. "Why can't we stay here, Ellie?"

"It's not safe. Let's go pack your things."

Patrick escorted them up the path, moving them as fast as he could. He kept an eye on the street while Elle unlocked the door, and then chivvied them inside. "I'll wait here. Don't take too long."

"We won't."

He watched as they headed up the stairs, their voices and footsteps echoing. A sudden thought occurring to him, he crossed over to the phone and checked the answerphone. No messages. Wrapping a hanky around the receiver, he pulled his sleeve over his hand and dialed one-four-seven-one to get the number of the last person to have rung the house.

It listed a mobile number calling at eight fifteen. He wrote it down and hung up.

Heavy footsteps sounded above him, followed by Abbie's hissed complaint. "I don't want to stay with him. He's bossy."

"He's paid to be bossy. And we don't have a choice," came Elle's reply. "It isn't *his* house anyway."

"I want to stay here."

"Well, you can't."

"Well, you're not my mother. You can't tell me what to do."

There was a pause before Elle replied. Her voice wobbled more than it usually did when she was upset. "I'm your sister and until mum comes home, I'm in charge. Patrick did you a favor by getting you out of the hospital. Don't be mean." She paused. "Abbie, it's been a bad day for all of us. You got in a car crash, Mum's hurt, you're hurt. Someone tried to kill you. Patrick just wants to make sure they don't try again."

He glanced up the stairs. They'd get nowhere fast by arguing. "Ladies? Time's up," he called. "We need to go."

"Coming."

"Why aren't we staying in your house?" Abbie asked.

Patrick smiled at them as they came down the stairs. "It's only got the one bedroom. The place we're staying in is much bigger. It has a garden and a swing. And my partner, Shay is staying there, too."

"Is Shay your girlfriend?" Abbie put her pack down on the floor by her feet and rubbed her arm above the cast.

"Abbie." Elle scowled at her. "Partner doesn't just mean girlfriend."

He smiled. "No, it's all right. Shay isn't my girlfriend. She's a colleague from work. I don't have a girlfriend."

"Why not? Did you get dumped because you're too bossy?"

"Not exactly. She vanished without saying goodbye." He glanced over at Elle and she ignored him. Just as well. This was one conversation they needed to have alone and not in front of her sister.

Abbie frowned, hugging her good arm to her stomach. "That wasn't very nice of her."

"No it wasn't."

"Bad enough she dumped you without at least saying bye or yelling at you first."

Elle blushed and Patrick hoped that Abbie wouldn't ask any more questions.

"Can I take your bag for you, Abbie?"

"Thank you." She picked up the pack and gave it to him.

Elle hefted the huge firebox in her hands. "Think we have everything."

He nodded. "That's good. Let me take that."

"It's fine, Patrick. I've got it."

"I'm taking it." Before she could argue, he took the box from her and eased Abbie's bag in his other hand. "OK, let me put this in the car first, then I'll come back for you."

"We'll come with you."

"No you won't," he said firmly. "Abbie come now, and I'll come back for Elle."

Abbie nodded, walking with him. "Why do you call her Elle? No one else does."

"I knew her a long time ago. When we were at university."

"Really? Maybe you could tell me about it some time. She never talks about when she was younger."

"Sure I will. Get in the car." He nodded to Shay, who eased up off the side of the car and opened the door.

"Thank you." Abbie slid slowly into the back seat, wincing as she did.

"Does it hurt very much?" Shay asked.

Abbie nodded.

Patrick looked at her. "I'll give you some of the meds the doc gave me when we get to the house." He put the box and bag in the boot of the car and went back towards the house. As he got there his phone rang. He ignored it as he caught sight of Elle standing in the hallway. She looked completely bereft. He crossed over to her. "Hey."

She moved into his arms, almost an automatic reflex. He hugged her tightly. Memories rushed over him, holding her, kissing her, just spending time with the only person, other than God, to complete him. His body stirred, feelings he'd long since forgotten springing to life. "Elle," he whispered.

She looked up, her lips inches away from his.

He leaned in, his forehead touching hers, her breath warm on his cheek. "I missed you. So very much."

"I missed you, too."

His lips brushed against hers. He hesitated, then pulled her close to him, kissing her. She parted her lips allowing him to deepen the kiss, her hands moving over his back.

Time stood still for a moment, transporting him back fourteen years to a time when all that mattered was Elle and her love for him. The phone vibrated again, it's ringing interrupting the moment.

Disappointment flooded him as she pulled back, her cheeks coloring and her fingers rising to her lips. "I...You better answer that."

He pulled out the phone. "Page."

"It's Nahum. Where are you?"

"Collecting clothes and things for Abbie from the Harrison's house. Why?"

"You didn't answer your phone."

"I had my hands full. What's up?"

"Jeanette Harrison died fifteen minutes ago."

"No." Shock speared him, numbing him. He turned to face Elle, not sure how he was going to tell her.

"You can take the daughters in tomorrow if they want to see her. For now just take them to the safe house."

"Will do. Thanks for the call." He hung up. "Elle..."

"What is it?"

"It's your mum. I'm sorry. She died a few minutes

ago." He wrapped his arms around her as she whimpered. Then held her as she cried.

11

Eleanor sat in the lounge at the safe house. The firebox stood open in front of her, papers strewn across the lacquered and stained surface of the table. Behind her, Patrick and Shay talked quietly. Abbie sat watching TV and sniffling. Frustration and helplessness filled her. She'd wanted to go straight to the hospital, but Patrick had refused. He promised to take her in tomorrow, but that was too late. Now was too late, but she wanted to see her mum, even if she wasn't there anymore.

The constant sniffing got on her already frayed nerves and she snapped. "Please don't sniff. Use a tissue."

"I'll sniff if I want to," Abbie muttered. "It's your fault she's dead."

Eleanor turned to look at her. "Mine?"

"Those men were looking for you. If you'd been at home instead of here..."

Patrick rose and crossed the room, sitting beside Abbie. "Speaking of those men, if I showed you some pictures, could you tell me if you've seen any of them before?"

Abbie nodded. "Ellie suggested I describe them. I've got an eye for detail. I could give you the make and model of the car, too."

"That would be really good. But first let's look at the pictures on my phone."

Abbie nodded, leaning down over his phone.

Eleanor tuned them out, concentrating on the papers. She was looking for this letter her mother mentioned, or a copy of a will or solicitor's letters. Anything that looked like it could shed some light on things or looked important. She pulled out an envelope with her name written in her mother's neat handwriting.

Her hands trembled as she opened the seal. Could this be the letter Mum mentioned? The one about her dad? She drew out two folded pieces of lined paper and what looked like two certificates. Carefully she opened the letter.

Dear Eleanor,

There is no easy way to say this, but I want you to know the truth. Your father was a criminal. He was not the man you thought he was. Although I was strict, and you resented me for it, you were my daughter and I love you. I just didn't want you to turn out like your birth mother, and like him. You have been a good daughter and although I didn't say it, you made my life happy when you brought Abbie into it.

Your birth mother's name was Rachel. I adopted you after her death…

Eleanor dropped the letter. Her insides knotted and a huge lump formed in her throat. She was *adopted*? The last conversation with her mother suddenly made sense. She unfolded the two official documents.

The first was her birth certificate. It named her father and a Rachel Foster as her mother. *Foster*…wasn't that the name Patrick kept mentioning?

The second was her adoption certificate.

A stifled wail ripped from her throat, her hand

clamping over her mouth in an effort to control it. Blood pounded in her head. She began to shake.

No wonder she hated me. I wasn't hers. Just a constant reminder of something Dad did.

Patrick looked at her. "What's wrong, Elle? Are you all right?"

Not wanting a fuss at all, never mind in front of Abbie, she inclined her head a little. "Yeah, I'm fine. Abbie, it's late. High time you were in bed."

"I don't want to go to bed."

"That's just too bad. You need to rest remember, and it really is late."

"I'm fine here, thank you very much. Watching the TV with Patrick."

"Please, Abbie, it's been a really long day."

Abbie folded her good arm over her chest and didn't move.

Elle looked back down at the letter, needing to learn more about this deep, dark secret. Learn more about this bomb that had just been dropped in her lap and exploded in her face. The words ran into each other as she read. Her stomach twisted and spun as her world, turned upside down since she got up that morning, disintegrated into a million tiny pieces.

Finally finishing the letter, she looked up. "Are you still here?"

"I have nowhere else to go," Abbie retorted.

"Bed."

"What if the men come back or something else happens? I want Mum."

Patrick got to his feet. "Abbie, I promise nothing is gonna happen tonight. How about I take you upstairs, and we find your room. I'll check it out, look in the wardrobe, under the bed. We can also leave your door open so the light from the landing comes in if you like. That way if you need someone you can just shout. Shay and I are both here all night along with another agent. You'll be perfectly safe while you sleep, I promise."

"All right."

"Come on, then. Say good night to your sister. We'll find your pain meds and get you settled. Your room is right across the hall from Elle's."

Abbie tucked her rag doll into her sling and got up slowly. She crossed the room and hugged her one handed. "Good night, Ellie. I love you."

"Good night, squirt. I love you, too."

Watching the two of them leave, her heart grieved for the life that never was. *How different things could have been if I hadn't left him.* She looked over at Shay. You and Patrick seem pretty close."

"We are, but we're just colleagues, nothing more. Patrick doesn't have time for anything other than work. Between you and me, it's like he's hiding from real life."

"He used to go out a lot. At least when..." She broke off. "It's just you two get on so well."

"Patrick's an easy bloke to get along with. He's charming, sweet, a real gentleman. It's not often you find someone in our line of work who's not tainted by what we have to do. His faith carries him through a lot. But even if he wasn't married to his job, I'm in love with my husband, and wouldn't break my marriage vows under any circumstances."

"Your husband doesn't mind you hanging with him or staying here?"

Shay smiled. "This is what I do. Kevin understands. Besides he's in the army, so he can be away for months at a time. Right now he's in Cyprus."

"That must be hard." She looked down at the letter in her hand.

"It is sometimes. But, Kevin was in the army when I met him. I knew what I was getting into. Just like he knew what I did. Neither of us would change it for the world. What about you and Patrick? I understand you've known each other a long time."

Her fingers traced the crease on the paper. "Yeah. We go way back. I knew him, rather went out with him, for a year at university. Then I left and never saw him again. Until now."

"Why not?"

"We didn't part on very good terms."

"What happened?"

She shifted, the letter creasing in her hand. "The kind of 'ruins your life' stuff I don't want to talk about."

"OK." Shay inclined her head and her eyes narrowed.

Had she said too much? She kept forgetting these people were spies. Besides what happened between her and Patrick was no one's business but their own.

"I'm going to go make some tea." Eleanor shoved the papers back into the firebox and locked it. She headed into the kitchen, Shay behind her. This was going to get tiring very quickly. At least Patrick didn't follow her everywhere.

If I could change things, I would. But I can't. It's too late.

As she sat sipping her tea, Patrick came into the kitchen. She smiled at him. "Is she all right?"

Patrick poured himself a mug of coffee and sat opposite her. "Yeah, she is. I told her you'd be up in a while."

Eleanor sat quietly. She looked at the custard cream biscuit and slowly pulled it apart. She scraped her nail through the cream filling. "Thank you." This was how it should be, Patrick tucking in his daughter at night, the two of them having time...

Patrick put a hand on her arm. "I need you to talk to me, Elle and tell me what's going on. All of it."

She shifted in her chair. "I'm not in the mood to talk."

"Elle, whoever is after you has killed your mother, hurt Abbie, and has threatened you."

"Don't you think I know that?" She sucked in a deep breath and lowered her voice, not wanting Abbie to overhear and get upset. "I know that they hurt Abbie and killed...Mum."

Trembling fingers snapped the biscuit in half. They needed to know and there was no easy way to say it, other than blurt it out. "Jeanette Harrison wasn't my birth mother."

Patrick and Shay exchanged shocked glances. "What?" he asked.

"Mum said to get the firebox, as there was a letter in there for me telling me about my father. I found it and... and there are papers in that box, my birth and adoption certificates. She wasn't my mother. And all this is my father's fault." The avalanche of tears she'd been holding onto for so long began to fall. She shoved her chair back, and ran from room.

****

Patrick sat there for an instant, before setting off after her, leaving Shay to clear kitchen. He took the cups with him. He knew Elle was still downstairs as he hadn't heard the front door open or the stairs creak. If he had to guess, she'd be in the lounge in front of the fire.

Peering into the lounge, he smiled as he saw her. "You're a creature of habit, Elle. You're sat in your thinking place, even if the fire isn't on."

"Yeah," she whispered. She held a letter in her hands, twisting it over and over. Tears streaked her face.

He sat beside her, setting her cup down on the floor next to her. He longed to put his arms around her and hold her, but he wasn't sure she'd accept it. "Talk to me."

"I was adopted. I didn't know." She handed him the envelope. "It says so in here."

He took it, pulling out the certificates, and reading them.

He hated the cold dread that washed over him. *Foster? No, it can't be.*

"It's your father's name, but who is this Rachel Foster?"

She waved letter slowly. "It's all written out in here in graphic detail. My father had a long standing affair with this Rachel woman. According to this, it began a year after he married Mum and just carried on. When she found out about the affair, Rachel was pregnant, so Mum threw him out. Rachel left her husband and twin sons and moved in with Dad. After I was born, Rachel's husband persuaded her to go home. She took me with her. Six months later, the house burned down. Rachel and her husband were killed."

"Oh, Elle." He put his cup down and wrapped an arm around her. "I'm so sorry."

"Dad collected me from the hospital. Mum

adopted me and Rachel Foster was never mentioned. Mum refused to have anything to do with the boys and Dad agreed as they weren't his, so they went into care. It was the only way she'd have him back. But I have brothers. Half-brothers," she corrected.

"I'm sorry. And you never knew?"

"No, not until I read this. She was very adamant I find and read the letter. It's almost as if she knew she was dying and wanted me to know the truth. That's why I picked up the firebox when we called in home for Abbie's things." She leaned against him, keeping her gaze on her hands as she held the letter.

His right hand moved slowly over her back, comforting her.

"It explains a lot. Why she kept telling me that I was the devil spawn. Along with the fact that all men are evil and not to be trusted. That they were only after one thing and once they got it, they'd leave you. She'd tell me that at least once a day. Growing up I wasn't allowed boyfriends, sleepovers, make up, or parties. I had a friend over once. She bought her makeup and we did each other's faces, copying an ad in a magazine. Mum wasn't best pleased. Make that livid. She told me I looked like a painted doll. She sent my friend home and scrubbed my face clean with a nail brush. Then told me I was a hussy who'd come to no good."

"None of that is true." He hugged her. "Not all men are the same and you are certainly not a hussy."

She looked down. "Yeah, I am. Anyway, you get told it enough and after a while you start believing it and figuring well may as well act like it."

Patrick smiled wryly. He knew there was no arguing with her right now. Her grief was clouding her judgment. Never mind the bombshell she'd just had dropped on her. "That explains a lot."

She tilted her head at him. "Huh?"

"At university," he explained. "Once you came out of your shell, you were always the first to do anything at parties. Try new things."

"The one exception to that being the charity bungee jump."

Patrick smiled. "I'd forgotten about that. You made me do it as you didn't like heights."

"You did it though. But, yeah, I rebelled. Call it freedom from the constraints of home."

"Freedom? Was it really that bad?"

"Yeah. At university I could be me or at least who I thought I wanted to be."

He finished his coffee. "Did you find yourself?"

"No."

"Do you regret any of it?"

"All of it," she whispered.

He stiffened. "All of it? Does that include me? Us?"

"I can't do this now." Eleanor pushed up from the floor and picked all the papers. "I'm going to bed. Good night."

"You didn't answer my question. Do you regret us?"

"Yes, Patrick. I regret all of it."

His throat tightened and he struggled to get the word out. "Me?"

"Yes. Especially you because I proved her right, Patrick."

He shook his head, trying to comprehend what she was saying. "I don't understand. What we shared was—"

She reached the door and turned around. A dark

sorrowful gaze pierced him, cutting him off. "What we shared was wrong. Good night."

12

Patrick watched her go and closed his eyes.

Lord, I don't understand this. I'm losing her all over again and I'm responsible either in part or in whole for her loss of faith and the way she's changed. I know I still love her and that I never stopped loving her. I've been hiding in my work for years now, trying to fill the gap she left in my life and not succeeding. Seeing her again has shown me this.

God, if it's Your will, please work things out between us. Help me to show her that whatever she's done or thinks she did, isn't unforgivable and it's possible to repair her relationship with You. She needs You, the same way I do. She needs the same forgiveness You granted me, so that she can move on.

Pulling out his phone, he sent a text to DI Nemec. He wanted everything the bloke had on Foster and he wanted it yesterday. All of it. If Elle was related to him…

He stood and began the process of locking up the house. He wasn't going to fail at protecting her a second time.

Looking back, he could pinpoint the one single moment, one choice that had changed his future. Not a bad choice at first, he'd had all the right intentions, but one choice in particular that had snowballed. Everything had changed after one weekend. If only they hadn't gone to that party.

Memories haunted him.

****

Lights and loud music blasted from the house as Elle parked. Patrick smiled at her. "See we made it. No more cats or logs."

She pulled a face at him. "You sure this is a good idea? There doesn't sound like there is much studying going on to me."

"Maybe not right now." He jumped out. "But I'm sure there will be. The grounds will be big enough for us to find somewhere quiet. Unless you'd rather go home."

"No." She pulled out the keys, sounding decisive for the first time since they'd left. "I crashed on the way here as it is. I don't want to drive all the way home right now, thank you very much."

"All right, then we stay." Patrick pulled the bags from the boot. Elle took hers and slid her hand into his as they crunched over the gravel to the front steps of the house. He rang the bell.

Garth smiled at them. He wore swimming trunks and his hair dripped onto his bare shoulders. "Hey guys. Glad you could make it. I put you both in the green room. Top of the stairs, turn left, then take the first hallway on the right. The doors are all labeled."

Elle didn't move. "Us?" she whispered.

Garth nodded. "You're a couple, so yeah. We're all sharing rooms. The bed's made up. We're out by the pool." He jerked his head towards the back of the house. "Dump your stuff, change if you want to get wet and come join us. Just follow the music." He headed back inside.

Elle took a deep breath. "I can't share a..."

Patrick squeezed her hand. "I'm not asking you to share a bed with me. I thought Garth might pull a stunt like this, so I brought my sleeping bag."

"OK." It sounded like an automatic response. The shock on her face telling him this was about as far from all right as they could get.

She followed him along the ornate hallway, with its patterned carpet to the door with their name on a card. The bedroom itself was huge, with deep pile blue carpet and massive paintings on the wall. A four poster bed took up space in the center of the chamber. An en-suite bathroom opened off to one side.

Patrick put his bag on the floor. "See, there's loads of space. A couple of pillows and I'm set."

"I'm not sure about this." Her hands shook as she put her bag on the bed. Her voice wobbled and she shifted uneasily from one foot to the other. "They'll all assume we're sleeping together and..."

"I don't care what they think. We know the truth and that's all that matters."

She nodded slowly.

He pulled her into his arms and kissed her. "I love you. Don't ever forget that."

She rested her forehead against his. "Love you, too."

The party was in full swing by the time they reached the pool. Huge lights both inside and outside the water lit the area, music blasted from the speakers and smoke rose from the burgers sizzling on a barbeque.

Elle hesitated. "I don't know..."

"Let's just go mingle for a few, then find a quiet spot somewhere and study. We should at least stay long enough to eat something and be polite. And if you're still not comfortable with this in the morning, we'll make our excuses and go home."

"Fair enough."

"Hey, Eleanor." One of the girls waved at her.

Patrick smiled. "Go say hi and I'll get you some juice." He watched her cross slowly to the other side of the pool and sent up a prayer for their safety.

He'd had a bad feeling since they left home. A warning bell had gone off in his head when Elle crashed. Another one at the shared room. And now a further one as he looked at the drinks table covered in alcohol of all kinds. They should leave now.

Garth grabbed his arm. "Come and play pool."

"I was going to take Elle something to drink."

"I'll do that while you break."

"Sure. One game" He looked over at Elle, but she seemed content, laughing at something one of the other girls had said. He headed in the direction Garth indicated.

One game turned into two, before he managed to get back to Elle. She was leaning against the bar, hair across her face, her skin flushed. Her eyes were sunken as she looked at him. He'd been to enough student parties in his time to recognize the effect of alcohol.

He put a hand on her shoulder. "Hey. Thought you were sticking to the juice tonight?"

"Hey you…" Her words slurred into each other.

He looked around for Garth, seeing him over by the pool. "I'll be right back."

He crossed swiftly over to Garth. "What did you give her?"

"Just something to relax her, man. To relax all of us. I put vodka in the punch. She never knew what hit her." Garth laughed "Anyway all that booze she drank will make it easy for you tonight as she didn't seem too keen on sharing a room with you."

Patrick lashed out hard and fast, his fist connecting with Garth's face, sending him flying into the pool.

Garth came up, arms flailing, spluttering. "What was

that for, man?"

"You figure it out." He went back over to where he'd left Elle. "We should go home."

"I got a better idea," she whispered, running a hand down his face. "How about we just go upstairs?"

"Sure, you can sleep this off, and I'll drive us home in the morning."

He led her inside, worry gnawing at his stomach. She didn't drink and it wouldn't have taken much to affect her, but this was just way off the scale. What else had Garth slipped in the punch?

"You are one very good looking man, Patrick."

"That's very kind of you to say so."

He got her up the stairs, into the bedroom, and shut the door. He turned and Elle was there. Her fingers running over his chest, unfastening his shirt buttons.

He stilled her hands. "Elle, no. Not like this."

She kissed him. "Please, I need you to show me how much you love me."

He picked her up and laid her on the bed. "You need to sleep this off." He pulled off her shoes and covered her. "Night."

He made a hasty retreat across to his sleeping bag.

"Patrick…" She reached for him. "Please."

Another alarm bell rang in his head.

"Patrick…"

Fighting the desire tugging at him, he remained on his sleeping bag on the other side of the room. "Go to sleep, Elle."

****

Just after seven in the morning, Patrick sat at the table, files spread out in front of him. He was no closer to finding out why Foster was involved and it was more than a little irritating. It was possible he wasn't the person who'd sent the threat, and it was pure coincidence Elle had received the letter from him on the same day. He glanced up as Elle came into the room. "How's Abbie doing?"

"Not good. She's complaining her arm hurts, but she's curled up tightly, rubbing her stomach." She sat down. "Can we get a doctor out to see her?"

"Of course we can." He pulled his phone from his pocket. "Actually, didn't the doctor at the hospital say to take her back if she wasn't feeling good?"

"Yeah."

He nodded. "Then we'll do that."

A panicked cry came from upstairs. "Ellie...."

As one, Patrick and Elle ran into the hall. Patrick got there slightly before her. He glanced up the stairs. Abbie stood at the top, bright red blood soaking the front of her clothes. Her good arm clasped tightly around her stomach.

A gasp came from behind him. "Abbie..."

With a small whimper, Abbie bent over, vomiting a stream of red blood onto the carpet.

Patrick glanced at Elle. "Grab a bowl from under the sink. We'll take her to the ED." He took the stairs two at a time and picked up Abbie, heedless of the blood covering him. "Shay!" he yelled. "Need you now."

Shay came out of her room. "What the dev—" She took things in with a single glance. "I'll drive."

Patrick nodded. "We'll call it in on the way to the hospital. We don't have time to wait." He gently cradled Abbie as he headed back down the stairs.

"Abbie, I'm here," Elle said touching her arm.

"Scared, Ellie."

"I know, me too. But the doctor will make you better."

"Let's go," Patrick said. He left the house, myriad thoughts running through his mind and none of them good.

Arriving at the ED, he and Elle got out and ran into reception. Prepared for a fight once again, he was relieved when the receptionist took one look at him.

"I need a doctor out here now," she yelled, as Abbie leaned over the bowl again.

A doctor immediately appeared. Patrick recognized Dr. Peterson from the previous day.

He focused on the girl. "It's Abbie, isn't it?" he asked.

Abbie nodded. "I'm scared."

"I know. It's all right to be scared. We'll find out what's wrong and fix you. Bring her through." He led the way into the Resus department.

Patrick laid her on the bed. Then he stepped back as a team of medics descended.

One of the nurses spoke to Elle, trying to get information from her but she wasn't willing to wait, demanding to be allowed to stay with Abbie.

"She was in here yesterday?" the nurse asked.

Patrick slid a hand into Elle's and squeezed it. "She's in good hands," he said. "Just tell the nurse what she needs to know. They can't help her without knowing what's going on."

"She was admitted yesterday following a car accident. She said her stomach hurt a bit last night, and she didn't eat anything. This morning she said the pain was worse so we were going to bring her in, but before we could leave she started throwing up blood."

"And Abbie is thirteen?"

"Yeah, she's fourteen in January."

"It says here that her mother...your mother died in the accident yesterday. It could be a bit sticky getting permission unless your mother gave you—"

Elle caught her breath, her whole body stiffening. "No, I can sign whatever forms need to be signed. That isn't going to be a problem at all."

"Maybe you don't understand. Abbie is your sister. You can't—"

Eleanor held up a hand, cutting the nurse off, and gazed up at Patrick for a long moment. Then she dropped her hand and looked back at the nurse. "I can. Abbie is my daughter, not my sister."

Patrick's heart stopped. He twisted to look at her. Elle's insistence on wanting to see Abbie, her reaction when Abbie went missing and over the accident yesterday, all slotting into place. "Your *daughter*?" he echoed.

"Yes," Elle repeated. "My daughter."

"Miss Harrison?" Dr. Peterson called.

Elle let go of his hand and moved over to Abbie. "I'm here," she said.

"Ellie..."

Patrick digested the information while Abbie's blood soaked into his clothes making them stick to him. He kept watch on the figures by the bed, not listening to what they were saying, his mind in turmoil.

Abbie was Elle's daughter.

Everything had changed. Whatever the reasons, it was essential the medical staff, and his boss, knew this turn of events. He moved over to one of the nurses and pulled out his ID. "I need to speak to whoever's in charge here."

****

Patrick stood to one side as Elle signed the consent forms for surgery if that was deemed necessary, and stood silently as the nurses wheeled Abbie away, closely followed by Shay. Abbie was already sedated. It had been horrible watching her go under the anesthetic.

He glanced down his chest at his blood stained clothing. He probably looked as bad as he felt. His emotions were all over the place. But however bad he felt, Elle must feel a hundred times worse.

He walked over to her and took her hand. "Where are they taking Abbie?"

Elle blinked hard, and wiped at tears. "She's going for a CT scan to find out what's going on. Then, if need be, they'll take her straight to surgery to try and stop the bleeding. The doctor said it'll be a couple of hours before they know anything. Then they'll take her to intensive care. They said Shay can stay with her the whole time. Even in the theater if she scrubs up and stays out of the way."

"How are you doing?"

"Scared." She rubbed a hand over her eyes. "Terrified. I feel sick, my stomach's in knots. She'll need some things…"

"I'll take you back to the house."

"Thank you. You can change as well."

He glanced down at himself and grimaced. "Yeah, I will. Elle, there's something I need to ask."

She shivered, almost as if she knew what he wanted to ask. "Go on."

"We need to talk about what you told the nurse about Abbie being your daughter?"

She nodded. "Yes. But, this isn't the place for this conversation."

"I disagree. But if you prefer we can have it back at the house." That wasn't what he wanted, but he knew not to push the issue right now. She might clam up completely. He led her outside and over to the car.

Neither of them said anything on the drive to the house. Once inside, Elle ran upstairs to gather Abbie's things. All the blood had been cleaned up, proving Nahum could work fast when he put his mind to it. But Patrick was relieved that there were no visible signs of Abbie being taken ill so violently.

Patrick quickly changed then crossed into Abbie's room. He paced back and forth across the carpet, watching Elle as she packed, trying to find an easy way of saying what he needed.

"Abbie is your daughter?" He asked as he reached the window again.

"You sound like a broken record. You're also going to wear out the carpet. Sit down."

He leaned against the window sill, hands gripping the edge of it. "Talk to me, Elle."

She took a deep breath and shifted. "Yes, Abbie is my daughter." Her apparent unease grew, the pupils in her eyes constricting and her voice wobbled.

His mind ran fit to burst, doing the math in his head. Whichever way he looked at it, the figures added up to only one conclusion. "She's thirteen? Almost fourteen?"

Elle nodded slowly, shoving things into the bag. "Yeah, her birthday is January twentieth."

"That would make it... Is that why you didn't

return after the Easter break?"

She hesitated for a long time, before finally looking up. "Yeah, it is. I couldn't do both."

"Is she mine?"

She stood up and walked to the window, her hands clenching and unclenching. He watched her, knowing she was wrestling with something.

Unable to sit and wait any longer, he stood. "For Pete's sake, Elle, it's a simple question. Is Abbie my daughter?" He voiced the question he hadn't wanted to ask.

"I want to go back to the hospital now. Abbie's alone and I need to be with her."

"I'm assuming no?"

"I can't talk about this. Just take me back to the hospital."

"With pleasure." He shook his head. He'd find out the truth one way or the other. This wasn't over by a long shot. Had she betrayed him? Been seeing someone else at the same time? Surely if Abbie was his, Elle would have told him. She knew how much he loved her. He would have married her on the spot despite any opposition from her parents.

And surely she'd have answered his question as well. He'd asked outright several times and she'd brushed him off. What other secret was she hiding? If not him or another bloke, then who? The idea was almost too painful to bear. He had to get out of here, get his head around this and to do that he couldn't be anywhere near Elle for at least an hour, if not more.

He pulled out his phone, dialing quickly. "Nigel, its Patrick. Can you do me a favor? I have somewhere I need to be for the next hour or so."

"Sure. What do you need me to do?"

"Pick Eleanor Harrison up from the safe house on Brook Street and take her to Headley General. Her daughter is in ITU. Shay will meet you there."

"On my way. Give me ten minutes."

"Thanks." He hung up. "Nigel will take you to the hospital."

"You're not coming?"

He didn't bother to hide the betrayal in his voice. "Not yet, no."

13

As soon as Nigel arrived, Patrick left without saying goodbye. He drove to the gym barely keeping to the speed limit. He changed into tee shirt and shorts, determined to take his frustration, anger, and fear out on the equipment. He headed first to the treadmill, running the fastest 3k he'd ever done in his life. Before long, sweat slicked his hair back against his head, trickling down into his eyes and soaking his shirt, as he made his way around the gym.

He reached the punch bag, not bothering with the gloves as he slammed his fists into it, over and over again.

A hand came down on his arm. He looked up, breathing hard. He blinked, not expecting to see his brother standing there. This wasn't his day to work out. "Liam?"

"In the flesh."

"What are you doing here?"

"Frank rang. Said you seemed intent on killing yourself. Figured I'd come and stop you before you really did do some serious damage to yourself or the equipment."

Patrick shrugged off his brother's touch and slammed his hand into the punch bag. Pain ricocheted up his arm, but he ignored it. Compared to the pain in his heart it was nothing. "She lied to me."

"Who did?" Liam moved around to hold the bag

steady.

"Elle." He thumped the bag hard, almost knocking Liam off his feet. "She lied and now I don't know what else she's lied about. How do I protect her when she won't be honest with me?"

Liam raised an eyebrow. "Protect her?"

"Forget I said that." Patrick winced as he hit the bag wrong, sending further shards of pain up his arm.

"I heard through the church email that her mother was killed in a car accident yesterday. Abbie was hurt, too. I'm guessing that's related. How is Abbie doing?"

"Not great. We rushed her back to the ED this morning. She was throwing up blood. They're running tests, talking surgery."

Liam grabbed his hand. "You are going to hurt yourself. Why are you so worked up over this? Your job has never thrown you out of whack before. Is it just because Elle has come back into your life after all so long?"

"Yes. No." He sucked in a deep breath, his chest hurting. "Because while I'm investigating the biggest drug dealer around not to mention trying to liaise with the Scottish police, I find Elle after all these years. And she works for the guy. There are just too many coincidences for these things to just happen at the same time. And I don't believe in fate either, just like you don't."

Liam held his gaze and his hand firmly. "Fate might not play a part in this, but don't forget God is in overall charge of everything."

"I know that, Li. Sure God may have brought Elle back into my life at this particular point in time for some reason I can't fathom, but she's mixed up in this mess somehow, and I can't figure it out. What I need is for DI Nemec to stop dragging his heels and get me the promised info on this Foster." He pulled his hand free and punched the bag again hard, this time splitting the skin on his knuckles.

Liam grabbed him again. "So call him and chase it up. Maybe, like you, he's working more than one case and it's sitting on his desk waiting to be sent."

"Maybe. But then today I find out that Abbie is Elle's daughter, *not* her sister, and it's possible that Abbie is mine."

His brother hesitated for a moment and let go of him. "Do you know for certain she's yours?"

Patrick shook the hair from his face, sweat streaming down his neck and chest. "I know the math is right."

"That doesn't mean anything."

"Elle's lied about being her mother since Abbie was born. What else is she lying about? And why didn't she tell me?" He swung at the bag again, only to have Liam grab his hand. "What, Li?" he demanded.

"Enough. You and I are going patch your hands up and we are going to talk this out."

"I can't talk about work stuff, you know that." Never mind the fact he'd just done that, hadn't he?

"Not the work stuff, just the personal stuff."

"It's a combination of the two things, Li, and careless talk costs lives." Patrick held his brother's gaze.

"I'm not likely to go telling anyone. But you *need* to talk to someone. It's me, your boss, or Pastor Jack. Pastor Jack's first aid is useless. I've seen him in action on a church camp. And your boss would go down the personally involved route and take you off the case before you could count to three and you know it. I also know that's the last thing you want. So I guess you're left with me."

Patrick sighed. He didn't have a choice, but perhaps Liam would listen without condemning him. Something he wasn't sure the others would do. "I will tell you *only* what does not relate to this ongoing investigation."

"I promise, whatever you tell me will go in one ear and out the other."

****

Sun streamed through the gap in the curtains. Patrick opened his eyes as Elle groaned. He smiled at her. "Feeling better?"

"No," she whispered. "My head and stomach are killing me. What happened?"

"Garth spiked the punch. You were more than slightly drunk. We need to get some food and coffee into you."

She looked green at the mere suggestion. "I don't think I could eat anything and keep it down."

"Not an option, I'm afraid." He paused. "What exactly do you remember?"

She sat up gingerly. Color rushed to her face. "I...oh no. I'm so sorry. I think I threw myself at you."

He hugged her. "It's fine, Elle. I was flattered, but nothing happened."

"I came onto you. What must you think of me?"

"Like I said, nothing happened. I got you into bed and you fell asleep. I spent the night over there, like I promised I would. I wasn't going to take advantage of you." He held out a hand. "Let's go find you some coffee and toast."

She groaned as he gently pulled her to her feet. "Stop the world. I want to get off."

Downstairs, Patrick noted with satisfaction that Garth's eye was bruised.

"What happened to him?" Elle asked.

"I hit him," Patrick replied. "It's sorted now."

Garth brought over two mugs of coffee. "I'm sorry for spiking the punch. Everyone else is mad at me, too. If you want to go home, I understand."

After breakfast, they took their books and found a secluded spot on the cliff top overlooking the bay. Patrick leaned against the huge tree, book balanced on his thighs.

"So why did you turn me down last night?" Eleanor gazed over her book at him.

"I told you, I wasn't going to take advantage of you."

"It's not that you don't fancy me then?"

"You know I do. I love you."

She leaned forwards. "Good, because I love you, too." She kissed him.

The books slid to the ground as Patrick wrapped his arms around her, kissing her back.

****

Patrick looked over the cup at Liam. "Anyway, she left midafternoon, without saying goodbye, and I caught the train home. But she just disappeared, didn't come back after the Easter break. No one knew why."

Liam sipped his coffee, not saying anything, just listening intently. Sometimes having a teacher for a brother was a blessing. He knew when to speak and when to listen and his advice was usually well thought out and made perfect sense.

Patrick sighed, gently flexing the fingers on his bandaged right hand. "She didn't write or anything. I persuaded the college office to give me her address, but it came back person unknown. I never saw or heard from her again. Well, not until I ran into her in the library one afternoon a couple of weeks ago. But anyway, yeah, the dates fit."

"That doesn't mean Abbie is your daughter." Liam put his empty cup down. "You need to talk to her, bro."

Patrick shook his head. "I tried. The words brick and wall spring to mind."

"You know, for someone with an IQ of a hundred and twenty, you have the brain power of a box of rocks at times."

Confusion twisted within him, compounding the complex mix of emotions. "Rocks don't have brains."

"Exactly."

"I don't have time for your riddles," he said bluntly.

Liam didn't let up. "I know you are many things, Pi, but I didn't think an idiot was one of them."

"What are you talking about?"

"Think about it from her point of view. Right now she's hurting. Abbie's sick, her parents weren't who she thought they were, some maniac is trying to kill her and you waltz back into her life after fourteen years. That's a heck of a lot for anyone to cope with on a good day. I'm not sure I could manage one of them. Never mind all at the same time. Maybe Eleanor had a good reason for keeping quiet about being Abbie's mum. You won't know until you sit down with her and hash this out."

"All right. I'll go back and talk to her."

"Good." He grasped Patrick's hands. "But first, we pray. You and I might not see a way out of this, but God will."

"See that's the other thing. She thinks she did something unforgivable." *Would that be she's working for a drug dealer or would it be her involvement with me...and having Abbie? Or betraying me by seeing someone else at the same time* "How do I convince her otherwise?" He paused. "And please don't breathe a word of this to Ni or Jacqui, until all of this is sorted out. Or at least until I get a handle on things."

Liam mimed locking his lips and throwing away the key. "Ask the Lord for the right words, bro. Let Him take control here and work all this for good."

****

Eleanor sat in the intensive care unit, machines beeping and hissing around her. Abbie lay unresponsive on the bed, almost as pale as the sheets. She pushed her daughter's hair back from her face. "I failed you, squirt," she whispered. "I love you so much and all this time I let you down. I should have been stronger and never let any of this happen."

The nurse sat down next to her. "Did you want to ask anything about what the doctor said?" she asked. "I know how confusing it can all be when the doctor is talking. Usually you think of things after he's gone."

"He said something about her liver. And he did a blood test on me to see if I was a match for something."

"The CT scan they did showed a mass on her liver."

"A...a lump? She's been having pain for a while. I was going to take her to the doctors, but never got around to making the appointment."

The nurse nodded. "The accident yesterday caused swelling around the mass hence the bleeding

Abbie had this morning. They did a biopsy and the mass is benign, but there is a lot of damage. She needs a liver transplant. Actually, the accident probably saved her life."

"Is that what the blood tests were for? To see if I'm a match?"

The nurse nodded. "Does Abbie have any brothers or sisters?"

"No, just me. Do you know why the mass is there?"

"No. We'll probably never know what caused it, but it looked like it has been there for a very long time. She could have been born with it."

"She was a sickly baby. Couldn't tolerate rich foods. She never pees a lot when we go out, sometimes all day without going at all." She paused. "Is it my fault? Did I do something wrong when I was pregnant? Take too many headache pills or not eat enough iron or folic acid?"

The nurse patted her hand. "No, it's nothing you did. Main thing is we've caught it now and can do something about it."

The machines beeped and for a moment the bed in front of her vanished and she was in another hospital room, surrounded by machines...

****

Sweat dripped down her face as pain wracked her body again. She'd refused pain killers, and gas and air. She had to pay for her sins. She cried out, barely aware of where she was. She wanted to go home, not be stuck in a hospital with only her mother and a midwife for company. Unless things went wrong, she wouldn't see a doctor at all during the delivery, as per hospital policy.

"Push, Eleanor," the midwife said.

"I...am..." She screamed as the wave intensified, never breaking, just going on and on.

"Almost there, one more."

Stars floated in front of her eyes as with a final cry something broke inside her and the pressure eased. The cry of a newborn baby filled the air.

"It's a girl. Congratulations. Do you have a name for her?" the midwife asked.

She'd agreed with her mother this baby would be brought up as her sister. No one would ever know the truth. But maybe she could name her, her one and only gift. She opened her mouth to speak.

Her mother silenced her with a glare. "Abigail," she said. "Abigail Harrison."

****

"Miss Harrison?"

The doctor's voice jerked Eleanor out of the memory. Since Patrick had come back into her life, the flashbacks of memories long suppressed kept happening far too often for her liking. "Do you have the results?"

"I'm afraid you're not a tissue match."

"But I'm her mother."

"You're thinking blood type only. Abbie's blood type is O positive. Although your blood type is O you're rhesus negative. It wouldn't have affected either of you. However, for any subsequent pregnancies you have will need to be monitored carefully for the Rhesus factor. It's not as bad as it sounds. We can manage the condition fairly easily these days."

"Oh…"

"If we could test Abbie's father, it's possible he'd be a match. Do you have contact with him? It might be quicker than waiting for her name to reach the top of the list for a transplant."

"Yeah, I know where he is. I'll ask him to take the test."

"If you can get him to come in within the next hour, we'll get the results back today."

"OK." She returned her gaze to Abbie. "I really messed up, squirt. And I can't even pray for God to heal you because He won't listen to me." She closed her eyes. She had to tell Patrick the truth before she asked him to take the test.

Far from the truth setting her free, it would only serve to condemn her further.

****

Patrick crossed the ITU, and stood there not wanting to disturb her. "Hi."

Elle glanced up, concern filling her eyes as she took in his bandaged hand. "What happened?"

He shrugged it off. "It's nothing. I picked a fight with the gym equipment and lost. How is she?"

"Not good."

He sat beside her, his left hand threading between her fingers. "What did the doctor say?"

"There's a tumor in her liver."

His eyes widened, his jaw dropped. His whole body resonated as if he were a clanging cymbal. "She has cancer?"

"No, they did a biopsy. It's benign. But the accident caused damage, too." She paused, taking a deep breath. "It's time I told you the truth. She's your daughter, Patrick."

His face worked madly, his stomach churned, and chest hurt. "My daughter?" He wanted her to say it again.

"Yes," she whispered. "Our daughter."

Joy flooded him. He had a daughter. He was a father. Then his joy tempered slightly by the thought that Elle had lied to him, never mind hidden the fact for the last thirteen years. The anger he'd felt in the gym over her lying, seeped back into him. "Why didn't you say anything? I asked several times and you brushed me off. Why tell me now?"

"Abbie doesn't know. She thinks she's my sister. She's right about the secrets in my family, there are too many of them. The thing is Abbie's dying. She needs a liver transplant as soon as possible."

His heart stopped and his breath caught in his throat. *Dying?* The words stuck in his throat, adding fuel to the fire filling him. "So arrange it."

"I'm not a match because I'm O negative. She's O positive. They want to test you to see if you're a match."

"I'm a match, can tell you that without a blood test. Though I imagine they'll need to tissue type me as well." He narrowed his eyes. Now it was all so clear. "So the only reason you told me is because you want something."

"No, I need..." She shook her head. Tears filled her eyes. "You can save her life, Patrick. Abbie needs you."

"I need to think about this."

"Patrick? She's dying! What is there to think about?"

He got to his feet and pushed a hand through her hair. So conflicted he didn't know what to do or think or say. "Not about the transplant, Eleanor. About you. Shay's outside. I'll be back in a bit."

She reached out to him, but he evaded her touch. "Patrick, please, don't go."

Lord, God, what do I do? I need to think, need time to get my head around this.

"I need to ring the office and speak to Abbie's doctor. I'll be back." Biting his lip, he headed to the door. He glanced over his shoulder. Elle sat on the edge of the chair, her face buried in her hands. For a moment he almost went back and hugged her. But he was too angry. She didn't need his anger or his feelings of betrayal right now. He turned away, almost bumping into the doctor. "Elle said you wanted to do a blood test. To see if I'd be a match for the transplant Abbie needs."

"Are you Abbie's father?"

"Apparently," Patrick muttered. "Would a blood test prove that one way or the other?"

The doctor looked at him quizzically. "It would help, but there are other, more conclusive ones. Why?"

"It's a long story. Do the blood tests and whatever DNA test you need to prove it."

"I'll need to speak to Miss Harrison…"

Patrick sighed. He pulled out his ID. As much as he hated doing it, sometimes pulling rank was necessary. "National security, doctor. Just hurry on the results."

"OK. Come with me and we'll do them now."

"I just need to make a phone call. Then I'm all yours."

14

Eleanor sat for an hour after Patrick left, her body numb and her mind in turmoil. Of all the ways she thought he'd react, walking out on her wasn't one of them. Although she deserved nothing less.

She took hold of Abbie's hand, gently stroking it. "Wish I knew what to do, squirt. I hoped he'd understand. Guess I was wrong. I'd hoped that one day things would be different. Past few days with him around, seeing him with you, I'd even hoped he could be part of our lives, but I well and truly put paid to that one. What do I do?"

"Hi, Eleanor. Can I be of any help?"

She looked up into the smiling face of Pastor Jack. "Oh, hello, Pastor."

He sat down beside her. "I heard about your mum. I'm really sorry."

"Thank you."

"I was going to come and see you today, about organizing the funeral, but I guess you want to leave it for a couple of days."

She nodded. "If you don't mind, yeah. How did you find out about Abbie?"

"Patrick rang me. How is she?"

Tears filled her eyes and a fresh cramp of pain squeezed her heart. "She's dying. She broke her arm in the crash and started vomiting blood this morning. They found a tumor on her liver and if she doesn't get a transplant, she'll die. The thing is, we've been...*I've* been living a lie the past thirteen, almost fourteen years, and now I've told Patrick the truth he's run out on me. I'm not a match and he could be because she—"

"Slow down," Pastor Jack said. "They found a tumor?"

"Yeah, when they did scans to find out why she was throwing up blood. There's a huge mass on her liver."

"Is the lump cancer?"

"No. Which, although I'm thankful for, it's still killing her." She took a deep breath. "The other thing is, I haven't been honest with you or with anyone. I'm Abbie's mum, not her sister. It's a long story, but Mum was ashamed of what I did, and insisted on bringing Abbie up as her own."

He nodded. "I see. Did you argue the point with her? Try to insist she was your daughter and you'd bring her up?"

"You don't argue with mum...*didn't* argue with her. She said I would be Abbie's sister, nothing more. It was a better option than having her adopted. This way I got to see her every day."

"Who's her father?"

Right on cue Patrick walked in and answered the question without a pause. "I am." He looked at her. "I've had the blood tests done. The doctor said he's going to rush the results."

"Thank you."

He looked past her. "Pastor Jack. Thanks for coming over."

"Thanks for the call. I was about to suggest that Eleanor and I go and get something to drink. It might be an idea if you joined us."

Eleanor looked at him. "Pastor…"

Patrick spoke over her. "If this is about what I think it is, then it affects us both." He looked at Shay as they left the room. "Can you sit with her while we're gone? My phone's on. Ring if there's a change."

Eleanor walked down the hallway with the two men, footsteps echoing, the clinical stench assailing her senses. To say she was uncomfortable would be an understatement. Yes, she needed to talk to Patrick, but surely this bordered on counseling and she didn't need that.

A small voice within her, one she hadn't heard in a long time, began to whisper. *Wouldn't it be nice to have faith like Patrick's again? To have a relationship with God? To be loved unconditionally? To be forgiven.*

They reached the café. Pastor Jack looked at them. "Grab a table and I'll get the drinks. You guys want tea or coffee?"

"Tea," they said in unison.

Pastor Jack smiled. "Tea it is. I'll bring it over."

She nodded, moving slowly over to the table in the corner. Sitting down, she pulled over the sugar bowl, listlessly moving the spoon through the small white granules, trying to ignore Patrick.

But the voice wouldn't let her. *He came back. He had the test. Surely that means something?*

"Elle?" Patrick's soft tone brought her head up to meet his gaze.

"Why did you call Pastor Jack?" she asked.

"Because he needed to know about your mum so he can help you with organizing the funeral and so on. Besides, I can't help you with this other hang up you have. I just thought if he explained—"

She pushed the sugar around the bowl. "I miss it,"

she whispered. "I miss reading and praying."

"So why did you stop?"

"Because…" She broke off as Pastor Jack put the tray onto the table.

"Tea and pastries. Cassie's answer to all life's problems." He sat and winked at them. "Which accounts for my expanding waistline."

Patrick smiled. "You could always join me in the gym."

Pastor Jack looked at Patrick's bandaged hand. "Perhaps one day." He pulled his Bible from his jacket and set it on the table. "Shall we start by giving thanks?"

She nodded, closing her eyes. The familiar words warmed her, almost as much as the cup she wrapped her hands around when he finished speaking. If only it were enough to warm the frozen heart and soul within her. Patrick had gone some way towards doing that over the last few days. But she wasn't sure whether she wanted this conversation or not. Did she really want to know for sure she was eternally damned?

Patrick studied his pastry, slowly pulling little pieces off and eating them. "So why stop reading and praying, Elle?" he asked, almost as smoothly as if they hadn't been interrupted.

"Because I didn't see the point." She pulled a corner off the pastry, the sugar making her fingers sticky.

"That's not a reason," Patrick said bluntly. "That's an excuse. A bit like, I'm too tired or the cat ate my homework."

"What was I meant to do?" Guilt tied her stomach in knots and she dropped the pastry to the plate. "I've forfeited my salvation. There's nothing I could ever do to atone for my sin. So as my redemption was lost, I had no relationship with God. That's why I work in the nightclub. I'm past help. So there's absolutely no point in reading or praying."

"But you've been in church every week since you moved here a few months ago," Pastor Jack said.

"Mum insisted we went as a family." She took a long sip of her tea. "I can remember as a child being taken to London. We stood outside Buckingham Palace as the Queen drove past and went up to the gates. They opened automatically and she went in and the flag rose on the pole to say the Queen was in residence. A bit later we passed the palace again. There was a long queue of people in their best clothes, hats, suits, pretty dresses. She must have been holding a garden party or something. They showed their invitation to the soldier on the gate and he let them in. I wanted to go, but Mum said without a personal invitation, the soldier would turn me away."

She drew in a deep breath. "Church is a bit like that garden party. It's full of people who have a personal invitation from the King, only I don't have one. Because I did something so wrong, so bad, that even He can't forgive me."

Pastor Jack handed her his Bible, his grey-green eyes catching the light as he moved. "What Biblical references are you basing this on? Can you show me?"

She took the Bible. It felt strange in her hands. Like an old friend she hadn't seen in years. Familiar, comforting, yet its cover burned her fingers. Her conscience flared up, yelling at her. She wasn't worthy to even hold this Book, never mind look inside it. She put it down. "I can't. I'm sorry. I—"

Patrick reached over the table and took hold of her

hand.

Pastor Jack put down his cup and gave a gentle smile. "We're all fallen. No matter how hard we try this side of heaven, we won't be perfect. Not even me. That's why Jesus came in the first place. To do what you and I can't do in a million years, please a Holy God."

Eleanor sighed. "I know all that. My point is I threw it away. I turned my back on God and now I'm lost for all eternity."

Pastor Jack paused. "There's only one thing stopping you from opening the Bible, Eleanor."

"What's that?"

"Satan. He doesn't want you finding out the truth. He'd rather keep you in his kingdom." He slid the Bible back to her. "Show me where it says you can't be forgiven."

Slowly, her trembling hands turned to the passage in Hebrews chapter ten. "Want me to read it?" she whispered. As the two men nodded, she took a deep breath. "Verse twenty-six: *If we deliberately keep on sinning after we have received the knowledge of the truth, no sacrifice for sins is left, but only a fearful expectation of judgment and of raging fire that will consume the enemies of God. Anyone who rejected the law of Moses died without mercy on the testimony of two or three witnesses. How much more severely do you think someone deserves to be punished who has trampled the Son of God underfoot, who has treated as an unholy thing the blood of the covenant that sanctified them, and who has insulted the Spirit of grace?*"

Pastor Jack sipped his tea for a moment, a thoughtful look on his face. "OK. There are various views about quite what the unforgivable sin is, although all agree it's a sin that leads to death, eternal death. Matthew twelve, Mark three, and Luke twelve refer to blasphemy against the Holy Spirit. Hebrews six calls it the enlightened falling away and crucifying the Son of God all over again, subjecting Him to public disgrace, and the passage you read, Hebrews ten, to trampling the Son of God under foot and insulting the Spirit of grace."

"What does it mean?" she asked.

"From what is said in the Bible passages, the unforgivable sin seems to be 'knowing and being convinced of the truth concerning Jesus, and *willfully* rejecting Him.' I would add that those who fear they may have committed it and worry that they have, actually haven't done so because their heart is clearly not hard enough."

"But..." Heat rose in her cheeks and she studied her hands intently. "I broke the commandments. I couldn't keep them."

Pastor Jack finished his tea, setting the cup on the tray. "We all break them. Jesus himself said that thinking something is the same as doing it. But what you have to remember is that there is forgiveness for all who repent of their sin and ask God for mercy. First John one verse nine says '*if we confess our sins, He is faithful and just and will forgive us our sins and purify us from all unrighteousness.*' And again, in Romans eight verse one it says '*therefore, there is now no condemnation for those who are in Christ Jesus.*'"

"But I can't atone for that sin."

"Eleanor, the price has already been paid." Pastor Jack smiled. "And doubts are just Satan reminding you and trying to tempt you into more sin. Almost like an open packet of chocolate biscuits and that little voice that tells you 'go on, one more won't hurt.' Once you confess your sins, God forgives you and forgets them. He throws them into the deepest sea. True repentance means turning away from the sin which is confessed. You don't need to keep apologizing, unless you're still committing it over and over. Even then, He won't give up on you, unless you harden your heart and no longer care about Him. The only things that still stand are the consequences of that sin which you have to deal with on a regular basis. But the sin itself is dealt with, wiped out and forgiven."

Tears pricked Eleanor's eyes. Was there hope? "So, it's not too late for me?" she whispered.

"No," Pastor Jack assured her. "He's waiting, arms open for you to turn and run into them. The key is in that verse you read. *Deliberately keep on sinning.* True repentance means confessing and turning away, turning your back on it and taking the forgiveness offered."

Tears ran down her face unhindered and, not caring she was sitting in a public place, she buried her head in her hands and sobbed. Chairs scrapped somewhere then she felt two hands on her shoulders and heard Pastor Jack's quiet voice as he prayed. She followed his words in her heart, and for the first time in fourteen years felt forgiven and accepted.

15

After Pastor Jack left, Patrick smiled at Elle across the table. Hopefully they could talk for a few minutes, sort some things out before going back up to ITU. "How are you doing?" he asked.

A huge smile lit her face, making her eyes sparkle for the first time in days. "I'm a lot better than I have been. Actually feels like a weight has been lifted from my shoulders. Or at least part of it."

"That's because it has. God took the weight of sin from you and tossed it into the abyss." He paused and winked at her. "And you know what the best bit is? He threw away the key, too."

"Good." She took a deep breath. "Need to tell you some things. I owe you an apology. I shouldn't have told you about Abbie like that."

"No you shouldn't. I'd honestly wondered, because although she had your mannerisms, she looked like photos of me when I was her age." He pulled a face. "Though she's far prettier than me, and I don't wear dresses or those low cut tops she favors."

"Tell me about it. She drives...drove Mum mad with them. She's so proud of her womanly figure. All I ever wanted to do was hide mine."

He shot her an appreciative glance that had her blushing from the tips of her ears down to where her slender neck vanished into her shirt. "There is nothing wrong with your figure, then or now."

"Yeah, right."

"Seriously, Elle. You are a very beautiful woman. Never let anyone tell you otherwise. And it's possible to dress to show off your figure without sending the wrong signals. Have to ask Niamh to take you dress shopping. Both you and Abbie. And before you say something, it's not an imposition. She loves shopping and has exquisite taste."

"I'd like that. Thank you."

He squeezed her hand. "You're welcome."

Her smile lit her face. "And I want everyone to call me Elle now. It's what you call me and I prefer it."

"Then Elle it is. There's something I want to talk through though, without you running a mile if possible."

"Ask away."

"You left all those years ago without saying a thing. Did I do something wrong or hurt you."

"No, you didn't hurt me." She piled the plates back onto the tray. "I wasn't sure how you'd react."

"I'd have married you," he said without hesitation. "But right now we just need to concentrate on Abbie and getting her well. We can pick this conversation up again later."

"I'd like that."

He glanced at his watch. "We should get back up to ITU. The results should be back by now."

She stood and walked with him into the hallway. "Can't we take the stairs? I don't like lifts."

Patrick shook his head. "It's eight floors, with three flights of stairs per floor. It's far quicker to take the lift. I thought you were in a hurry to get back up to Abbie."

"And I thought you had to keep fit in your line of

work." She winked at him.

"Women," Patrick moaned half-heartedly.

"Secret agents," she replied in the same tone. She pointed to the bank of lifts. "Oh look, it says out of action. What a shame. I guess it's the stairs after all."

"Fine. The stairs it is."

She grinned and headed to the stairs to find a janitor standing there.

"Stairs are closed, love. I've just mopped them. You'll have to take the lift."

"Oh. But it says out of action."

The janitor pointed. "Those three service lifts are in general use."

She looked at Patrick.

"We'll be fine. Come on." He took her hand and led her to the bank of lifts. "Pick one."

She pressed the button for the elevator and winked at him. "It doesn't work like that. It's random. But I tell you something that isn't."

"What's that?"

"The way I feel about you. It hasn't changed."

Patrick grinned. "Nor has the way I feel about you."

"Even after all I did to hurt you the past week...years?"

"Yes."

He pulled her into the elevator as the doors opened. Fortunately they had it to themselves. He hit the button for the eighth floor and pressed her against the wall of the lift and lowered his voice. "There is something that I've always wanted to do in a lift."

"Really?" She held his gaze. "And what might that be?"

He ran his fingers down her face, aware of the

spark of electricity that passed between them and of the way she shifted slightly so her body was touching his.

Elle ran her hands over his arms. Did she realize how cute she was when she blushed?

Patrick pulled her closer, one hand running over her back, the other resting on her waist. He lost himself in her gaze. Her scent was overpowering, sending shivers down his spine and curling around his stomach. Slowly, he inclined his head towards hers. "This," he whispered, his lips brushing against hers.

Her eyes widened as a jolt of electricity passed between them. "Ohhh," she gasped.

Patrick pulled back. "I'm sorry."

"Please," she whispered. "Don't be. Kiss me again." She slid her hand around his neck and kissed him again. His hands moved in response, sliding through her hair.

The elevator shuddered and began to drop.

Elle cried out falling to the floor.

Patrick landed beside her, grabbing her hand and pulling her close, in the vain hope of protecting her. He closed his eyes tightly waiting for the final thud as the lift hit the bottom of the elevator shaft.

16

Elle felt Patrick's hand touching hers as they fell and she gripped it tightly. She cried out as the elevator stopped with a stomach twisting jerk.

"It's all right. We've stopped. The emergency brakes have kicked in. We're not going anywhere." He sat up and looked up at the doors. "We're on the fourth floor. Are you all right? You're not hurt?"

"I'm fine. How far did we fall?"

"I don't know. I wasn't paying much attention."

Elle backed into the corner and pulled her knees to her chest, wrapping her arms around them, feeling the panic starting to set in. She looked up at Patrick. Did anything ever rattle him? Her voice shook as she tried to control her breathing. "We should have taken the stairs."

"All eight floors? Besides they were blocked off." Patrick hit the alarm and the bells began to echo through the elevator shaft. He shot a smile over at Elle as he opened the phone box, grabbed the phone and put it to his ear. "Hello? Yeah, there are two of us. The lift number is zero five. OK, thanks."

He looked over at her as he put the phone down. "They'll call the fire brigade and the lift engineers. We just have to wait."

Elle shook her head. "Yay. Stuck in a lift, just what I wanted to do for the rest of the day. I need to get back to Abbie."

"She'll be fine." He pulled out his mobile phone and checked for a signal, relief crossing his face as he found one. "Yeah Shay, it's me. We're trapped in a lift. I've rung for rescue, but wanted to let you know we won't be appearing any time soon." He smiled reassuringly at Elle. "I'll tell her. Bye."

"Tell me what?"

Patrick moved over and sat next to her. "Shay says she'll sit with Abbie 'til we get back." He eyed her with concern as she tightened her arms around her knees. "You didn't mind my company a few minutes ago. What's changed?"

Elle closed her eyes for a moment, the silence broken by the ringing of the alarms. "Is this a good time to mention I suffer from claustrophobia? Always have. It's like the walls are closing in on me here."

Patrick put an arm around her. "I'm here with you."

She shivered. The fear was totally irrational, but felt real none the less. "Least I don't die alone."

"We're not going to die," Patrick responded.

"Really?"

"Really. They'll get us out." He paused. "Besides its Saturday."

Elle looked at him confused. "What's that got to do with anything?"

He winked at her. "I have it on good authority that no one ever dies in a lift on a Saturday. I'll give it to you in writing if you like."

"If you want to, but like you keep telling me, you lie for work all the time. That's when you're not shooting people."

"I only shoot the bad guys, and I use cover stories when I have to in order to keep the country safe."

The elevator cables creaked. "How strong are those cables?"

"Those cables could break completely in two and we'd stay right here. The emergency brakes are on two huge poles on either side of the lift. We're not going anywhere."

"I see." She took a deep breath. "Does the 'not going anywhere' mean we don't get rescued either?"

Patrick pointed up at the roof hatch. "They'll come through the roof. They'll lower down from the next floor up and get us."

Elle frowned. "On the TV it always stops by the doors and they just pry the doors open. Why'd they have to come through the roof?"

"They might not. We might be near enough the doors. But I promise they will get us out."

"All right." She sighed and hugged her knees closer. She was suffocating, but couldn't let him see. "So, since we're stuck here, tell me about your life the past fourteen years."

Patrick looked at her. "You want my life story?"

"You know about my past, yet I know next to nothing about yours."

He let out a deep breath and mirroring her, pulled his knees up to his chest, resting his free arm on them. "Honestly there's not much to tell. I finished the course and then went to America for three months, sightseeing mostly. Then I spent three months in Australia doing the same thing. Came back here, joined MI5 and the rest as they say is history."

"Have you ever killed anyone?" she asked more out of curiosity than anything else.

Patrick studied his nails. "Yeah."

Elle rubbed his arm. "I'm sorry. That must've been

hard."

"It comes with the territory. We shoot to wound, to take them down before they get us or the general public. Sometimes it works, other times not so much."

"Have you ever been shot?"

"I've had more than a few scrapes in the past. Shot once." His brow furrowed and he gnawed his bottom lip. "Anyway, I'm married to my job, for better and worse and usually poorer rather than richer. The only girls I meet are ones I'm protecting, chasing, partnering or investigating. Or worst case scenario, pushing them up against a wall, slapping handcuffs on and reading their rights to. Kind of ruins any chance of a relationship."

He paused and shook his head. "That last bit sounds dreadful if it were taken out of context."

"I know what you mean."

"The short story is, even if I'd had time for a relationship, no one would want me."

Elle shook her head. How could anyone not like him? "There's nothing wrong with you."

"Uh huh." He looked away.

Elle elbowed him until he looked at her. She ran her gaze over his figure slowly, running her tongue over her lips. "Seriously. You're fit, good-looking, and talented. Plus you know how to give a girl a good time."

Patrick scoffed. "We're stuck in a lift."

Elle nodded. "See, you defiantly know how to give someone a good time."

He smiled slightly. "You're silly. So, since we're now on the subject of my job, let's talk about you and the case for a bit. I've been trying to work out what this bloke has on you."

"I don't know. Does it matter?" she said. "I mean…at first I thought he wanted to expose I was Abbie's mum, now I'm wondering if maybe he found out about Dad…" She took a deep breath. She couldn't tell him, not yet. Not until she'd had chance to think it through. "Doesn't matter. I just need to get out of here."

****

Half an hour passed and the alarm finally fell silent. Elle kept her arms wrapped tightly around herself battling with the emotions and rising panic inside her. She was hot and couldn't stop shaking. "They're not coming."

"They'll come. Elle?"

"Patrick," she replied in the same tone.

"Are you OK?"

"Yes, fine, never felt better." She pushed her hands through her hair. Her chest tight and her throat raw, she looked around wildly.

"Talk to me."

She shook her head. Jumping up, she started pacing. "I need to get out of here. There's no room in here."

Patrick stood. "It's an eight person lift. Just sit down. It won't be much longer. Look, I'll call them again."

"I can't sit any longer. I can't breathe in here. I have to get out." She hit one hand on the elevator doors. "Help! Get us out of here!"

"We're fine." He moved over to her and put his hands on her arms. "Just take a deep breath. Come on, calm down. They'll be here any minute."

Elle pulled herself free. "I don't want to calm down. I want out of here." Banging on the doors again, she yelled, "Let me out!"

Patrick grabbed her wrists gently, maneuvering his body between her and the doors. "We're fine. I'm here. You're OK."

Her breath came in gasps. "I can't...do this..."

"Elle, look at me."

She glanced at him, his eyes full of concern and worry and something else she couldn't quite put a finger on. "I'm...looking..."

"Tell me about my daughter." His hands were gentle on her arms and his intense gaze held hers fast.

"You just trying to take my mind off the fact we're stuck."

"Yep." He grinned. "But I want to know everything."

She took a deep breath. "I was sick for almost the whole pregnancy. Day and night..."

He pulled a face. "OK, not quite everything." He slid down to the floor, wrapping an arm around her.

"She was born almost 9 months to the day after that night. I named her after you."

"Her name's Abbie."

She glanced up at him, one brow was raised. "Actually it's Patricia Abigail. As soon as she was born, Mum named her Abbie, but I registered her. Figured if she was used to Abbie all well and good, but it would be her middle name. And yes, you are named on the birth certificate as her father, but Mum insisted on saying she was theirs. I wasn't happy about it, but the only other choice they gave me was giving her away and I wasn't about to do that."

Patrick raised an eyebrow. "Why?"

She shrugged. "It doesn't matter. But this way I got to be around for her all the time. We moved a few times. No, make that a lot. We moved every couple of years or so, never having our own place, always renting. Then Dad died and since Mum had no marketable skills, I had to work all hours to support them. No boyfriends, no dates. Pretty boring life really."

"What about Abbie? Does she know?" His hand moved gently over her arm, his light touch keeping her grounded.

"No" She smiled wryly. "It's kind of ironic in a way. I kept from her the very thing that had been kept from me."

"Did they adopt her as they were insisting she was theirs?"

"They wanted to. But no, they didn't. I refused to sign the papers. I still have them. I never showed them the birth certificate, so they never knew who her father was and I wasn't going to tell them."

"Do you know where the certificates are?"

She nodded. "Yeah, why?"

"Just a hunch. Soon as we can I want to go to your place and find them."

She shivered, the panic surfacing again. "If you figured it out, maybe someone else has. Maybe...maybe...I need to be with her. She's alone out there."

"Shay is with her." His hand cradled her face. "Elle, stay with me."

"Patrick, I can't breathe." She was terrified, filled with the need to get out.

"Yes, you can. You can talk therefore, you can breathe."

"No..." She shook her head, rocking now as he wouldn't let her pace.

"Yes, you can. Look at me."

She opened her eyes. "No."

"No, you can't look at me? You just did."

"I—"

"Now breathe with me. In...out...in...out..."

She struggled to inhale, wanting to please him as much as she wanted out of the tiny space. The walls were closing in, but she kept her gaze on his, trying to breathe with him.

"That's better. We'll get out of here in a few." Patrick kissed her forehead, slowly working his way down to her mouth, his lips warm against her cold skin. He looked at her, gazing deeply into her eyes. "You're beautiful." His lips touched hers again as he pulled her gently towards him.

She slid her hand around his neck and kissed him again, finding his lips soft and warm and responsive.

He pulled her closer, his body firm and safe.

When his mouth touched hers, nothing mattered apart from him. She kissed him back, no longer afraid.

Patrick broke off as something hit the roof and the escape hatch opened. He looked up into the flashlight, shielding his eyes against the brightness. "Hello?"

"Fire brigade. Is everyone all right?"

Patrick grinned. "We're fine, Jared. Glad to see you guys though."

Elle straightened up, breathless but for the right reasons. "*Jared*? Do you know the entire fire department by name?"

"Only one. Jared is my brother-in-law. It's always nice when family comes to the rescue."

A firefighter in full gear, dropped down to them.

He moved over to Patrick and hugged him. "Though rescuing my own family is beginning to become a habit I'd rather ditch. Are you both sure you're OK?"

"I love it when family drop in for a visit." Patrick returned the hug. "We're fine, Jared, but definitely ready to get out of here. Elle didn't like lifts before we got stuck in one."

Jared smiled and held up the harnesses. "We'll strap you in and take you up through the shaft to the next floor."

Elle shook her head, liking that idea even less. "I don't think so. Can't you just pry open the doors?"

Jared shook his head. "The lift is stuck mid-way between two floors. Until we know why the cable failed, we can't risk taking the lift up or down the shaft."

Patrick rubbed her arm. "You *can* do this, Elle. It's either that or you stay in here, and we both know that's not an option."

Elle shivered, trying not to flinch as they attached the harness to her.

Patrick took a deep breath as another firefighter dropped down through the roof. "Elle, look at me." As she looked up, he continued. "You want out of here, right? Well, the only way out of here is up."

Jared finished attaching the harness to Patrick and double checked it. "OK, let's get out of here."

"Take her first," Patrick insisted looking at him.

Jared nodded. "Sure thing."

Patrick turned back to Elle. "Look at me."

Elle looked at him as she felt the ropes passed around her and fastened to the harness. Tears filled her eyes. As much as she wanted to get out, she couldn't do this. "Hmmmm?"

"You can do this. Abbie needs you and she's up there." He leaned forwards and brushed his lips across hers. "You go first and wait at the top."

She parted her lips, disappointment overriding her embarrassment as he pulled away. She looked at him her face falling. She hesitated.

Patrick winked. *"The only way is up,"* he sang. Was he deliberately off key? He brushed his finger over her lips. "Wait for me at the top. Else I'll start singing, again."

Elle nodded as the firefighter gently lifted her into his arms. She kept her gaze on Patrick's face as she was hoisted upwards. Once she could no longer see him, she shut her eyes tightly. The shaft walls closer than the lift ones were, despite the fact logic dictated they had to be wider. Then the movement stopped and something solid appeared under her feet. She opened her eyes. "Where am I?"

"Fourth floor. How are you doing?" Another fire fighter with an Australian accent asked as he ushered her to a nearby chair.

She took a few shuddering breaths. "All right, I think."

"Good. Your friend will be out in a few."

She pushed herself back into the wall, sliding down on it, hugging her arms to her chest.

Someone pressed a bottle of water into her hand. "Here, drink this."

"Thank you." She looked over at the door waiting for Patrick.

****

Patrick let Jared rope him up and then winch him

up the elevator shaft. He was immensely relieved the firefighters had arrived when they did, as Elle had been on the verge of losing it completely. He totally understood where she was coming from, but panicking wouldn't have solved anything. She'd been through too much these past few days. She was barely holding it together. Although effective, slapping her to snap her hysteria hadn't been an option, but kissing her seemed to have worked.

"Thank you," he said as Jared set him safely on the floor.

"Welcome. Wait 'til I tell Niamh about this tonight."

"I'll never live it down. Agent 3.14 being rescued from a lift."

Jared grinned at him. "Your secret is safe with me."

As soon as he was unhooked, Patrick moved over to Elle. "Hey, how are you doing?"

"OK," she whispered.

Patrick nodded, pulling her to her feet, hugging her. It felt so good to have her in his arms. He never imagined in a million years he'd feel this way again, but Elle made him feel alive. "You are one of the bravest women I have ever met."

She looked at him and raised an eyebrow. "Ri-ight."

"I mean it. Yes, you got upset, and yes, you panicked, but you know what? You still let them take you out of there, despite being scared stiff."

A faint smile crossed her lips, making him want to kiss her again. "I did, didn't I?"

Patrick smiled at her. "You did." He caught her mouth with his, kissing her.

"There are people here," she protested. "Including your brother-in-law."

"I don't care." He stood there, his forehead touching hers, able to hear a pin drop, despite the noise going on around them.

For a moment, they were the only two people in the world. He studied her face, for a moment, then kissed her again.

17

Breaking off for air, Patrick pushed a hand through her hair. "Are you feeling better?"

She nodded. "Yes, thank you." She cupped his face with her hand.

Jared came over to them. "We're off. Not every day I get to rescue MI5." He stuck out a hand. "Guess I have time to say hello properly, though. I'm Jared Harkin, Patrick's brother-in-law. I'm also guessing you two know each other rather well."

She shook his hand. "Elle Harrison. We go way back." Patrick smirked and she glanced curiously at him. "What?"

"If only he knew he'd just shaken the hand of his favorite singer," he grinned.

Jared frowned. "Huh? Think being stuck in a lift has gone to your head, mate."

Patrick lowered his voice. "This is Lisa Bellamy."

Jared did a double take and took a step back. "You're kidding."

Elle shook her head. "Nope. Guess that's two firsts for you today then. Rescuing a secret agent and a singer."

Jared nodded. "We've got all your CDs. Niamh, my wife and Patrick's sister, wants the new one. Don't suppose you could give me an autograph, please?"

An autograph was the least she could do for them. Perhaps when Abbie was better, and Mum was buried, and she wasn't being hunted by a killer, she'd go visit and let Patrick take her photo with them all. Funny how being stuck in the lift had blocked all that out. And, like surviving the lift, she'd just take all the horrible things in her life at the moment one at a time. God was with her.

She looked at Patrick. "Have you got some paper?"

He pulled out a notebook. "Here you go."

"Thanks." She took it and winked. "Pen?"

"You didn't ask for a pen," he laughed. He pulled one from his pocket and handed it to her.

She smiled and looked at the paper. *To Jared, thanks for being my knight in shining armor, Lisa Bellamy* she wrote. She looked up. "What fire station are you based at?"

"Cedarwood Fire Station, Green Watch."

She nodded and wrote on another piece of paper. *To the heroes of Green Watch, with grateful thanks, Lisa Bellamy.* She held them out to Jared. "I'll bring a signed picture in later on. But now, I need to get up to ITU."

Patrick's phone rang and he turned to answer it.

Jared nodded. "Thank you so much for these. The guys are going to be rapt."

"Welcome."

Patrick gripped her arm. "Yeah, you're right Elle, we need to go. The docs want to talk to us. I guess the test results are back."

Jared looked at them concern in his eyes. "Is everything all right?"

"Not really. Just pray for a teenager called Abbie, will you?"

"Sure." Then Jared leaned closer. "I haven't finished up the investigation, but I want you to stop by the station when you get the chance. I'm quite sure the lift mechanism had been sabotaged, but I'll know more when I get the inspector's report."

Patrick frowned. "We were prevented from using the stairs. They were being cleaned. And the other lifts were having maintenance done. The janitor told us to use the service lifts."

Jared frowned. "Hmmm, they weren't being serviced when we arrived. I'll look into it. See you later."

"Sounds good. Thanks again, bro." Patrick glanced around for Elle. She was standing by the stairs.

"Come on," she said. "Thought you said we had to go."

"I'm coming." He took three long strides to the door and grabbed her hand. "I'm here."

She smiled. "Good. What did the doctor say?"

"It was Shay on the phone. She just said the doctor was looking for the both of us." He pushed open the fire door and started up the stairs with her.

"That's not good."

"Don't worry. Shay didn't sound stressed or upset and she's pretty good at reading situations. And if something had happened to Abbie she would have said."

"OK." She glanced down at her feet. "These stairs don't look very clean to me."

"No, they don't. I was just thinking that, myself."

His hand was warm in hers. Now things were right with God, could she make things right with Patrick, too? Was he a match? And if so, would he agree to the transplant? She didn't dare to hope he'd want to be part of her life. Part of Abbie's yes, that was understandable.

She could be reasonable about access, couldn't she? As long as he didn't want Christmas, every weekend and all summer long.

She took the stairs two at a time, anxious to get back to Abbie as quickly as possible. She'd wasted enough time in the lift as it was. Half way up, she heard Patrick's breath coming in gasps. She glanced at him. Was he was out of breath?

"Patrick, are you OK?"

"I'm... fine."

She shook her head, deliberately playing with her words. "How can someone so fit be so unfit?"

He *harrumphed*. "That's nice. You just managed to compliment and insult me in the same breath. Is that some special ability or something?"

"Yeah. You have a problem with that?"

"Nope." He looked at her. "And I'm perfectly fit, just been a long couple of weeks, is all." He started climbing again.

And getting longer especially with Mum dead and Abbie so ill... She broke off, not wanting to think it. "Have you decided what you're going to do?"

"About what?"

"The transplant?"

"It depends on what the doctor says. Presumably it'll mean more tests, even if I am a match." He paused. "I also need to protect you. And find out who's behind the letters. They already tried to take your family out once. I'm assuming that was a warning and you'll get a follow up letter or phone call."

"But I don't have my phone. You took it away, remember?"

"I know. I'll send Shay to pick it up, along with any mail from the house. You can have it back to check for messages, but I'd rather you didn't make any calls."

"OK."

They reached ITU and she noted the worried look Shay and Patrick exchanged. "Is Abbie all right?"

Shay smiled. "Abbie's doing fine. I sat right by her bed, the whole time you were gone. Read to her."

Elle smiled. "Thank you."

"Just hopes she likes the celebrity gossip column." Shay winked.

Elle's smile widened. "That's right up her street. That and boy bands."

Patrick grinned. "She's a teenager, what do you expect? Go on in, I need a quick word with Shay, then I'll be there."

She went inside the unit, leaving the two agents to talk quietly. She washed her hands and crossed over to the bed where Abbie lay, surrounded by machines.

She sat and took hold of Abbie's hand. "Hey, squirt. I'm back."

Abbie stirred and opened her eyes. "Hi..." she whispered.

Elle smiled, her heart jumping for joy. "Hey, you're awake."

"You weren't here..."

"I went to get some tea and we got stuck in the lift and had to be rescued by the firefighters. Just like on TV."

"We? Is Patrick here, too?"

Elle squeezed her hand. "Yeah, he is. How are you feeling?"

"I want to go home."

"I know, but you have to stay here for a little while longer. Has the doctor been in?"

"Looking for you, then he went away again. I'm

scared, Ellie. I really don't like it here." Her voice wobbled and her eyes widened and glistened.

"I'm right here. I'm not going anywhere."

"What if I die, like Mum did?" Abbie squeezed her hand so tightly it hurt.

"The doctors won't let that happen."

"But I might. This is where they put the really sick people, right?"

Elle nodded slowly. "Yes, but not everyone in here is going to die. And neither are you," she said, praying she was right. There'd be time for the other conversation later, assuming Abbie didn't ask too many questions now.

Patrick came over to the bed. "Elle?"

She looked up. "Hey, Patrick, look who's awake."

He glanced down at Abbie and smiled. "Hello. How are you feeling?"

"Not great," Abbie said. "I want to go home."

"I know. Me too. Can I borrow Elle for one minute?"

Abbie tightened her grip on her hand. "Don't leave me."

Elle squeezed her hand. "We won't. We'll be right over here, so you can see us."

Patrick reached into his pocket and pulled out his work phone, making sure it was switched off. "Look after this for me. I'm not allowed to be without it."

Abbie gripped the phone tightly. "OK."

He smiled and took Elle's hand, pulling her to one side. "I'm a match. They want to do a few scans today if possible."

"Like what?"

"Chest X-ray, ECG, CT scan, MRI. Enough to keep me occupied for a while. Oh, and a chat with the counselor and a nurse, to make sure I know the risks and am sure about what I'm doing."

"You'll do it?"

He held her gaze. "She's my daughter, Elle. Of course I'll do it. How much does she know?"

"I haven't told her anything. I won't until they've confirmed it's going ahead."

"I didn't just mean the transplant. She's going to want to know why I'm a match and you're not. She's also going to need to know you're her mum."

"I know, but not yet. Mum just died and someone tried to kill her. We'll cross that bridge when we get to it."

"Try crossing it before you get there."

She tilted her head. "How do I do that?"

He smiled. "You're clever, you figure it out. Now I have a date with several large needles and even larger pieces of equipment."

She reached up on her tiptoes and kissed his cheek. "Be careful."

He kissed her back. "I will. Tell Abbie to look after my phone for me." He raised a hand and waved to Abbie before leaving the ward.

Elle watched him go then went back to Abbie, now new trepidation filling her. *Could I lose them both to this? Just what are the risks involved? And I thought those letters and being stalked was scary. That is nothing compared to this. Help me.*

Abbie looked at her. "Where's Patrick gone?"

"He's got a doctor's appointment," Elle told her honestly. "He asked that you look after his phone until he gets back."

"Why me?"

"So you'll know he's not leaving."

Abbie winced as she moved. "He likes you and I think you like him. I saw you kissing him."

Her cheeks warmed. "Yeah, I like him."

"Has he asked you out?"

"Not in so many words."

"But he kissed you back. He must like you to do that."

"It's complicated, Abs. There's a lot of history."

Abbie took her hand. "Tell me about when you first met him."

"All right. I was at university..."

****

Eleanor struggled to hold her books and the Styrofoam cup filled with hot tea with the same hand, while dodging chairs. She was almost at the only free table in the campus restaurant when the strap on her bag broke, sending the contents flying across the floor and the tea smashing down next to it. Her books and papers slithered after them.

Bright red with embarrassment, she dropped to her knees to pick it up. Tea turned her papers into a brown soggy mess, and her brand new textbook would never be the same again.

A tanned hand, with long, sleek fingers and well-manicured nails caught the rest of her books before they slid to the floor. "Oops-a-daisy."

She followed the hand up the arm to the owner of the chocolate-smooth Irish accent. Wow. Light brown hair, sparkling blue eyes and the most infectious, beaming smile she'd seen since she arrived at Sunderland University, three years previously. His blue V-necked sweater, white shirt, and brown cords showed off an almost perfect body.

"Let me help."

She blushed harder, his deep voice turning her knees to jelly and her voice to a squeak. "Thank you."

He knelt in the mess and helped her scoop up tissues, perfume, and assorted bits and pieces from her bag. He grabbed a pile of serviettes and helped dry each item, setting them on the table above him.

Someone else tossed a couple of cloths for the floor. "Thanks, Jerry," he called and continued cleaning.

Eleanor knelt beside him, tears of embarrassment filling her eyes. She was useless, as always. She gathered the last of her books. There was no way she could replace them. She needed what little money was left in her account for food and rent and there was barely enough there to cover that as it was.

The man, her knight in shining armor, smiled, his hand touched hers, his fingers lingering slightly longer than they should. "May I buy you a drink to replace the one you spilled?"

She blushed again. "There is no need, but thank you." She just wanted to get out of the café.

"But I would really like to."

"I don't…"

"Accept drinks from strange men," he finished with a cheeky grin and a wink. He held out a hand. "Patrick Page, post-grad history and politics."

Eleanor shook his hand. His skin was warm and sent shards of heat straight through her. His grip firm, despite the softness of his hands. "Eleanor Harrison. Third year history and politics.

"Pleasure to meet you, Eleanor. So, now I'm no longer a stranger, may I buy you a drink?"

"Thank you. That would be good," she managed.

He led her to his table and pulled out a chair for her. "What's your poison?" he asked and then blushed himself.

"Sorry, that's what I say to my brother and sister."

She managed a smile. "My mother says the same thing. Herbal tea please." She gave her bag the once over as he crossed to the counter. The strap was irreparable. More money she just didn't have. She couldn't ask her parents for extra, they'd say no anyway. Maybe she could get another shift waiting tables this weekend.

"Here you go." Patrick slid the tea across to her and sat opposite. "So how come I haven't seen you around before?"

"I don't usually come here. But I'm meant to be meeting my student mentor for this year in half an hour and didn't have time to go back home for lunch."

He nodded pointedly to her cup. "That's not lunch."

"It's all I can afford..." She broke off. "Forget I said that."

"No." He stood. "Wait there."

Eleanor didn't move. Her mother used that tone when she meant business and she was afraid of what would happen if she left. Part of her immediately rebelled against that idea. She was in a packed cafeteria. What did she think was going to happen? And she wasn't alone with him. She'd already established that.

Patrick came back with a plate of steaming sausage, eggs, and chips. "Here," he said.

"I can't..."

"Thought you'd say that, so I got two forks. We'll share it." He paused, his deep penetrating gaze holding hers. "Please. You don't look like you've eaten properly in days."

She took the fork. "Thank you. No, I haven't." She started eating, relishing every mouthful.

Patrick ate as well. "Did your grant money not come through?"

"I don't have a grant. Just what my parents send me." She paused. "It's either pay the rent or eat this week. Next *week who knows how I'll...?" She broke off. "Why am I telling you all this? I don't even know you."*

"It's part of my irresistible charm," Patrick replied. He winked at her. "My brother, Liam, says girls don't stand a chance around me."

She withdrew into her shell. "Really?"

"But then he's far more handsome than I, and has way more girlfriends than anyone I know, including me." He stabbed the fork into a chip and dipped it into the egg yolk. "Mind you, that isn't hard. I've always concentrated on my studies rather than anything else."

"Oh?"

His smile lit his eyes. "I like studying and I passed my degree with first class honors."

"Really? I'm struggling to get a two point two."

"Probably why they've put you on the mentor scheme." He pushed the plate towards her. "Here, finish it."

"Are you sure?" She didn't want to take advantage of him, but she was starving.

Patrick nodded. "I'm sure."

"Thank you." She started eating before he changed his mind.

He picked up her drowned textbook. "I've still got my copy of this in my room. Do you want to borrow it, save buying a new one?"

"Really? That would be great, I mean..."

"It's fine. I wouldn't have offered if I didn't mean it. It's just sat on the bookcase gathering dust, which is a waste of a book. What time's your next class?"

She checked her watch. "Three. Right after this mentoring meeting. I'm meant to be getting paired with someone who can help me."

"I have a free then. I'll run home and get it and meet you after your class."

"Only if it's no trouble."

He smiled. "No trouble at all."

Eleanor nodded and finished off the plate of food. For the first time in days, her stomach was comfortably full and she felt warm. "Thank you for that."

"You're welcome."

She shoved as much as she could into her broken bag and tucked it under her arm.

"Let me take the rest. I happen to be going to this mentoring meeting as well. Professor Malcolm is hoping some of my brilliance will rub off on someone. His words, not mine. He thinks I'm some kind of genius." Patrick gathered his books and balanced hers on top. "Let's go." He stood and smiled at her.

Eleanor walked with him. Would she be fortunate enough to be paired with him? Not that anything good ever happened to her. She just hoped her mother never found out she had dinner alone with a bloke. She would be forever condemned for it.

18

Patrick sat outside the counselor's office. He'd been poked and prodded and had countless scans and x-rays. All he could think of was Elle and Abbie. Now he knew the truth, he wanted to be a part of their lives. Abbie's life definitely, but would she want a father who suddenly appeared out of nowhere?

Would he be any good as a father? He didn't know the first thing about raising a child, let alone a young teen. Sure he could interrogate any boyfriend she might have in the future, but what good would he be otherwise? Actually thinking about it, Abbie might never have a boyfriend once word got out her father was armed at all times. Not to mention being a crack shot.

"Mr. Page?"

He glanced up. "Yes."

"Come on in."

He rose and followed the woman into the office.

"Take a seat. My name is Corrine Downton. This is Betty Willis, the transplant coordinator and John Brown, consultant surgeon. It's our job to make sure you understand the risks involved and answer any questions you may have."

"OK." He settled uneasily into the plastic chair and crossed his right ankle over his left knee. "I'm assuming that means I'm a match?"

The surgeon looked at him. "Physically you're a

perfect match. There are no indications as to why surgery can't go ahead."

"Good. Why do I sense a 'but' coming?"

"Being a live donor isn't as easy as it sounds. It's major surgery for you as well as for Abbie."

"I know that." From the corner of his eye, he could see the counselor scrutinizing his every movement and word. He relaxed his hands, calling on the interrogation aversion techniques he'd had drummed into him. He could do this. It wasn't as if he was being tortured with buckets of water and electric cables or being beaten whilst blindfolded, was it?

"Surgery itself for you will run concurrently with Abbie's. It will take approximately seven hours. The surgeon and his team will remove the left lobe of your liver, whilst another team works on Abbie. The donated piece will then replace her liver. You'll be in intensive care for upwards of twenty four hours, spend another five to seven days in hospital after that. After two, maybe three days post op, you can get out of bed, but will need assistance to begin with. You will be left with three large scars." The surgeon demonstrated across his stomach. "Here, here and here."

"OK. What about returning to work?"

"No work or home activities for a month. Then part time for another month after that. No driving for six to eight weeks."

"I see." That was going to make protecting Elle impossible.

"The surgery comes with major risks to your health. There is a chance of blood clots and a two percent chance you could die."

Patrick shrugged, keeping his poker face, despite the way his insides were churning. "I face death on a daily basis at work."

"This is different."

"I know that too," he snapped. "Look, I've made up my mind and there is nothing you or anyone can say to make me change it." He sucked in a deep breath. "Sorry, go on."

The surgeon continued. "Your liver will regenerate within about six weeks to its original size."

"What about Abbie?"

"Her surgery will take upwards of ten hours. She'll spend about five days in intensive care and another three weeks on a general ward. She'll need to be monitored for rejection, but within about three to six months she'll be able to do everything she can now. The transplanted liver will grow to the size of her original one within six weeks."

"OK. Where do I sign?"

The counselor cleared her throat. "Is anyone coercing you to do this?"

"What kind of a question is that?" he asked, shifting in his chair.

"Are you being offered payment for it?"

He sighed. "Abbie is my daughter. I'm exercising my parental right to save my child's life. Where do I sign?"

The surgeon handed him the form. "The surgery will take place in a week's time."

Patrick glanced up from reading. "Can she wait that long?"

"We think so."

"You *think* so? She has a massive tumor inside her and you *think* it can wait a week?"

"Right now, Abbie isn't strong enough to survive surgery. She has a fever which we need her to recover from first."

"And if she deteriorates?"

"We'll rethink. Until that time we wait until she stands a better chance of surviving than she does now."

Patrick returned his attention to the form, reading it carefully. *Lord, am I doing the right thing here? Is this why things happened the way they have? Elle comes back into my life so suddenly, in order that I can help Abbie. Would they have found the tumor without the car accident? Are You keeping Your promise in Romans of working everything for good?*

A sense of peace filled him and, knowing he was doing the right thing, he signed the form and handed it back to the surgeon. Once Elle was safe, he could run the desk at work for the time being. That wasn't exactly strenuous. Nor was protecting her while sitting next to her on the sofa. "Now what?"

"Now, I go and talk to Abbie and Miss Harrison and explain to them what will happen."

"I don't think Elle said anything to Abbie yet. She doesn't want her told."

"Abbie is thirteen, old enough to understand how sick she is. Without the transplant she'll die."

Patrick jerked as if stabbed. He recalled Elle saying that, but she'd been hysterical at the time. "I'm sorry?"

"Abbie's dying. She's got a month, maybe two."

"And you want to wait a week before surgery?" Panic filled him. "If she's dying anyway, then surely it'd be better to operate sooner rather than later, fever or no fever."

"Mr. Page, I understand your concern, but right now, Abbie wouldn't survive the anesthetic never mind the surgery. For yourself, you need to take care over the next few days. Avoid getting sick or injured as much as you can."

Patrick nodded. "OK."

The surgeon looked at his notes. "I'll book a tentative date for Friday."

"The tenth?" Patrick asked looking at his personal phone.

"Yes. You'll need to come in the day before for a final set of x-rays and blood tests."

He shook the surgeon's hand and left the room, his mind whirling. First he didn't know about her at all. Then in a few short hours he'd been given a daughter and now he was losing her.

He fumbled for his phone and dialed Liam. The answer phone picked up and he sighed. "Li, it's me. I really need to talk to you, Ni and the parentals. Give me a call when you get this. See if we can all get together tonight for a few. Bring Jared and Jacqui."

Pressing the button briefly, he dialed the police station in Tannoch. "Can I speak to DI Nemec? It's Agent Page with MI5."

There was a brief pause, then the call connected. "Nemec."

"Sir, it's Agent Page in Headley Cross. I don't have much time, but things are moving a pace down here. I really need to see those files."

"What's up?"

"Turns out the woman I'm protecting, Elle, was adopted. Her mother was Rachel Foster…"

Nemec cut him off. "Foster?"

"She has twin brothers, but all I know is what Elle found out a couple of days ago. Since then we've been in the hospital with our…her seriously ill daughter."

"*Our* daughter?" The American voice hardened.

Patrick closed his eyes. He'd slipped up there. "Forget I said that. But I really do need whatever information you have. I won't be in the office for a bit though. I'm working in the field on protective detail."

"I'll do what I can from this end and get down to London before the end of the week. Will your office know where to find you?"

"They will. Thank you. See you when you get here."

He hung up and went back up to ITU. Shay stood outside the door. "How's things?" he asked.

"Fine. The doctors are in talking to Elle and Abbie. You don't look so good, what's up?"

"Bad news, that's all. I'm going to go in, see what the doctor's saying."

"It's family only, Patrick."

"Still going in."

She grabbed his arm. "Patrick, if there is something between you and Elle, beyond the obvious attraction which can be seen a mile off, then I need to know and you need to back off this case."

"Abbie is my daughter."

"She's *what*?"

"You heard. DI Nemec is collating info before flying down with it. I really think there is a link between his Foster and ours. Now if you don't mind I'm going to find out what my daughter's doctor has to say."

He shook her arm off and headed into the ITU, aware of her stunned face behind him. He washed his hands and then crossed over to Abbie's bed, sliding into the seat beside Elle.

She shot him a grateful smile, and gripped his hand tightly.

Abbie looked at him. "The doctor said you're a match," she whispered.

He nodded. "Yeah."

"So I get part of your liver because mine is seriously messed up."

"Sounds about what they told me." He smiled at her. "If that's all right with you."

She nodded slightly. "Ellie said they tested her as well, but her blood's wrong."

Elle looked at him. "They explained all about the matching and told her basically that she and I are positive and negative."

"And we all know that positive and negative attract not repel, right?" he winked, knowing Abbie would have done that in science at school.

She smiled faintly. "I know science. We do all three sciences at school. We actually broke the Slinky in a physics experiment."

He laughed. "How did you manage that?"

Abbie tilted her head. "We were studying wave motion. Only we got too enthusiastic and ended up putting a kink in the Slinky."

He snorted. "Oh, I bet I can guess what you guys called it. Have you done the Maltese cross experiment yet?"

"Last week."

"We blew it up. Well, imploded it."

Abbie looked at him in awe. "That beats breaking a Slinky hands down."

"Certainly does. So, yeah I know a lot about science too. Comes with being a..." he broke off and put a finger over his lips.

Abbie raised a hand and shielded her mouth so only he could see. "Secret agent," she mouthed with a laugh.

He winked at her and gave her a thumbs up.

"When can I go home?"

The doctor looked at her. "I'd rather you stayed in."

Abbie pouted. "I don't want to."

"Unless there is a need for her to be here, it would be better to have them both at a safe house." Patrick looked at her and then at the doctor. "If I move them into my place, there are no stairs and she'll do nothing but rest. I can guarantee it."

"Please," Abbie added. "I promise if I get sick again, I'll come back in."

"If the scans are clear. If they're not, then you stay in."

Elle looked at the doctor. "I don't want to put her in any danger, no matter what anyone says."

"Nor do I. Let's see what the scans show and go from there."

Patrick nodded. He didn't want anything to happen to Abbie, but more than anything he wanted to get her to a controlled safe environment. If someone could walk in and disable a lift, then the security in this hospital needed a lot of work. And it definitely wasn't anywhere near safe enough for his daughter.

19

Patrick held Elle's hand tightly as they walked down the hallway to the hospital café. Abbie was sleeping, finally agreeing to stay overnight on the condition they both stayed with her. Shay had promised to stay with Abbie until they got back on the ward. He'd pulled strings and several armed officers stood at various points in the hallway and on all the exits.

And the conversation he was about to have with his family would be far easier with Elle at his side. He glanced at Elle as they walked. "Are you sure you're all right with me talking to them now? We could wait until all this is over."

She tightened her grip on his hand. "I'm not looking forward to it. But I do understand you need to tell them. You're planning on having major surgery and they have a right to know about it."

"Actually, I want to tell them everything." He stopped and pulled her to one side of the corridor. "Elle, because Abbie's my daughter, by default it makes my parents her grandparents, my brother and sister her aunt and uncle. She's part of my family. She's not alone anymore. And nor are you."

"What if they think like my mother? Assume I've led you astray and that I'm trying to trick you into child support or steal your liver or something else."

He gently put his fingers over her lips. "They

won't."

"How do you know?"

"Elle, trust me. They'll love our daughter and you the same way that I do. They will love her and pray for her and the surgery. And yes, they'll pray for you, too. I promise."

"OK."

"Come on. Don't want to be away from Abbie for too long." He led her down the corridor and into the small café.

He caught Elle's small gasp as she saw the only crowded table in the room. He squeezed her hand. "It'll be fine. Besides, we can shock them into silence by telling them your stage name."

Liam stood as they came over. "Hey, bro. Your message sounded urgent."

Patrick nodded. "Yeah, it is. Thanks for rounding up the troops."

"Welcome. Sit," Liam said. "We got drinks in already."

Patrick pulled out a chair for Elle. "Everyone, this is Elle Harrison. Elle and I go way back. She's a good friend of mine. Elle, this is Mum and Dad. Jared, you already met earlier today and this is my sister, his wife, Niamh. My brother, Liam, and his fiancée, Jacqui. Don't worry, there won't be a test on names later."

"Hi," Elle said.

Patrick sat and took her hand tightly as everyone said hello and introduced themselves again.

Niamh smiled. "Jared was telling us about rescuing you both from the hospital lift in the car on the way here." She rested her cup on her swollen stomach. "It must have been scary."

Patrick nodded. "Yeah, it was. And you be careful

my nephew doesn't kick that cup off."

"Who says it's a boy?" Niamh gave a sly smile. "Jarrie also hinted at something else, but wouldn't say what."

Patrick grinned. "That would be Elle's secret identity."

Liam tilted his head at Elle. "You do look familiar and I don't just mean from church. Are you...?" He broke off. "No, can't be."

Jared winked at Elle. "I didn't tell them. I figured you should have that right."

She smiled slightly. "I'm a singer. My stage name is Lisa Bellamy."

Patrick laughed as the faces dropped a mile around the table. "Told you that would silence them, didn't I?"

Elle smiled. "Yeah, you did."

"*The* Lisa Bellamy?" Mum asked.

"The one and only." Patrick grinned as silence reigned supreme.

"You're dating Lisa Bellamy?" Liam finally managed.

"Not exactly, dating. Well, not yet. I'm protecting her and her daughter."

Jared snorted. "Aye, I protect Niamh the same way you protected Elle outside the lift sometimes. But don't worry, that secret is safe with me...and the rest of the lads at the fire station."

Patrick shook his head, noting the way Elle's face flamed. "You're embarrassing the lady."

"You did that yourself this afternoon, when you snogged her in front of the entire watch." Jared winked at Elle. "And you, Elle, are braver than you let on."

She smiled faintly at him. "I was scared out of my

mind. But with everything else that's going on right now, it seems a minor hiccup."

"Yeah, Patrick alluded to something, but wouldn't say much."

Liam added. "I'm sure he didn't invite us here, just to meet you."

"No. I'd pick a better way to do it. Not to mention someplace nicer than a hospital canteen. But something *is* wrong. That's why we need to have this conversation." Patrick lowered his voice. "What I'm about to tell you goes no further."

Elle tightened her grip on his hand.

"Here we go," Liam said. "More secret agent stuff. I did my bit last summer, thank you. Elle, did he tell you he sent me and Jacqui to Africa and almost got us killed?"

Patrick sent him a withering look.

Dad coughed. "OK, that's enough. Let Patrick explain."

He took a deep breath. "In a way, Liam is right. It is secret agent stuff. But there's more to it, which means I have to bring you guys into the loop. It's imperative you tell no one else. To cut a long story short, we were involved when we were at university. Elle and I have a daughter called Abbie. She's thirteen now."

Shock passed over the faces in front of him, except Liam who already knew.

Elle studied her hands, her face turning red. When she looked up, a sea of smiling faces greeted her.

Niamh smiled. "I have a niece. And my baby will have someone to play with."

"What's my granddaughter like?" Mum asked.

Patrick looked at Elle. "You know her best."

"She has blonde hair, blue eyes. Looks a little like Patrick, but he insists she flicks her hair back like me." Elle's voice was quiet. "She loves singing, plays the flute really well. I have a photo if you'd like to see."

His parents smiled. "Of course we would."

Elle pulled the photo from her pocket. "It was taken six months ago." She gripped Patrick's hand tightly under the table.

He squeezed her hand back, wishing he could do more to put her at ease as the photo was passed around the table.

"How long have you known about her, Patrick?" Dad asked.

"A few hours," he said evasively. "It's a very long and complicated story. I'm not going to go into all the details now, that'll keep until a better time. The thing is, Abbie's really sick—she's dying. She's in ITU, which is why we're meeting here. Her only chance is a liver transplant."

The faces around him fell.

"Surgery is scheduled for this Friday coming. I'm going to be a live donor."

"Come again?" Niamh said.

"Abbie needs a new liver," he repeated. "Elle isn't a match. I am. We don't have time to wait for one to come up via normal means. So, I'm it. I'm convinced that meeting Elle again, the car accident revealing the tumor, all has God's hand on it. He's taking a bad, a very bad situation and working it for good. If Abbie hadn't been in that accident, they wouldn't have found the tumor until it was too late. Without the transplant she has two months to live. And before you jump in and say Elle only told me because she had to, it was a conversation we'd intended to have. We just hadn't found the time to sit down and discuss it before Abbie got taken ill."

"What are the risks?" Liam asked slowly.

Patrick hesitated and looked down. "What makes you ask that?" he hedged.

Liam continued. "It's major surgery, not a walk in the park. Besides, I'm guessing there must be risks otherwise you wouldn't have told us."

"He could die, too," Elle said, finally looking up. "Either during surgery, or just after, from a blood clot, complications, infection and so on."

Patrick looked back up to meet his brother's gaze. "I know the risks, but like I told the doctors and the counselor they made me see, I want—need to do this for Abbie. She's my daughter, and I'm not going to sit in the intensive care unit and watch her die when there is a good chance that I can save her life. I'm putting my trust in God to see this thing through and bring the three of us out the other side."

There was silence for a few moments.

Patrick took a deep breath. "I'm not asking you to give your blessing on this, just wanted you to know. And ask you to pray for Abbie. That she'll be strong enough for the surgery on Friday and that she won't reject the liver."

"That goes without saying," Mum said. "And of course you have our blessing. Why wouldn't you?"

Dad handed the photo back to Elle. "She really is beautiful. Would it be possible to see her?"

Elle nodded. "She's sleeping now, but..."

"Sure, I'll take you up in a few." Patrick glanced at his parents. "Abbie doesn't know I'm her father, yet. Like I said, it's complicated. Once she's well again, then we'll tell her. She probably won't wake until morning."

Liam put his cup down. "You said you're protecting her. So you're working?"

"Yeah. I can't say much about that, but you know Elle's mum died a couple of days ago?"

Mum nodded. "We're really sorry for your loss, Elle. If there is anything we can do to help...organizing the funeral or anything, let me know."

"Thank you."

Patrick paused for a moment. "The car crash wasn't an accident. It was murder, so yeah...I'm protecting them both right now. And that is all I can say. And all this I've told you goes no further."

Dad looked over at them. "I can't speak for this lot, Elle," he said slowly. "But Abbie is our granddaughter, and by default that makes you family, too. You need anything, don't hesitate to ask."

Elle's eyes glistened. "Thank you."

"I do suggest we begin by praying," his father held out his hands. "Perhaps we lay hands on Patrick and Elle and take turns to commend them to the Lord's care." Patrick wrapped his arms around Elle and looked over at the bowed heads of his family. Praying like this was instilled in them, but he'd never been the focus of it himself before. His heart swelled and his eyes burned. Then they were surrounded, hands touching them as one by one everyone prayed aloud for them and for Abbie.

Afterwards, Jared caught Patrick's eye. "Let's get another round of tea in."

Patrick got up. "OK." As he headed across the room with Jared, he heard his Mum start asking Elle about Abbie.

Jared picked up a couple of trays. "I thought I

should bring you up to speed on the lift incident investigation. There was no stair cleaning scheduled for this morning. Or lift maintenance for that matter."

Patrick stopped dead. "What?"

Jared handed him a tray. "The cables to all three service lifts had been tampered with. As had the brakes. It was providence that neither of you were killed today. God must have sent an angel to watch over you both."

"You have proof?"

"Cast iron. I've already handed copies of the file to both DS Nate Holmes and your boss. Just thought I'd give you a heads up."

They rejoined the others and Elle looked at him. "I was thinking about Mum's funeral. After all that's happened, I can't get my head around it. I don't—"

"She was your mum," Patrick said. "She loved you in her own way. Deep down, you know that."

Elle nodded. "I thought just at the crematorium and before the surgery if possible. Otherwise, it can't be for months. It'll only be me and Abby. We moved so often, we never really knew anyone."

Dad nodded. "I can sort that for you. I'll give Pastor Jack a call. We've done services there before. Let me know what hymns you want and I'll do the rest. And it won't just be you and Abbie. Like I said, we're your family now. We'll all be there."

****

Two days later, Elle sat in the crematorium, Patrick on one side and Abbie on the other. Patrick's family sat in the row behind them. An email had gone around the congregation and several of the church folk had also come to support her. But mostly everyone else in attendance were either police or spooks. Pastor Jack led the short service.

Elle sat wishing she could feel something, anything, some shred of remorse or grief, but there was none. Patrick assured her it was normal and that grief would come. But she wasn't sure. All she could think of was the lies that had been told to her over and over again.

Abbie sat beside her in a wheelchair, pale and drawn, tears running down her face. She still didn't know the truth and it was going to stay that way for a while longer. Until she was well enough to deal with it and accept Patrick, things had to stay as they were.

Elle looked down, tears filling her eyes. That made her guilty of the same sin she was blaming her mother for. Huge sobs welled up and overwhelmed her.

Patrick wrapped an arm around her, pulling her towards him. She buried her face in his black overcoat, crying for what she had lost and the secrets that now threatened to overwhelm her and steal what little she had left.

20

Patrick glanced up as Abbie padded into the kitchen of his small flat. Nahum hadn't liked the idea. He'd wanted them back in the safe house, but Patrick had talked him around. The girls had his bedroom and he slept on the sofa. Shay was around all day, and another two agents sat in the kitchen overnight. Three days out of hospital and still Abbie looked awful. Why hadn't anyone noticed this mass on her liver before?

Elle had said she'd wanted to take Abbie to the doctor's but her mother wouldn't let her go, saying Abbie was faking. Liam assured him that kids were notorious for having stomachaches or headaches in order to get out of P.E. and any other classes they didn't like at school. Maybe if the Harrisons hadn't moved every few months the school would have picked up on Abbie's constant absences and the same doctor would have realized something was wrong before now.

He was glad they had been able to have a funeral for Mrs. Harrison. That part was over. But the day had been a strain for both Abbie and Elle.

He smiled at her. "How are you feeling this morning?"

Abbie shrugged, slowly sitting down. "I hurt. Ellie's sleeping. She woke me with a nightmare. But I guess it's time to get up anyway."

He took her over a glass of juice and sat next to

her. "You sure you're OK?"

"Yeah. Ellie was talking in her sleep. She does that a lot."

"I learnt a lot of my brother's secrets like that," he said, winking at her. "Learn anything interesting?"

"Other than a lot of weird stuff? She's scared of someone called PJ. Kept saying she didn't want to do it." She paused. "And she mentioned you as well."

He raised an eyebrow, and picked up his coffee. "Really?" He tried to sound as nonchalant as possible, but still knew Elle wasn't telling him everything. DI Nemec was flying in today. Hopefully, his intel would fill in some of the gaps in this operation. Patrick swallowed the hot coffee and replaced the mug. "Do I want to know what she said?"

Abbie grinned, her newly-cut hair making her look like a pixie. Elle had restyled it at her request. "She wanted you to kiss her. Or was she scared of you and wanted this PJ guy to kiss her? Could be either."

He pulled a face at her.

She tilted her head. "Do you like Ellie?"

"I always have, but it's up to her who she sees and who she doesn't. And anyway, I'm working right now. Have to keep the two of you safe."

"Why? Because of the bad guys after her?"

"Yes. If she wants to carry on seeing me after we've caught and locked them up, then that's up to her."

"But do you want to see her again?"

"I'd like to know that, too." Elle's voice made them both look up.

Patrick grinned. He put a hand over his mouth to shield his words. "I think we've been sprung," he said in a stage whisper.

Abbie returned the gesture. "Oops."

Elle winked at her and sat down. "Well, I'm waiting. I mean, it doesn't matter what I want, if you just want to run away and hide once this is over."

"I'm not the one who ran away," he teased. "But yeah, I'd like to keep in touch. Tea?"

"Sure."

He got up, giving his hands something to do. "I still feel the same as I did all those years ago. I never stopped loving you, Elle."

Abbie wolf whistled.

Patrick grinned as Elle shushed her. "But, like I told Abbie, the balls in your court." He glanced over his shoulder. "Did you sleep OK?"

She nodded slightly. "Didn't expect you to have a double bed though."

He laughed. "I always have done since I got my own place. I prefer the room. Sides, it makes it easier when I have guests sleeping over like I do now."

Abbie stiffened. "Do you have a girlfriend?"

"Nope. I just like lying diagonally across the bed, which I can't do on a single one."

"No, cause you'd fall out or your head and feet dangle off the edge." She paused "But then you're so tall, you'd fall out anyway."

He chuckled. "Exactly." He brought over Elle's tea. "Here you go."

"Thank you."

He sat and winked at Abbie. "So, once we've run around the block, what shall we do?"

"Neither of you are running anywhere," Elle said shooting him a fierce look that had Abbie doubled over with laughter, before it turned into a wince and a gasp of pain.

"I'm OK…"

"Fine, no running for you," Patrick said, unable to hide his huge grin. "Being serious for a moment, can I add my mobile number to Abbie's phone? That way she can contact me should the need arise."

"Sure."

"Cool." Abbie pulled her phone from her pocket. "I'm almost out of credit though."

"I'll top it up for you." Elle put the cup down.

Patrick took the phone and scrolled to contacts. He added his name and number. "OK, send me a text so I can add you back."

Abbie tapped rapidly. "OK, sent."

Patrick winked at Elle. After a couple of seconds his phone chimed. *'I've got a text and you can't see it.'*

Abbie screamed with laughter. "Oh, send it to me."

He grinned and added her number to his phone. "Or do you want this one." He pressed a few keys and his phone screamed *incoming, pnueeeeeeeeeewwww, banggg.*

"Oh, that's brilliant. Can I have them both?"

He laughed. "Sure."

Then her face grew serious. "Can you grant wishes as well as save people?"

"What kind of wishes did you have in mind?"

"If Ellie's going to be my stand in mum, I want a dad, too. Only I'd like one like you."

He tilted his head. "Like me? I'm not perfect, you know."

Abbie nodded. "I know that. But you're tall, you have the same color eyes as I do, the same blood type, and you make me feel safe. And now I don't have a mum or a dad. Just Ellie."

He didn't know what to say. What could he say? Patrick held Elle's gaze for a moment. "Well, now you've got my number, any time you need me you can call. I'll be your stand in dad for a while. How does that sound?"

"Sounds good." Abbie smiled at him.

Elle smiled. "Abbie, go do that English assignment your teacher sent over. Let me talk to Patrick for a few."

Abbie stood and took her juice from the room.

Elle's expression changed to ice. "I don't want you making any false promises to her."

"I meant what I said. She needs someone and I'll be there. And that goes for you, too." He rubbed his fingers over the back of her hand. "Don't hide any more. And you don't need to run from me anymore, either. Let me in, Elle. Let me care for you and Abbie. She's my daughter…"

"Shh." She put her fingers over his lips. "I haven't even told her about me."

"Don't you think you should?"

"I know I should, but what do I tell her?"

"The truth. She deserves that."

She took a deep breath. "I will, just not today. Once she's better, I promise."

"So, shall we spend the day doing nothing, then? As we can't go running."

She laughed. "Go help Abbie with her English. I'm going to go have a bath. She can bring it in here and do it at the table."

He stood, and kissed her cheek before heading from the room.

****

Elle watched the two heads bent together. They'd passed the morning with Abbie's school work, doing first her English assignment and then doing her online maths homework. They'd eaten a sandwich lunch on the floor on a rug. Now Abbie listened as Patrick read aloud from the novel her literature class was reading. One dark and the other fair, but both with matching eyes and senses of humor.

Lord, is it presumptive of me to ask a favor of You? I love him. I always have. Please, work things out so we can be together. I'll do whatever it takes. The first thing being to stand up to Zeke and tell him no more. Make him listen this time. And find out from PJ the truth about Dad. I know that's really Patrick's job, but I'd rather him not know. I'll go in tonight. Tell PJ no more deliveries as well as give him the package back.

The chapter finished, Patrick smiled up at Elle. "Your turn."

"To do what?"

"The maths homework we couldn't do for a start. Then you can read the next chapter. Or... Oh, I know, you could write something."

Abbie nodded. "That's a way cool idea, Ellie. Write a song for Patrick."

Elle sighed. "I told you both, I gave up writing a long time ago."

Patrick winked. If she didn't know better, she'd say it was a conspiratorial wink. "Maybe she'd agree to write one for you instead, Abbie."

"Why me?"

"Because, squirt, A comes before P."

Abbie laughed. "Please, Ellie. Write me a song."

Elle put her hands on her hips and pretended to be

shocked. "He called you squirt and got away with it. How come I can't do that?"

Abbie shrugged. "So write me a song."

"Agent Page he had a squirt..." Elle began to the tune of old Macdonald, then broke off laughing realizing what she'd just said.

Patrick threw a cushion at her. "Way TMI," he complained in between laughing.

Abbie held her good arm across her stomach as she giggled. "Please a proper one, a song to sing in church." She tilted her head. "I know you worked it out with God. You settled things, didn't you?"

"Yes." When had Abbie gotten so astute?

"Then write one for Him, that we can sing in church when I'm better."

"OK, I'll try."

"Do it to the tune of *Danny Boy* and I can play that on my flute. Shall I show you?"

"I'd like to hear you play."

Patrick stood. "I'll go and get your flute."

Abbie waited until he'd left the room before gripping Elle's arm tightly. "He's nice. You really should date him."

"What is it with you and dating today? Patrick and I were together a long time ago."

"He likes you."

"He likes you, too, Abbie."

"Yeah, I know but..."

Oh, she was her father's daughter to a tee. "But?"

"I saw you kissing in the hospital. He really, really likes you. Go ask him out. Or are you chicken?"

"Noooo."

Abbie clucked like a chicken and flapped her arms like wings.

Elle grinned and threw a cushion at her. "Not chicken."

Patrick came in with the flute case. "Who's chicken?"

"Ellie is."

"Oh really? I like chicken."

Elle sighed. "I'm being ganged up on."

"Ask him."

"Ask me what?" Patrick asked, handing Abbie the flute.

"Can I speak with you? In the hall?" Elle poked her tongue at Abbie and went into the hall.

Patrick followed her. "What's up?"

"Abbie saw us kissing in the hospital and has it in her head that we should go out and said I should ask you."

Patrick grinned and put his hands on his hips. "And are you going to ask me?"

"No she won't, cause she's a chicken," came Abbie's voice from the lounge.

"Abbie…" Elle started to shut the door.

Patrick took two steps towards her "Kid sisters tease all the time. She'll get over it. So ask away."

Instead she grimaced. It wasn't her place to ask him out and she needed to sort everything else out first. And it was better to just out and say what she had to quickly. "I need to go to work at some point tonight."

The smile left Patrick's face instantly and Elle's heart sank. Then she steeled herself for a fight. She had to do this.

****

"Why not just call in? Tell them what's happened." A red flag went up in Patrick's mind as he spoke and he went into agent mode. What would make her need to go to work? With Abbie on the brink of major surgery, he needed to keep them both inside and away from danger as much as possible.

"It's not feasible. I have to go in. It's better to do this sort of thing"--she waved her hands in agitation--"in...person."

"We squared it away with the library on the phone. Besides they close at five, you know that."

"No, I need to go to the club."

"You realize I cannot protect you and Abbie in two different places."

"So get Shay to stay a bit later tonight and keep an eye on Abbie. Please, I wouldn't ask if this weren't important."

"Do you need the money that badly? I can pay child support or whatever you need."

"It's not the money. Please just let me go tonight. It's important." She shifted her weight from one foot to the other telegraphing her unease. "There's a lot depending on this." She added.

What aren't you telling me, Elle? He was still on this case until Thursday, or until the boss pulled him off it. He could still wrap this up. The agent in him had to let her go...

But the man who was in love with her wasn't going to let her go... not without a fight. And on his terms.

Patrick scowled. "I'll set it up." He headed into the kitchen, letting the door shut firmly behind him.

Shay looked up. Worry creased her face. "What's up?"

He crossed his arms and met her gaze.

"Can you watch Abbie for a couple of hours, while I escort Elle to work at the club? She's insisting on going despite how sick Abbie is."

"I'm sorry?"

Shay read the situation as he had. And as much as he hated to believe it, Elle *was* involved in this investigation.

"That's what I thought." He'd lowered his voice so only Shay could hear. "There is something going on. Something she's not telling me."

"You know protocol."

He nodded curtly. "That's why I'm going to put a bug in her bag and let her go in alone."

"Alone? You know what this man can do."

"I'll be in the bar, but she'll have to go into the office on her own—assuming he wants to see her tonight. When we leave have someone sent to guard the front and back door. Oh, if DI Nemec gets here before I get back, make him coffee. His plane landed at two, and I'm hoping he'll come here tonight."

"Will do." Shay reached into her bag and pulled out a listening device. "Here."

Patrick grinned. "Girl scout in a former life, huh?"

Blinding afternoon sunlight filtered in the kitchen window and Shay pulled down the shade. "Of course."

Patrick crossed to where Elle's bag sat on the counter. He unzipped it and stopped short. He pulled out the package. "What on earth is this?"

Shay's gaze met his. She didn't need to say anything.

Drugs

Patrick picked up a knife and slit the package open. Several small packets fell out, each containing white powder. He closed his eyes. *Lord God, what do I do now?*

He picked up two of the packets and handed them to her. "Get them to the lab. I'm going to put the rest of this in the safe."

"Pat—"

"Until she has been to the club, and I know how far she's involved in this, no one else is to know where they came from." He pushed a hand through his hair, feeling as if he'd just been punched in the stomach.

Shay looked at him long and hard. "If it were anyone else asking me this, I'd refuse. But I'll agree on one condition. If we have to arrest her—"

Patrick swallowed hard. "We'll do it. But after the surgery. Not before. Who she is, isn't going to stop me doing my job and upholding the law." He wired up Elle's bag and then went over to the larder. Swiftly he pulled everything from the right hand side of the lower shelf.

"Your safe is in the larder?" Shay snorted.

He rolled his eyes. "Last place you'd think of looking. And it's a little less obvious than behind the family portrait over the fireplace." He winked. "Or in the knicker drawer."

Shay snorted again. "Darn, now I have to hide the family heirlooms and my passport someplace else."

With the package hidden, he went to find Elle.

Elle sat with Abbie.

"It's all set. Let's go then."

She looked at him. "Everything all right?"

"Fine," he said curtly. "Sooner we go, the sooner we get back." This had to end and end now. If this meeting didn't further his investigation, he was going to confront Elle tonight.

Elle turned to Abbie. "I won't be long. Just going to the club for a bit."

"What about my song?"

"I'll write it when I get back. You be good for Shay."

"OK. Can I watch what I like on the TV until then?"

Patrick crossed the room and turned on the TV. "Nope. You can have...the kid's channels."

"Oh, wow. Thank you." She took the remote and settled back happily to watch.

"Since when have you had the kid's channels?" Elle asked him. "I didn't think you needed them."

"I upgraded to the full package this morning. Figured it'd give her something to do the next few days."

"And when we leave here?" she whispered.

"Then I cancel them."

21

Elle felt Patrick's hand on her lower back as he hurried her into the club. The rain, which began as a drizzle when they left, had turned into a downpour. Patrick's umbrella had saved her to some extent but he looked like a drowned rat. A very angry drowned rat. She had the feeling she'd done something to upset him, but despite her best efforts to draw it out of him, he'd just grunted and ignored her.

He led her through the back.

"You'll need to wait by the bar," she began.

"I'll wait where I want to," he snapped. "Let me get you to your dressing room."

Zeke stood by her dressing room door. "Where have you been?" he snarled. "You're not answering your phone, either home or your mobile. And what's he doing here?"

"He drove me in. You know my mother died a few days ago. And Abbie's been in the hospital. You're lucky I'm here —"

"We start recording tomorrow at six in the morning. The car will pick you up from your place at four thirty."

"I'm not doing it. I have Abbie to look after."

Zeke jerked his head at Patrick and lowered his voice. "I'm sure lover boy here could look after her."

"No." She would not sing in a bar or for either of those men again.

His hand tightened on her arm and he pulled her to one side. "You will do it," he hissed.

"No. Zeke. I quit. No more." She tugged free and went back to Patrick, gripping his hand tightly.

"Lisa, if you quit, you leave now. No money, no recording contract, no nothing."

She nodded grateful Zeke had used her stage name not her real one. "Suits me fine. Patrick, take me home, please."

Zeke's brows furrowed and rage sparked from his eyes. "Don't you dare walk away from me."

The office door flew open. PJ stood there, shirt sleeves rolled up, dragon tattoo plainly visible on his arm. "What is going on out here?"

"Lisa finally showed up. I was just explaining to her why she can't quit."

PJ fixed his ice stare on Elle. "Get in my office now."

Patrick took a step to go with her.

Elle shook her head. "Wait here, this won't take long."

PJ pointed at Zeke. "Zeke, stand here and watch him. He so much as blinks and you know what to do."

Zeke nodded. "It'll be a pleasure."

PJ glared at Patrick, jabbing his finger in his direction. "You don't move from this spot. Is that understood?"

"Crystal." Patrick eyes were as icy as his tone. He looked at Elle. "I'll be right here. Yell if you need anything.

"OK." She eased past PJ and into the office.

PJ slammed the door behind him. Expletives fell from his lips as he glared at Elle. "Where have you been?"

"I called in. My mother died. My sister has been in the hospital."

"I asked you to take care of something for me."

"Yes, but like I said, things happened, and I wasn't at home when they came to collect it, apparently. Then what with the accident and Mum dying and Abbie getting sick, honestly the whole thing just went right out of my head."

He held out a hand. "Give it to me."

"Sure, it's right here." She opened her bag and moved things around. Her stomach fell into her shoes. Her throat dried and her voice stuck. "I...I...it..."

"What?"

"It's n...not here."

PJ drew himself up to his full height. "Then where is it?"

"It's probably at home. Or at my friend's house. I'm staying with a friend for a few days." She backed away, terrified of what this man would do.

"The bloke in the hallway?"

"Yes. Let me go back with him and look for it. If I find it, I'll bring it back tomorrow."

"Tip the bag onto the desk."

"Why?"

"Just do it."

With trembling hands, Elle tipped the contents of her bag onto the desk. She cringed as PJ rifled through her bits and pieces. Nausea flooded her. Where was it? Had Patrick found it? Is that why he was so angry with her? What on earth did the parcel contain to make PJ this upset with her? When he nodded, she scraped everything back inside and zipped it up.

"Find it. I want it on my desk in the morning."

"Or what?"

"Being fired will be the least of your worries."

"You don't need to fire me. I already quit. I don't want your money or your help or your packages anymore."

PJ's face changed. It was as if he suddenly sprouted a pair of horns. His skin reddened, and a look of pure evil shone from his eyes. "No one quits, Eleanor."

"I just did. At least twice."

He leaned in, his face inches away from hers, his nails digging into her arm viciously. "If you love your sister at all, you will keep working for me in whatever capacity I deem fit. Is that understood?" He shook her hard, yelling at her. "Is it?"

"Y—yes," she whispered.

"Good. Numbers fourteen verse eighteen. Go."

Not needing to be told twice she left. She had to get out of this mess. The only way was to tell Zeke she wasn't coming back and trust Patrick to keep her safe and away from this place. PJ wasn't the man she thought he was.

Patrick's concerned eyes held hers as she scurried from the room. "Elle, are you OK?"

She nodded and looked at Zeke. "By the way. I quit. You can tell PJ that. He wasn't listening to me."

Zeke reached out for her.

Patrick formed a wall between her and Zeke.

"Back off." Patrick looked down from his substantial height advantage.

Zeke's eyes widened a little as his gaze went to Patrick's shoulder. He'd seen the holster. "Fine, you take her then."

Taking her hand, Patrick exited the building. He didn't say a word until he'd ensconced Elle in the safety of his car. He leaned down as he pulled the door closed, and held her gaze. "Elle, what are you doing?"

"What I should have done a long time ago. Quitting."

He shut the door and quickly ran around the car. He got in and looked at her. "Are you going to explain?"

"Yeah, but I got something while I was there." She reached into her bag and waggled a flash drive between her fingers. "PJ made me empty my bag and when I put everything back, I took it off of his desk. Give me a while to look through this and I might figure this out."

"No. That has to go to evidence." He snatched it from her fingers, pocketing it.

She sighed. "Fine. Oh, by the way, did you find a package anywhere in your house? A brown padded envelope?"

He narrowed his eyes and frowned. "Why? Did you lose one?" He started the car and turned on the lights. Across the car park, lights blinded them.

Irritated, she turned her face away, putting a hand up to shield her eyes. Then she settled back in the seat as Patrick drove out of the space. "No of course I didn't," she said sarcastically. "That would be why I asked." The car opposite did the same. She pulled down her sunshade, watching the car follow them.

"This discussion will have to wait." Patrick kept checking the mirror as he drove. "I think we have a tail."

"You think?"

He changed lanes and turned right onto the main road. He reached up and activated the Bluetooth earpiece for his phone. "This is Page. I've picked up a tail. I'm currently driving east on the London Road heading into Headley Cross. I'm going to try to lose him on the back roads." He glanced at Elle. "Hang on."

Elle closed her eyes as Patrick began driving like a madman. He took corners too fast, and although she didn't normally get car sick, she definitely was nauseous now.

She hit the seatbelt as Patrick slammed on the brakes, performing a hand brake turn. She stifled a scream and braced herself.

"Sorry. Are you all right?"

"Yeah." She closed her eyes and hung on tightly.

Another two or three sharp turns later and Patrick sighed. "Lost him. Heading home now."

She kept her eyes shut until the engine finally turned off. She opened the door and quickly darted up the path to the house, gulping huge breaths of fresh air.

Patrick ran after her. "Elle?"

"I'm fine." She headed inside as soon as the door was unlocked.

Shay came into the hall. "Everything all right?"

"Not really," Patrick huffed. "Where's Abbie?"

"She's lying down in your room, watching TV. She said she was tired. DI Nemec is staying in the Rainbow Lodge Guest House tonight. He'll be over first thing in the morning."

"OK. Thank you." Patrick caught Elle's arm as she headed for the bedroom. "Lounge, we need to talk."

"Tomorrow, please. I'm tired."

"I want to talk about this now."

"I don't." She wrapped her arms around her stomach, willing herself not to throw up. By the time he knew the truth, he wouldn't want anything to do with her.

"You just quit your job for a reason, and I have a feeling it has something to do with why you're being protected. Not to mention the fact we got tailed. So sit down and wait for me while I bring Shay up to speed. It's time you told me the whole truth. And that includes the package full of drugs from your bag."

Bile rose in her throat. "What?"

"Don't tell me you didn't know." His blue eyes turned to ice. "By rights I should arrest you here and now, but I'm prepared to hear you out first. Go into the lounge and stay there."

Elle looked down. "Can't I check on Abbie first?"

He shook his head. "Shay just said she's fine. Get in the lounge, and wait while I bring Shay up to speed."

****

Patrick finished filling Shay in just as the phone rang. He sighed. "Now what?" He answered it. "Page, I'll be with you in one moment."

Shay looked at him. "Want me to stay 'til the night shift get here?"

He shook his head. "No. I'll see you in the morning." As she headed out, he turned back to the phone. "Sorry about that."

"Did I call at a bad time?" Liam asked.

"Not the best time," Patrick said. "What can I do for you?"

"Actually, I was reading my Bible and study notes and had a feeling I should share it with you. I need you to listen because this isn't coming from me."

Patrick angled himself so he could see Elle sitting in the lounge. "OK."

"I was reading Numbers eleven. *'Is the Lord's arm too short?'* You need to pray before you do anything else tonight, bro. It doesn't matter how screwed up things are right now, no matter what's happened and gone wrong today. You can't fix things. Only God can..."

"Wait a minute," Patrick interrupted. "How did you—"

"This isn't coming from me. I have been told to pass it on. You can't fix things, only God can do that. You have to put your own desires aside and submit to God's will. God's reach is so great, there is no situation that He can't turn around and work for good. Even if we can't see a way out, God can. It might not be the path we want or would choose for ourselves, but God put you in this very set of circumstances for a reason. You just have to trust Him."

Patrick sagged against the wall.

"Does that make any sense?"

"Yeah, it does," he whispered. "Things have gone pear shaped. I don't know what to do..."

"Pray. Let God handle things as He sees fit."

"Thank you."

"Welcome. So, how's Abbie?"

"Doing OK. She's in bed. I need to have a conversation with Elle. It's not going to end well...and I'd value your prayers."

The smile on his brother's voice resounded down the phone line. "I'll do that now. Talk to you tomorrow. Night."

"Night." Patrick hung up and took a deep breath as he slid the phone into his pocket. *Thank you, Lord, for the reminder that You are in control here. I don't know what to do, how to fix it. But You do. Help me.*

22

The lounge door opened and shut as Patrick came in and sat down. "It's time we had this conversation. You've been changing the subject on me long enough."

Elle shifted in the chair. Patrick watched her carefully, every sense on full alert. Her skin was pale and clammy and her arms clenched her stomach tightly. Was what she had to tell him that bad? Or was she sick from the ride home? Or because she'd been caught out? Either way he didn't intend to let her go until he knew the truth.

He changed his tone and spoke gently. "And start from the beginning at the house party." For some reason that seemed to be the starting point. No matter which way he looked at it, everything stemmed from the choices the two of them had made that weekend. A decision that had not only produced Abbie, but sent Elle on a path to seeming destruction, and him on one to total solitude.

"Over break, when I found out I was pregnant, I thought my life ended. Everyone was disappointed in me. Except mum, who did nothing but gloat because I'd proved her right. We moved house so that no one would know us. I'd write songs to take my mind off being sick and I'd sing them to Abbie before she was born."

Patrick listened as she spoke. Tears glistened in her eyes and her voice was hard to make out at times.

She sat on the edge of the chair, her skin a mottled white and from the way she gulped for air, she felt as bad as she looked.

"Then Dad brought home a bloke he knew from work one evening—Zeke. Got me to sing for him. Zeke took me on, became my manager. He arranged everything, or so I assumed. I started getting jobs in all these clubs. I made enough money to buy things for Abbie. Dad worked as an accountant." Elle took a deep breath.

"Until my mum's letter I never put it all together. We never owned a house. Always rented, moved frequently. Soon as someone recognized me, we'd move or at least that's what Dad and Mum claimed. It was hardest on Abbie. With us constantly on the run, Abbie didn't have time to make friends or settle into any school."

"What about your manager, Zeke?"

"He arranged the housing. He set me up in clubs and so on. Actually this is the first time we've been at the same club. Before that he'd come over and visit once a week or so, hear me sing a couple times a month in the clubs. But it goes deeper than that."

Her tale had more than unsettled him. Alarm bells were starting to sound, and he had the uncomfortable feeling in his gut that always accompanied his moment of clarity when working. The pieces were starting to fit into place and he had a horrible feeling he knew, finally knew, where he'd heard the name PJ. *Lord, please, let me be putting them together wrong.*

"So, if Zeke doesn't own HC1, then who does?"

"PJ. I met him for the first time the other day. He owns a whole chain of clubs up and down the UK. Zeke works for him too, and I only ever sing in his clubs. I've delivered packages for him. He's my boss. But I swear, I didn't know what was in them. I did this, because he said if I didn't do what he asked, I'd regret it. I found out the other day my father worked for him, for years. When I was in his office he said that being fired would be the least of my problems, and then said Numbers fourteen verse eighteen. I don't know what that is."

Patrick grabbed his Bible from the end table. He flicked through it. "The sins of the father," he said holding her gaze. "'*He punishes the children for the sins of the fathers to the third and fourth generation.*' So, it must be something that your father did, that you are paying for. You and Abbie. The question is what? How long have you been living here?" Patrick pulled out his phone and sent Shay a text asking her to confirm who owned HC1.

"Here in Headley Cross?"

He nodded. "Yeah."

"Four months." She took a deep breath and at a noise from the doorway, turned. She held out a hand. "Hey, Abbie. What's up?"

"I can't sleep." Abbie looked shattered, her dressing gown hanging open over her baby doll pajamas and her sling. She held her mobile phone. "Can I download a new game for it? I found this really cool one."

"Sure, come here and show me."

Abbie slowly crossed the room and sat down.

Patrick looked at her and then at Elle, knowing the conversation was, for the moment, paused. "So, who wants some cocoa with cream and sprinkles and a flake?"

"Yes, please," came the answer from them both at

the same time.

Patrick smiled. "Coming right up." He stood and headed to the kitchen. His phone beeped as he pulled the milk from the fridge.

Shay's message read *'PJ Foster owns HC1 and twenty-five other clubs in the UK.'*

'Something's not right' he replied. *'She moved every six months yet still worked for him. Why?'*

After a minute the reply came. *'Ask her, not me.'*

He grinned and punched in Shay's number. He tucked the phone under his ear, making the cocoa as it rang. "Hey, figured this would be easier than texting. I did ask her. Her mother insisted it was because she was Lisa Bellamy. Every time she was recognized they'd move."

"Being recognized comes with the territory of being famous, surely. I mean, Hiram Davies gets it all the time, but he doesn't move house constantly."

"Exactly. And Hiram Davies doesn't work two jobs to make ends meet. Something else is going on, but not sure what. She quit her job at the club tonight."

"I bet that went down well."

Patrick stirred the cup and added the cream. "That's putting it mildly. Dig into PJ Foster. His name set off alarm bells in the back of my mind. He's got something on her, said if she didn't deliver the packages he'd make sure everyone knew. I'm giving her the benefit of the doubt as far as the drug connection goes, at the moment. I've got a feeling it's the bloke DI Nemec is after. Same surname, same first initial."

"What are you thinking?"

"Just check. There has to be more to us protecting her than she's letting on." He glanced towards the door and smiled as flute music drifted through the hallway.

"...Are you listening?" Shay sounded irate.

"Sorry, got distracted. Can you say that again?"

"I asked if you want me to ring DI Nemec now."

"Yes please. This PJ has sent out some pretty big messages. But he's never threatened her life. He owns the clubs and she works for him. He doesn't want her dead. She's had near misses, but these guys don't miss. At least, not unless it's intentional."

"Got you."

Patrick set the microwave going to heat the milk for the last cup. "He quoted the sins of the father verse at her and how the children pay to the fourth generation."

"But why threaten to kill Elle? Like you said, that makes no sense."

"Did you see the actual letter she came in with? I don't remember it being in the file." Patrick added a flake to the two cups and set them on a tray.

"It wasn't. Hang on...the sins of the father. Maybe it's nothing Elle did at all. Maybe it's something her father did."

"My thoughts exactly. Dig up what you can on Elle's father."

"Will do." Shay paused. "How are things going other than that?"

"Just making cocoa, then planning on an early night. Have to be at the hospital at four tomorrow afternoon."

"You got enough back up for tonight?"

"Yeah. Nigel is in his car out the front. Martin should be here in the next half hour. Abbie and Elle are in my room same as last night, and I have the couch. We're fine—"

Shattering glass resounded in the other room. Patrick dropped the phone and the cup. The cup spun on its edge for a second, then tipped, spilling cocoa all over the table.

"I need back up...now." Patrick raced to the lounge, as Abbie's scream pierced his soul.

"Nooooooo. Patrick...." Elle's cry struck him in the heart.

He pulled his gun from its holster, as he ran. "Elle..."

Abbie screamed again.

Elle's voice echoed. "Don't hurt her. Leave her alone."

The anguished cry had him pounding the hall and bursting into the lounge, gun drawn and held in front of him in both hands.

Two masked men stood in the middle of the room. One held Abbie, the other Elle. Elle had a gun pointed at her head. Rain and wind poured in through the shattered front window.

Adrenaline and terror filled him. The personal and professional sides of him battled it out for an instant before the professional won.

"Put the gun down," Patrick ordered.

"I don't think so."

There was a swift arm movement.

A flash and a bang.

Pain spun him around, as he got off a shot of his own.

"Patrick..."

As he fell, he saw the men back out of the room, dragging the two girls with them. He struggled upright, gripping the gun in blood soaked fingers. "Elle..."

He ran into the hall, turning his ankle. He cried out involuntarily, getting to the door in time to see a car pull off the drive and screech off into the darkness, leaving a cloud of exhaust behind. He memorized the plate. *Lord, God, please protect them. Forgive me for failing.*

Where was Nigel? Why hadn't he stopped them?

He limped over to the car on the grass, his stomach plummeting as he registered Nigel slumped over the wheel, covered in blood.

Pain, guilt and stomach turning nausea churned inside him. He clutched his arm and limped towards the front door. He needed to get to a phone and call this in. Salt burned his eyes. He'd failed them.

Screeching rubber and brakes came from behind him. He spun around, gun up and ready to fire. They weren't going to take him without a fight.

23

Elle clutched Abbie tightly as the car swung away from the house. Images of Patrick caught by the bullet and spinning around before falling, played over and over in her mind. He was hurt and it was her fault. *Please, don't let him be dead. I need him. Abbie needs him. Now he's back in my life, I want him to stay.*

Abbie whimpered as she clung to Elle.

"Shut her up," hissed the tall man. He clutched his arm. Perhaps Patrick's one shot had hit him after all. "Or I shut her up permanently."

Abbie screamed.

Elle hugged her. "Shh, it'll be all right. Just sit quietly."

"It's not OK. We've been kidnapped." Abbie's words struck deep into her core.

The man with the gun turned around in his seat. "Listen to your mother and be quiet."

"She's not my mother. She's my sister."

"I said shut up." He waved the gun at them. "You do know how to shut up, don't you?"

Abbie nodded, her face white and pinched. "Yeah," she whispered.

"Then obey your mother and be quiet."

"Where are you taking us?" Elle asked.

"Mr. F wants to discuss a breach of contract with you."

"Like I told Zeke, I quit. There is nothing to—"

"Mr. F doesn't like being told no. His patience has run out."

"So why bring Abbie if he wants to see me? He doesn't need her. Please let her go, she's sick."

"She doesn't look sick to me. She stays as insurance."

Elle looked down at Abbie, holding her tightly. The beginnings of a plan formed in her mind. "I guess we're going to head office in Wokingham, then?"

"Of course."

She nodded and leaned down to whispered in Abbie's ear. "When I tell you to jump, I want you to get out of the car and find help."

"While it's moving?" Terror flickered in her eyes.

"If you stay here, they'll hurt you and I don't want that."

"Jumping out will hurt, too. And they'll hurt you if I leave."

"Hush up all that whispering." The man glared at them. "Or else."

"They won't hurt me." Elle hugged her. "We need to work together here. I need you to go and get help while I pretend to do what they want."

"I'm scared."

"Me, too." She kissed her forehead. "When I get home we need to have a long talk. But God will keep us both safe until then."

"You promise?"

"I promise." The car slowed down as it approached a junction. "Soon as it stops get out. Run to the nearest shop…"

"Everything's closed. It's too late."

"Do you still have your phone?"

Abbie nodded. "It's in my pocket."

"Then ring Patrick or dial 9-9-9. Find a policeman. Get help. Scream if you have to." The car stopped. Elle opened the door and pushed Abbie out. "Go. Run."

Abbie glanced at her and cried out as she hit the ground. Then she pushed up and ran away from the car, screaming.

"You stupid—"

Elle shut the door. "Let her go. I'll do whatever you want, just, please, let her go."

The two men hesitated. The car behind sounded its horn several times. "What do I do, Rick?"

"Go, leave her. I can always pick her up again."

Elle turned as the car drove off. She could just make out Abbie limping into the darkness, heading back the way they'd come. She had no idea where they were. *Please, God, keep her safe. Let her find Patrick or someone who'll keep her safe. As long as she and Patrick are OK, it doesn't matter what happens to me.*

****

Patrick winced as the nurse bandaged his arm. He had gone to the hospital under sufferance. All he wanted to do was find Abbie and Elle. The longer he sat here, the colder the trail was getting. Shay and DI Nemec had arrived at the hospital shortly after he had, and he was also desperate to talk to the American. But the nurses had prohibited it while he was being treated.

The bullet hadn't done any major damage and having it removed hadn't been as bad as he'd thought. He'd refused pain medication of any kind, not wanting his brain dulled and his thoughts addled. He glanced up at Mr. Brown, the transplant surgeon. "Is this going to affect the surgery on Friday?"

Mr. Brown looked up from the notes. "It shouldn't. So long as you keep the wound clean and keep out of any more trouble. I will want all the tests to come back clear, however."

"Good." Relief filled him. Now all he had to do was find Abbie and Elle. "You still want me to book in at four tomorrow afternoon?"

"I'm tempted to make you stay in now."

"I can't do that." Patrick paused as Nahum pushed through the curtains. "Did you find them?"

"No. Every cop in town and the rest of the county is looking for the plate you gave us. Nigel's fine. They're keeping him in overnight."

Patrick pulled down his shirt sleeve and buttoned it. "So, Doc, as staying in isn't an option, can I go now?"

"You need to wait here for the prescription meds. I'll see you at four in the afternoon for those tests. You and Abbie can share a room tomorrow night." He nodded and left the cubicle.

"Assuming we find her," he muttered. He winced again as the nurse fastened his arm into a sling.

"I'm sorry?" The nurse looked at him.

"That's how I got shot." Patrick ignored the black look Nahum gave him. "Trying to prevent her and her mum from being kidnapped. But that comes under patient confidentiality."

"Of course. I'll get you those meds." The nurse said and vanished.

Shay and DI Nemec came in. Shay looked at him. "Patrick, you need to hear this."

Luke Nemec held out a hand. "Nice to meet you at last, Agent Page. Shame it's like this."

Patrick shook his hand. "Likewise, Inspector."

Nemec nodded. "Agent Williams brought me up to speed and we compared notes. Your PJ or Mr. F is my guy—Philip Joseph Foster or Phil Baines. He was responsible for the kidnap of his sister-in-law along with helping run one of the biggest drug cartels in the country." He drew in a deep breath. "He and his brother killed their parents in a house fire when they were twelve. They went into care."

Patrick went cold. What had Elle said? After her mother died in a fire... "What were the parents' names?"

"Rachel and Daniel Foster."

Patrick closed his eyes. "Rachel Foster was Elle's birth mother." He filled Nemec in on what Elle had told him a few nights earlier. "So this is revenge pure and simple. Mr. Harrison just took his daughter, leaving the Foster boys to social services."

Shay looked at him. "The sins of the fathers. Elle and Abbie have to pay."

The nurse came back in. "Here are your meds."

"Thank you." The phone vibrated in his pocket and he pulled it out.

"That should be switched off," the nurse scolded.

"I'm on duty, sorry." He looked at the screen. "It's Abbie's phone. Inspector, I assume you'd like in on this?"

Nemec nodded. "And it's Luke."

"Patrick." Answering the call, he strode from the cubicle, heading to the exit. "Abbie, is that you?"

"Patrick?" Her voice was faint, her breathing heavy as if she were running.

"Yes, it's me, honey. Where are you?"

"I don't know. They've got Ellie. They said they'd

kill her. She pushed me out of the car, told me to get help. But it's dark and I don't know where I am."

Patrick looked at Nahum. "Get a trace on her phone." He pushed open the doors into the chilly night air, trusting his boss to do as he asked. Pain ricocheted from his arm through his whole body as he and the others ran to the car. "Did they follow you, Abbie?"

"No. They shot you." Sobs echoed down the phone. "I thought you were dead."

"I'm OK. The doctor bandaged my arm. I'm more worried about you and Elle."

"Please help me."

"I'm almost in the car now, sweetheart. We're tracing the call, so stay on the line."

"I'm running out of credit."

"Another minute or so and then I'll call you back." He got in the car, struggling to do his belt up one handed. "Tell me what you can see."

"It's dark. There aren't many street lights. Some big houses."

"Can you see a street name or a shop name?" The phone went dead as Shay began driving. *Please, Lord, some help here.* He redialed, hoping Abbie had the sense to end the call. "Did you get a trace?"

"Not yet."

"Try again." The phone rang and was picked up almost immediately. "Abbie?"

"I'm still here. I'm cold, Patrick. And scared."

"I know. I'm trying to find you. Can you see a street sign or a shop anywhere?"

"No. There's something coming."

"Flag it down, sweetheart. Give the driver your name and then give him the phone so I can talk to him."

"K." Her voice faded for a moment. "He didn't stop."

"It's all right." He looked at Nahum. "Anything?"

"Yes, she's in Arbor."

Patrick allowed himself a slight smile. Arbor was a suburb of Headley Cross, albeit on the other side of town. "Abbie, I need you to do something for me. We know where you are, but it'll take us a little while to reach you. About fifteen minutes."

"What do you...want me...to...do...?" Her voice was faint and Patrick could hear her shivering.

"Keep walking until you find a road sign."

"OK." There was a long pause. "It says Willow Hill."

Patrick sighed in relief. *Thank You, Lord.* "That's great, honey. Now turn into that road and keep walking until you come to house number seven."

"Who lives there?"

"My parents. They'll look after you until I get there."

"Is it safe?"

"Yes, sweetheart, it's safe. You met them in the hospital, remember?" He looked at Shay. "Did you get that?"

She nodded. "Yeah."

"Can I borrow your phone, Nahum?" He took the outstretched handset and dialed his parents, holding it to his other ear. He winced in pain. "Hey, Dad, it's Patrick. Abbie is about to knock on your door. I need you to find her or if she gets there first, let her in, keep her safe. I'll explain when I get there."

"OK."

He heard the door chime in both phones. "Dad, I'm hanging up." He gave Nahum back his phone.

"Abbie, my Dad knows you're coming." He heard the door open.

"Patrick sent..." The teenager's voice tailed off.

"Abbie? Abbie answer me."

Silence.

He caught Shay's gaze in the mirror and shook his head. "Go faster. Abbie? Abbie, speak to me."

"Patrick?" A deep male voice with a familiar Irish lilt echoed down the phone.

He sucked in a deep breath. "Yeah, Dad. Where's Abbie? Is she all right?"

"She passed out on the doorstep. Mum's with her. She's stirring now. But she's very cold. We'll get her warmed. Do you want me to call an ambulance?"

He shook his head. "No, don't do that. We're no more than fifteen minutes away. Do me a favor, Dad?"

"Anything."

"Lock the house up tight. Turn on every single light and don't open the door until I get there. I'll phone before I ring the doorbell. If anyone other than me turns up, call the police."

The drive was an eternity. Worry for Elle gnawed at his gut. Every bump in the road sent rivers of pain coursing through him. Perhaps not taking the meds was a stupid move after all. Pain, although it usually sharpened his senses, was now beginning to cloud his judgment.

He closed his eyes. *Forgive me for failing in my duty. Please, keep Elle safe until I can find her. Thank You that Abbie is safe. Please don't let her be harmed or too sick for the transplant to take place in two days' time.*

"Patrick."

He opened his eyes. "Yeah, Shay."

"We're here. I'm going to get someone to come

and stay here. That way we don't have to move Abbie again."

"At least until we need to take her to the hospital." Patrick got out of the car and ran up the path as fast as he could, dialing the phone. "Dad, it's me. We're here."

The door opened. "She's safe," Dad said. "What happened to you?"

"I got shot. I'm fine. Where is she?"

"In the lounge with Mum."

Patrick strode down the hallway and burst in. "Abbie?"

"Patrick..." She bolted off the sofa and ran into his outstretched arm.

He held her tightly with his good arm, ignoring the pain soaring through him. His eyes burned with the tears he wasn't going to let fall. He'd never realized that being a parent could hurt this much. "I got you." He sat down, pulling her onto his lap. "You're safe now."

24

Abbie didn't move off his lap. Despite his desire to go searching for Elle, Patrick had to comfort his daughter for as long as she needed it. Besides, right now he had no idea which way to go and where to look. Luke and Shay were making phone calls, tracking Foster's movements and trying to work out where he'd take Elle. Abbie sipped the cocoa his Mum made and snuggled against him.

He kissed the top of her head. "How are you doing?"

"Better now." She looked down at the cup. "But Ellie's still out there."

"I'll go and find her, but first I need to ask you some questions. The more you can tell me, the quicker I can find Elle."

"I'll try."

"Did they say where they were taking her?"

Abbie's face creased in thought. "I don't know. I was scared."

"It's scary having a gun waved at you." He hugged her. "But they can't hurt you anymore. I can find Elle a lot faster if I knew where they went."

"They mentioned a Mr. F. He was mad at Ellie, wanted her to see him."

"Did they say where they were going?"

"Wokingham. To the head office."

Patrick hugged her. "Thank you, sweetie." He

glanced over. "You get that?"

Luke nodded. "Give me a minute and you'll have an address."

Abbie tugged at his sleeve. "Are you going to find her now?"

"Yes, I am."

She twisted her head, her eyes wide with fright. "Can I come with you?"

"No, it's too dangerous. I need you to stay here in the warm. Besides, we don't want you getting sick before the surgery on Friday."

"OK. But am I safe here? You said we were safe at your house. Did they find us because the man followed you?"

"How did you know about that? You were asleep when we got in."

She shook her head. "I was pretending to sleep. I do that a lot."

He winked at her. "Don't tell my Dad, but I used to do the same thing."

"Heard that," came the comment from the other side of the room.

Abbie smiled slightly. "You need to work on your stage whispers. For a spy, you're useless."

A chuckle spread around the room, the tension lessening slightly.

"But yes, we were followed back to my place. However, I promise you'll be safe, this time. No one knows you're here." He hugged her again. "I want you to stay here until I come back. My mum and dad will look after you until then. And you see that man over there?" He nodded to Nahum. "That's my boss. No bad guy would dare take you away with him here."

"OK. Does your arm hurt very much?" She lifted a

cautious hand and touched the fingers poking out from his sling.

Pain rocketed through him, but he hid it, not wanting to scare or upset her further. "A little, but you know what hurts more?"

"What's that?"

"Not having Elle here with us. So I'm gonna go find her."

Abbie nodded. "You will come back?"

He kissed the top of her head. "I promise." He managed to slide his watch off his wrist and put it over her hand. "Will you look after this for me until I get back?"

She fingered the clock face in a caress "Don't you need this for spy stuff?" She flipped it over. "Isn't there a mini gun or camera inside?"

He smiled. Abbie had watched way too many spy movies. "Shay has hers so we'll be all right." He lowered his voice. "Besides I still have my pen."

"OK." Then she looked up at him. "I'm scared."

"I know," he whispered. "Me too."

Dad came over and sat next to them. "How about we pray before Patrick leaves to find Elle?"

"Please." Abbie snuggled into him and closed her eyes.

Patrick looked gratefully at his dad over the top of Abbie's head. "Thank you," he mouthed.

"Dear Jesus. We ask that You keep Elle safe wherever she is. Send one of Your angels to watch over her and protect her until Patrick and his team can find her and bring her home. Please be with Abbie as she stays here with us tonight. We also ask that You go with Patrick now, protect him, and give him the strength and guidance he needs to do what has to be done. Amen."

"Amen." Abbie looked up. "Will Jesus really send an angel? Aren't they all busy in heaven singing hymns?"

Patrick smiled. "Some of them are, but the rest are busy doing what Jesus needs them to do. I'm sure He'll send one to look after Elle."

"Can I stay up until you get back?"

"You need your sleep." He tucked a finger under her lowered chin. "But we'll be here when you wake up in the morning. Or if we're not, very soon after."

****

Elle dragged her feet as the driver, Rick, forced her down the corridors to the office. He was gripping her arm so tightly she knew she'd be bruised in the morning. The one hope running through her mind was she'd signed into the building. There was a record of her arriving her, if nothing else.

She tried to tug free. "I can walk on my own."

"I don't trust you. Mr. F wants to see you."

"So you keep saying."

"He won't be happy your kid isn't here."

"I told you, Abbie is sick. She needs to be home in bed."

"Maybe she is now. He may want me to go and get her again."

"You leave her alone." She screamed finally losing the last bit of her composure.

Rick dragged her into office and pushed her towards the desk, letting go of her.

Staggering forward, she lost her footing and landed on her hands and knees, catching her head on the edge of the desk. Stars danced at the edge of her vision and she closed her eyes tightly.

"Careful, don't damage the merchandise. Her face is worth as much as the rest of her now." PJ gripped her arm, pulling her upright, before sitting her in a chair. A hanky was pressed into her hand.

She blotted her face with it. "What do you want?"

PJ smirked. "I want you to honor your side of the contract. You either pay for those drugs you kept or you bring them back."

"I don't think so." She caught her breath.

PJ looked at Rick. "Leave us."

The door shut behind her and PJ gripped her face, jerking it upwards. She held the dark gaze, as his hand slid to her throat and squeezed. She couldn't breathe or swallow. Her eyes felt like they were popping out of her skull. Stars floated before her, darkness creeping around the edge of her vision.

"You're nothing like our mother." he hissed. "But you're the only family I have left."

Then the pressure eased. She leaned forwards, her hands cradling her throat, gasping for breath.

"What?" she whispered.

"Yes, dear sister. Your father had an affair with my mother...our mother. She left *us* to be with him when that Holy Roller he was married to kicked him out. She must have told you—"

Elle gasped. "Then Mum knew you..."

"Jeanette Harrison was not your mum, and of course she knew me. Our mum, yours, RJ's and mine, wasn't so...righteous. She had an affair with one of Dad's accountants and left. Then after you were born, Dad persuaded her to come back home. But it wasn't the same. She kept threatening to walk out and leave with her little princess. Baby EJ, who could do no wrong. Dad hated you, hated what you stood for. A constant reminder of the sin she committed against him. There is no betrayal greater than that of a wife against her husband. You know that? Unless it's with his brother...but that's a different story."

Elle watched him pace as he spoke. His hands gesticulating, his steps firm, ice shooting from his eyes and all the time the underlying tone of hatred directed solely at her. She held her arms tightly across her middle, trying not to shake and show the fear flooding her.

"Have you any idea how many times RJ and I stood over your crib, took the blows he meant for you. So what if you weren't his...you were still our sister. It was going to be so great. The three musketeers. RJ, PJ and EJ."

"RJ?" she whispered.

"Robert James, my twin."

"Where is he now?"

He shook his head. "Only things got worse and soon Mum treated you with the same contempt. You'd be left in your crib for hours to cry, while she and Dad got as high as kites. So we killed them. And your *father* took you. After all we did to make sure you were safe, RJ and I were left to rot in care home after care home. Only EJ was good enough for him."

"I'm sorry..." Maybe if she placated him, he'd let her go once all this was out of his system. "It must have been hard—"

"Hard?" His voice rose and his face reddened. "You don't even know the meaning of the word. You got *everything*, and we got *nothing*. But we are family, you, me, and RJ. So we rebuilt our mother's business and we tracked you down. Your father really was a clever accountant and as dirty as they come. It didn't take much to entice him back. He laundered money for us for years."

"But as he grew older he lost his edge, got sloppy. I had to keep moving him in order to keep him a step ahead of the cops. He didn't die in a hunting accident, by the way."

"You killed him?"

"I did. It was my pleasure. And Jeanette Harrison, too. And now you will keep working for me. Either singing or delivering the drugs or both."

She shook her head. "I'm not working for you."

"EJ, this is a family business, always has been." He put his finger on her lips, silencing her. "And you don't have a choice. This is the way it's going to be. You will continue to work for me, in whatever capacity I deem fit, and Abbie goes to boarding school. You can see her during the holidays."

"Or?"

"She dies and you work for me anyway. What was it you said when you first came to me for a job?"

"I didn't come to you. You came to me."

"Technically, your father came to me. Kept raving about how proud he was of you. What a wonderful singer you were. I sent Zeke to the house, and you said if it paid enough, you'd sing. For Abbie."

She closed her eyes. She'd do anything for her daughter, almost, but what he was asking was one step too far. She'd face the consequences with Patrick, assuming she ever got out of here. If she went to prison, so be it, but she wasn't going to do this anymore.

She wasn't going to compromise herself or her

faith any longer.

So long as Patrick looked after Abbie. No matter what, Abbie had to be kept safe and protected.

A hand around her throat forced her mind back to the angry man in front of her. "—and pay attention when I'm speaking. If you don't work for me, I will kill Abbie."

"Why? What have I done? What has she done?"

"Because you were Mum's favorite," PJ yelled. "She loved you more than me. More than RJ. You were all that mattered and you weren't even born a Foster."

Tears she refused to let fall burned her eyes.

Lord, please, get me out of here, somehow. I don't want to do this, don't want to dishonor You. But he said he'd kill Abbie if I didn't. I read somewhere about angels being sent to preserve the saints. Lord, I'm no saint, so I don't ask for protection for me. But please, please protect Abbie. What he wants me to do is wrong. It doesn't matter what happens to me, because I'm nothing. But don't let him get ahold of Abbie when I stand up to him and say no.

****

Patrick strode across the impressive lobby of Foster Towers to the desk. Shay and Luke walked close behind him. He stood in front of the bored looking security guard.

"We're closed."

"I can see that. I can also see your boss's car parked out the front of the building."

"Mr. Foster doesn't like to be disturbed when he's working late. He's in a meeting…"

He pulled out his ID. "Now we can do this the easy way or the hard way. Personally, I'd prefer the hard way. Where is he?"

"In his office. Fifth floor. I'll let him know you're here."

"Don't bother." Behind him more footsteps sounded as the rest of his team joined him. He pulled Elle's picture from his pocket and waved it in the guard's face. "Have you seen this woman tonight?"

"No."

Patrick spun the signing in book around and looked at it. "So, who was on the desk two hours ago when she signed in? Where is she?" There was no answer, but then he didn't really expect one. "Arrest him. Charge him with accessory to kidnapping and obstructing an official inquiry."

One of the agents vaulted the desk and twisted the guard's hands behind him. "You can't do this," the guard protested as metal cuffs were clapped on his wrists.

"Looks like we just did." Patrick frowned seeing the gun on the guard's belt. "Put in a call for CO19 to get here ASAP." He and his team were armed but having the Armed Response Unit as backup wouldn't hurt. Especially if he was right about this place. "Right, we tear this place apart looking for her. She signed in so she must be here somewhere."

He headed to the bank of lifts. Perhaps Mr. Foster would be a little more co-operative.

"Agent Page," called one of the other agents. "Wait a second."

He spun around. "What is it?"

"Come and look at this."

He crossed the lobby in six long strides to the back of the desk and surveyed the bank of CCTV screens. "What am I looking at?"

"L6. Isn't that her?"

He peered at it. A heavily paneled office, an angry man and Elle tied to a chair, her shirt sleeves torn and bloodied.

Patrick pulled out his gun and vaulted the desk. He ran across to the guard being escorted from the building. Pulling his arm from the sling, he ignored the pain, pushing the guard up against the wall and held it to his head.

"Patrick!" The warning cry came from both Shay and Luke at the same time.

Patrick didn't falter. His hand tightened on the guard's throat, the gun pressed firmly against his temple. "I can see her on camera L6. Where is the feed for that coming from? I'm not going to ask again."

"Mr. Foster's office." The man before him paled and his voice quivered. "Take the lift to the fifth floor, turn left. It's the suite right at the end of the corridor."

"Thank you." Patrick ran to the lifts, praying hard. *Please, keep her safe until I get up there.*

25

Elle pulled on the ropes tying her wrists, waiting for her brother to hit her again. How could this monster be her brother? But as she looked at him she saw the similarities in his eyes and hair. But that's where the comparison ended.

"I provided for you. I sent you to college. All that time you thought it was your father.

"Dad?"

"Yeah, your father." PJ spat the word out. "He ran the whole club side of the business for years, not just the accounts until he died, then that idiot Jeanette thought she was in the clear. You see he got greedy. He cooked the books, skimmed off the profits from the club, and tried to get into the drug racket as well. So he had to die. Then I worked on Jeanette. Told her that if she kept you singing, I wouldn't press charges against her, because she knew what he was doing. After that, you only received a pittance from your sales and singing. I had to get my money back."

"I don't want any of your money."

He raised a hand.

She closed her eyes, reciting the verse from Psalm ninety-one in her mind.

For He will command his angels concerning you to guard you in all your ways; they will lift you up in their hands, so that you will not strike your foot against a stone.

Her head slammed sideways as PJ's hand made

contact.

Bright light filled the room and she closed her eyes tightly to avoid being blinded. The brightness faded enough for her to open her eyes.

A huge figure stood over her. Clad in trousers and a shirt, he held a sword in his hand. Easily standing over six feet tall, with long golden hair that fell over his shoulders, the stranger's physique put PJ to shame. Brightness shone around him and what looked like wings extended from behind him, wrapping around and over her.

"You will not harm her." The voice filled the room, yet his lips didn't move.

PJ froze. "What the—" The blasphemy died on his lips.

"You will not harm her." The voice was louder.

Elle struggled against the ropes, desperate to get away. PJ raised a gun and aimed at her point blank. The bullet missed. He aimed and shot again.

"You. Will. Not. Harm. Her," the voice boomed, resonating so the light fittings quivered. The empty glass vase on the table shattered.

The bright light increased around her and a breeze wafted her hair. A sense of peace filled her.

The sound of running footsteps made her look towards the door. Several armed men burst in, all shouting at once.

"Put the gun down."

"Armed police."

"Put the weapon down."

"Elle?"

The light faded and the figure vanished.

"Elle?"

She looked around, relief filling her. "Patrick."

Clare Revell

Tears ran unbidden down her face. "I thought they'd killed you."

His trembling fingers tried to untie the rope that bound her. "No."

"Where's Abbie?"

"She's safe." His fingers worked at a frantic pace, until the rope gave. He pulled her against him, holding her tightly against his chest and injured arm.

She clung to him, hardly able to believe he was there. "Did you see him?"

"See who?"

"The tall blond man. He was right here. He wore a white shirt and tan slacks. He had a sword."

"Sword?" Patrick's head jerked up, scanning the room. "Is there another armed man we need to worry about?"

"No. He appeared when PJ hit me. He repeated over and over 'you will not harm her.'"

Patrick looked down at her. "Elle, love..." He slid out of his jacket and wrapped it around her. "Did he hurt you?"

"No, few bruises, that's all." She took a deep breath. "Did you just call me love?"

"I did." His voice faltered for a second. "Is that all right?"

"It's very much all right. I like it."

"Then I shall keep doing it. So, this other man?"

"Didn't you see him? He was stood right over me. There was a bright light around him and he had wings and—"

A smile crossed Patrick's face and lit his eyes. "Wings? That sounds like the angel that Dad prayed for." His gaze held hers.

"Angel? That's what I thought, but doesn't that

256

make me crazy or something?"

Patrick kissed her cheek. "Not at all. Now let's get you checked over and take you somewhere safe. "

"Take me where Abbie is." She leaned against his chest. His strong heart beating in time with hers. Her skin warmed where his lips pressed against it.

"That, my love, goes without saying."

He closed his eyes as he kissed her. His hands ran over her arms, goose bumps rising on her skin in response. Stars exploded around her. She never dreamed so many different feelings could come from such a small touch as this. What had once been between them was still there. Perhaps she could rekindle it, have him become part of hers and Abbie's lives.

When he broke off, she leaned against him and watched the officers pull PJ to his feet. A tall man she didn't recognize held PJ firmly.

"Nice to see you again, Foster." An American? What was an American doing here? Was she in deeper than she realized and caught up in something international?

PJ snarled. "Nemec. So how are my niece and nephew doing?"

"Doing great and will be doing so much better now you're back behind bars where you belong. You have the right to remain silent..."

Elle tuned them out. *Niece and nephew?* She didn't understand. Did she have more family she hadn't been aware of?

****

Patrick held Elle tightly in the car as they were

driven back to his parent's house. He thanked God over and over for delivering her. Apart from rope burns on her wrists and a small cut on her forehead and left arm, she was unharmed. She'd fallen asleep almost as soon as they'd left Wokingham, not that it was a restful sleep. She whimpered and tossed against him, repeating something about family over and over.

He kissed her forehead, determined not to lose her again. She was his new obsession. If she'd let him. He wanted to be part of her and Abbie's lives. A big part if he had his way, although he'd settle for weekends and holidays if he had to.

Elle's eyes flickered open. "Are we there yet?"

"Almost." He smiled at the childish statement. "I'm sorry. I didn't mean to wake you."

"It's all right." She shifted in his arms, resting her head higher up his chest. "You make a really comfy pillow."

"Thank you. I think."

She ran her fingers down his shirt buttons. "Is Abbie really safe?"

"She's fine. I've seen her. We'll be with her soon."

"Where is she?"

"She's at my parent's place. I have six agents staking out the house. We're going there for the night. We have to be at the hospital at four tomorrow afternoon." He glanced out at the rising sun and smiled. "OK, this afternoon. There's not much left of tonight." He stifled a yawn.

"You should sleep a little."

"I'll spend most of tomorrow and the following day asleep. Elle, you mentioned family in your sleep."

A wry smile crossed her face. "Something PJ and that American officer said. About kids and a sister-in-law. It's possible I have more family out there. That's if they want anything to do with me."

"Why wouldn't they?"

"I don't know. Let's see I have a psychopathic brother named PJ and apparently another just as bad named RJ and my father "cooked the books" for drug dealers. How long will it be until RJ comes looking for me to pick up where PJ left off?"

"You don't have to worry about RJ. He's dead." Then he paused. "Sorry, I guess."

"Don't be. I don't want to talk about my family anymore." She raised a hand and ran it slowly down his face. "You're my hero. My tall, dark, handsome, stubbly hero."

Patrick turned into her touch and kissed her fingers. "You leave my stubble out of it." He hugged her as the car pulled up outside his parent's house. "Knowing my mum she'll have made up a bed for you. You should try to get some sleep."

"I will, once I know Abbie's all right."

Patrick slid out of the car and ran around to open the door for Elle. He wrapped an arm around her as soon as she got out and then headed into the house with her.

The door opened as they got there. He smiled at his father. "Dad."

Dad smiled. "Come in. Are you both all right?"

"I will be. Is Abbie OK?" Elle asked.

"She's sleeping upstairs in Patrick's old room. I'll take you."

"Thank you." Patrick kept an arm around Elle as they followed Dad upstairs to the small back bedroom. He pushed open the door.

Elle left his side and hurried to the bed, curling up

behind her daughter. Tears ran silently down her face as she held her.

Abbie opened her eyes. "Ellie?"

"Yeah, it's me."

Abbie turned over and clung tightly to Elle, sobbing hard.

Patrick leaned against the doorframe, longing to hold them both, but having the sense to hold back for a few minutes.

His mother appeared at his side. "Here," she said, holding out a glass and two pain meds. "You should take these. Shay said you refused anything at the hospital."

"I needed to think. I still do."

"Patrick, you're exhausted and in pain. I can see that just by looking at you. Take them. They're just aspirin."

"Yes, Mum." He swallowed the pills and then rubbed the back of his neck. "It was close," he said quietly.

"But you got her back."

He nodded. "Yeah." Handing the glass back to her, he went into the bedroom and sat on the bed next to the two most important women in his life.

Abbie looked at him. "Thank you for bringing Ellie back," she said, hugging him.

He hugged her back. "I promised, and I keep my promises."

"Speaking of promises." Abbie looked at Elle. "You said we needed to talk?"

26

The silence was deafening. It was as if the whole world held its breath waiting for her next move. Elle looked at Patrick, then at Abbie. "I—"

"Please, Ellie. You said you'd tell me what that man meant."

She'd dreaded this moment. Yet, she was partly glad the time for secrecy was over. There would be no more secrets in this family. *Lord, give me the right words to explain this to her.* "All right."

"I'll leave you to talk." Patrick started to get up.

"Stay, please." She ran her tongue over her lips and took a deep breath. "Yeah, the man in the car was right. I'm your mother and not your sister."

Abbie pulled away and sat bolt upright. "What? So you, Mum and Dad all lied to me?"

She shook her head. "There were a lot of other things going on, things that you were too young to understand. Some things I've only just found out about myself."

"Don't give me that 'you were too young to understand' codswallop. I am not too young," Abbie yelled. "I'm almost fourteen. I'm not a kid anymore, Ellie. I have a right to know the truth, don't I? You've just admitted I've been lied to all my life. Yet, you all told me never to lie. To always be honest even when telling the truth hurt and got me into trouble. What is this? One rule for me and another for the adults?"

Elle studied her hands for a moment. "Yes, I did lie. I'm not denying that. I wish I knew how make it better, but I don't."

Abby took a long breath. "You can't make it better. But you can at least tell me the truth now. All of it."

"There were a lot of things going on. Things aren't always black and white." She twisted the cross on her chain. "First, you are my daughter. I got pregnant when I was at university. I didn't intend...it just happened. After you were born, Mum and Dad insisted that they brought you up as their child. It wasn't what I wanted."

Abbie face crumpled, tears fell from her eyes. "So I'm a mistake that wasn't meant to happen. Oh, this just gets better and better, doesn't it?"

Elle shook her head. She reached for Abbie, then dropped her hand as the child pulled away. "That's not true. You were very much wanted. I wanted you. I loved you from the moment I knew about you. Getting rid of you was never an option. Ever." She looked at Abbie. "I promise that I would never do that to you or any other child I may have in the future. Life comes from God. From the minute the baby is conceived, it's alive and needs caring for. I just had no choice in who brought you up."

"Course you did."

"Abbie, you know what Mum was like. It's ironic. Neither of us were hers and she loved us so much. I just never knew she had secrets, too."

"What do you mean?"

"Dad had an affair. I was the result of that relationship. Mum adopted me when my birth mother was killed. I found the papers in her things the other night."

Abbie pushed up off the bed and crossed the room. "But why did you do it? Why lie to me?"

"I didn't think I had a choice." Tears filled her eyes. "I was young and couldn't see any other way. It was either give you up, which I wasn't prepared to do under any circumstance, or agree to their plan."

Abbie scowled. "So you agreed?"

"I worked every hour I could for you, held down two, sometimes three jobs at once. I gave up university, my degree and hope of a high powered career. Nothing mattered except you. Everything you have, every trip you went on, I paid for. It was all I could do, all I had to give. It hurt so much watching you grow up, hearing you call her Mum and knowing you had no idea who I was."

Abbie folded her arms tightly. Her eyes narrowed and she looked so much like her father that Elle's heart broke. *What have I done? I just made things ten times worse.*

"Were you all ashamed of me? Is that why we kept moving?"

"No, Abbie, I could never be ashamed of you. Dad was an accountant for a drug dealer." Tears fell slowly down Elle's face. "Mum tried to protect us." Until she knew the truth about her mother's involvement she wasn't going to say anymore.

"Why didn't he marry you?"

"What do you mean?"

"The deadbeat who knocked you up. Or didn't he want anything to do with you after you did it with him?" Abbie glared at her, using language designed to shock. "Did he leave you like Cori's father did? Decided he didn't want the responsibilities of being a father, so he left when things got tough?"

"Abbie." This wasn't how she'd imagined the conversation going. "Your father is a good man. I left him, OK? I didn't see him again or contact him. I wasn't allowed to. It's something I have regretted every day since."

"So who is he? Or don't you know?"

"You shouldn't speak to Elle like that," Patrick said.

"This has nothing to do with you, Patrick."

Elle sucked in what should be a deep calming breath, but wasn't. "It has everything to do with him," she sighed. "Abbie, this isn't the way I wanted to do it, but Patrick is your dad."

Abbie's face became a snarl. She pushed to her feet, putting her good hand on her hip. "So where were you all my life, then?"

"I didn't know about you." Patrick's face dropped. "If I had, I would have been there every step of the way."

"Is that the reason you agreed to the transplant? To try to make up for not being there all my life?"

He shook his head. "No, far from it."

Abbie took two steps backwards away from both of them.

Patrick held up his good hand. "It's all right to feel the way you do now."

Abbie glowered at him. "And how do I feel?" she spat. "You have no idea what I'm feeling, so don't you start to patronize me."

"I don't intend to. Right now, you're mad and that's a perfectly natural reaction. You should be upset and angry."

"I just found out my entire life is a lie. I'm an illegitimate waste of space neither of you wanted in the first place."

"You are wanted. Very much so, which is why your mother had you. Just don't let your anger blind you to that fact, and above all don't let your pride get in the way here."

Abbie rolled her eyes. "Get in the way of what?" she muttered.

Elle sagged onto the bed. This wasn't how it was meant to go. Abbie's anger was just escalating and there was nothing she could do. Perhaps Patrick could calm her—he did this for a living after all. Well, not deal with angry kids, but stand offs and negotiations.

"Your family." Patrick looked at Elle and then back at their very angry daughter. "We all make mistakes and…"

Abbie exhaled sharply. "What family?" she interrupted. "I have a liar for a mother, who didn't even want kids and a father who was never around and pretended I didn't exist. I must be the biggest mistake you two ever made. You wouldn't even acknowledge me. And to top it off the man who I thought was my father was a criminal—" She paused. "Is that why someone's been trying to kill us?"

Patrick shook his head. "We are still working on the why someone tried to kill you. But I need you to listen to me very carefully for a couple of minutes now. OK?"

Abbie shrugged. "Why?"

"Because you've had your say and so's Elle. And now it's my turn. Some of what you said true, but not all. You are *not* a mistake. No child is a mistake. Children are important. Not only are they a gift from God, they are the legacy of the love between two people. Your mum and I were very much in love and you are the proof of that love." He paused. "We aren't perfect; no one is. Even though most people like to think they are."

"She lied to me," Abbie insisted. "She tells me never to lie no matter what and in the same breath lies to me. When did she tell you about me?"

Patrick's face creased in pain and exhaustion. He rubbed the sling across his chest. "I didn't know about you until you needed the transplant and Elle wasn't a match. If I had known about you, things would have been different, I promise you that. I would have married her and fought tooth and nail for you."

"Yeah, right."

"And don't you give me the 'she hurt you so you are gonna hurt her back' line either, because that doesn't work. It just makes things so much worse for everyone involved. Including you."

Abbie glanced sideways at him and then looked back at the wall. "And how would you know?"

"Abbie, the last few days have turned everything we thought we knew on its head. Elle found out she was adopted and her father, birth mother, and brothers were all involved in the drug trade. Cut her some slack, will you? She's a victim, too."

He took a step closer and Abbie didn't move this time. "I found out I had a daughter I didn't know about. You found out your parents weren't who you thought they were." He knelt in front of her, his hands on her shoulders. "You've been shot at, kidnapped, lost your grandmother. We are all hurting right now, but what you don't want to do is throw away your family, because in the end they are all you have."

Her face softened, then the hard mask came down again. "Whatever. Just go back wherever you came from. I managed almost fourteen years without you. I don't need you now." Abbie pushed past him, running to the stairs.

Elle stood. "Patricia Abigail Harrison, you get back here now."

"Get stuffed," came the angry reply. "And my name is Abbie." Her footsteps thudded down the stairs and away from them.

"I'm sorry," Patrick said, leaning heavily against the wall. "I thought I'd gotten somewhere."

"So did I." Elle moved after her daughter.

Patrick's father appeared as if from nowhere and caught hold of her arm. "Let her go," he said. "She can't get out the front door and the garden is enclosed."

"I can't just let her go," Elle said, looking at Patrick and back to his father.

Mr. Page nodded. "That's exactly what you have to do. I know from bitter experience that the last people she is going to want to see or talk to right now are you two. Just give her time to think all this through. She's just had a huge bombshell dropped on her." He looked at Patrick. "You both know exactly how she feels at this precise moment."

"That is why I should go after her, Dad."

"No. Give her some space. Otherwise it will turn into a fight with both of you saying something you end up regretting for the next twenty years."

Elle looked at Patrick for a long moment and nodded.

Mr. Page nodded. "Now, the two of you need to eat some breakfast. That should give Abbie enough time to calm down."

"Thanks Dad. We'll be down in a few."

Elle studied her hands, tears sliding unbidden down her face. "Made a mess of that, didn't I?"

Patrick wrapped his arm around her. "We both did. I guess she's just got to work through this for herself."

"She was right. I used double standards on her. The old 'do what I say not do what I do' routine." She leaned into him heavily. "What have I done?"

"You did what you had to," he told her. "But it's where we go from here that matters."

"Guess only God knows that," she managed, trying to swallow the huge choking sobs.

Patrick nodded. He held her close, starting to pray.

****

Patrick opened his eyes. He had dozed on the couch, Elle resting against his good shoulder. Pain and a cramped arm woke him, but he didn't move. He flicked his gaze first to the clock and then to the patio window. Abbie was still on the swing where she'd been when his eyes closed on him.

Liam smiled at him. "How are you doing?"

"Not great. Sorry, I hadn't intended to sleep for three hours."

"It's fine, bro. You needed it."

"I guess. So tell me, why is it I can talk down terrorists and gunmen holding women hostage, but can't cope with a thirteen year old?"

"Kids are a minefield. Take that from one who works with them on a daily basis. Abbie's a good kid. I've sat with her, talked with her a little."

"And?" Patrick allowed a spark of hope to burn.

"She's still pretty upset, hence being out there and

not in here. She's reached the 'I'm worthless' stage. Give her another hour or so and she'll be ready to listen to you."

"Maybe."

Elle shifted and sat up slowly. "I'm sorry. I didn't mean to fall asleep."

"It's fine, love. I did too."

"Where's Abbie?" Elle got up and turned around wildly.

"She's in the garden," Liam said. "Three of Patrick's team are with her."

Elle moved stiffly over to the window. She stretched slowly and leaned against the glass.

Patrick rose and joined her. "If she went any higher on that swing, she'd end up flying."

"Like someone else I know," Liam said from behind him. "Every time Patrick got into a strop over something, he'd be out there on that swing as hard, fast and high as he could. He even broke it once, do you remember?"

"Yeah. The swing went one way and I went the other. I landed in the roses and the swing ended up on Dad's runner beans."

Patrick wrapped his arm around Elle, pulling her tight against his chest. He leaned his head against hers. The scent of shampoo and perfume filled his senses. How could things have gone so wrong? A simple case had become a nightmare.

He watched Abbie as she moved back and forth on the swing, holding tightly to the rope with one hand. She kicked fast, going higher and higher until she was flying. Tears streamed down her face, visible even from here. She glanced over at them, then looked away, kicking harder. Liam was right, she was like him in that respect. He'd spent hours doing just what she was doing now. The others would storm off to the bedroom and slam doors. He'd run to the swing and go as high and fast as he could.

He remembered the freedom he'd felt in that—

Abbie's head lolled back and her hands fell to her sides. Her thin body flew through the air before landing hard on the ground.

"Abbie…"

Patrick ran down the path, Elle at his side, Liam behind them.

She lay motionless, a trickle of blood coming from her mouth.

"Abbie…" Elle screamed. "Abbie, open your eyes."

Patrick felt for a pulse, raw terror twisting within him. "Liam, call an ambulance," he yelled. "Elle, don't move her."

"Abbie…"

He stilled her hands. "Don't move her, love."

She looked at him, tears running down her face. "Patrick…"

"I know. But everything's in place. If need be we just do the transplant a little earlier."

27

Patrick sat with Elle next to Abbie's bed in ITU, Elle's cold hand clasped tightly in his clammy one. He felt sick. Abbie still hadn't regained consciousness and her life signs were a lot lower than the doctors were happy with. He glanced up as the surgeon came over to them. He wore scrubs and had a stethoscope around his neck. The doctor's serious expression sent chimes of doom resonating though Patrick and judging by the way Elle stiffened, she felt the same way.

"Doctor?"

"It's not good. The MRI shows the fall did additional damage to her liver." He opened the file and went into more detail.

Elle gripped Patrick's hand tightly, leaning against him.

"Then we operate now," Patrick said.

"Mr. Page, even if we do, she only has a twenty percent chance of making it."

"And if you don't?"

"She'll die."

Elle gasped. "No."

Patrick looked at her, then looked back at the doctor. "Then do the surgery now."

"You are in no fit state to do anything yourself. Your arm is..."

"Doc, I'm not going to argue with you. It's not my arm you need, it's my liver."

The surgeon nodded. "I thought you'd say that. I have the theatre standing by." He nodded to the nurse. "We'll take Abbie up now and get her prepped."

"What do I need to do?"

"We'll need you about ninety minutes after we start Abbie's surgery. The nurse will show you where you can shower and change. Then we'll take you upstairs."

Elle leaned over the bed and kissed Abbie's forehead. "I love you. I'll see you soon."

Patrick stood numbly then leaned over and kissed Abbie too. He held Elle as they wheeled Abbie's bed from the room.

"What if I lose both of you?" she whispered as they followed the bed into the hallway.

"It takes more than a little surgery to get rid of me," he whispered. He tilted her face to his. "I'm not giving up just yet."

Elle held his gaze. "Promise?"

"I promise." He closed his eyes and kissed her, his good arm pulling her tightly against him.

She clung to him, responding to the kiss, accepting every ounce of love he poured into it.

Breaking off, he brought his hand up to cradle her face. "I love you."

"I love you, too."

If only there was a way to prove to her just how much he loved her. He glanced past her to see Pastor Jack standing next to his parents. An idea struck him so quickly, and with the force of a thunderbolt, that it could only have come straight from God. "Pastor, can I have a quick word?"

"Sure."

He moved over to him and whispered quickly.

Getting the response he was hoping for, he smiled and looked at the nurse. "The doc said ninety minutes. Is it all right if I spend an hour or so with my family?"

The nurse nodded. "You can have an hour, but no longer."

"Thank you." He returned to Elle. He took her hand and dropped awkwardly to one knee. "Marry me."

Her eyes sparkled with tears. "Patrick?"

"Marry me, now" he repeated. "We wasted the past fourteen years, I don't want to be without you a second longer."

"Now?" She glanced around. "Right here?"

"In the hospital chapel. Pastor Jack can do it."

"What about Abbie? Shouldn't she be here?"

"Love, with all the risks this surgery entails, I want you to know how I feel. We'll do it again with Abbie as chief bridesmaid once she's better."

"Then, yes, I'll marry you."

He gripped Elle's hand tightly. He nodded to his parents and the others to follow them down the hallway to the small chapel.

He led Elle to a pew at the front and twisted to face her.

"Can we do this? Is it legal?"

Pastor Jack nodded. "You'll need to do it again once the banns have been posted, but yes. As far as God and the church are concerned, you'll be married."

Patrick looked at her. "I love you."

Elle smiled and stood with him, repeating the vows Pastor Jack said.

Patrick pulled his college ring off his finger and, wincing, gripped her hand in his injured one. "With this ring, I thee wed. With my body, I thee honor and all my worldly goods I thee impart." He slid the ring onto her finger.

"It's endow." Elle giggled.

"Is it? Oh, OK. In that case, all my worldly goods I thee endow."

"I don't have anything to…Oh, wait, yes I do." She reached up and pulled the scrunchie from her hair. She slid it over his wrist. "I give you this scrunchie as a sign of the covenant made between us this day and a pledge of our mutual love."

A guffaw came from in front of them. "I assume you'll do it properly when I marry you next time."

Patrick winked at Pastor Jack. "Of course. She'll have a gold plated scrunchie next time."

Laughter came from behind them.

"Sounds good to me," Elle said.

"Now that Patrick and Elle have given themselves to each other by solemn vows, with the joining of hands and the giving and receiving of a ring and a scrunchie, I pronounce that they are husband and wife, in the Name of the Father, and of the Son, and of the Holy Spirit. Those whom God has joined together let no one put asunder. Amen. You may kiss the bride. And then we'll pray and ask the Lord to watch over all of you and for the surgeons."

Patrick wrapped his arm around Elle and pulled her close. "I love you, Mrs. Page," he whispered before his lips joined hers.

****

Patrick stood under the shower, the plastic razor in his hand. His hand shook and he prayed desperately he wouldn't cut himself. The nurse had offered to do it for him, but he refused. That was one thing he'd never allow anyone to do. He just hoped his chest hair would grow back. Five minutes later, clean, completely shaven and dressed in the very fetching open-backed gown they'd given him, he wrapped the robe over the top and padded out into the hallway.

His entire family stood there. Elle looked like she'd been crying, as did Niamh and Mum. He stood there and looked at them. "All I need now is the last meal and the last rites," he quipped.

Pastor Jack shot him a wry smile. "I can do the Baptist version of the last rites if you want."

He shook his head. He moved over to his mother and hugged her. "Don't cry," he said. "This isn't goodbye."

One by one, he hugged his family and kissed them. By the time he got to Elle, he had tears burning his own eyes.

She looked at him, her eyes red and tears pouring down her face. "Pat…"

"Elle, please." He wrapped his arm around her. He closed his eyes tightly, a huge lump in his throat. "I'm not scared for me, but for Abbie," he whispered.

"Me, too, but for both of you. Maybe my guardian angel will watch over you and Abbie for a few hours."

"Maybe."

"I love you so much."

"I love you back. I always have." His lips found hers and he kissed her, not caring who was watching.

The door opened and the surgeon came out. "We're ready for you."

Patrick nodded and slowly let go. "See you later," he said. He forced himself to leave Elle and follow the surgeon through the double doors.

His mouth dried as he looked at the gurney with all the equipment next to it. He took off the robe and sat down. His heart pounded and he shivered. Then a heavenly peace descended over him. He glanced up and for an instant saw a bright figure in the corner of the room with a sword and wings. It could only be the angel that Elle had described.

He winced as the nurse removed the sling and his arm dropped.

"You ready?"

"Yeah, let's do this." He lay down and looked up at the ceiling. *Please, God, don't let this be for nothing. Let it work and heal Abbie.*

****

Tears blurred Elle's eyes. Two theaters containing the two most important people in her life and there was nothing she could do to help either of them. Except pray.

"Elle?"

She turned towards Mr. Page. "I'm OK."

He put a gentle hand on her arm. "No, you're not. Let's get you back to our place. It'll be a long while before we hear anything."

"I should wait here."

"It'll be at least seven hours before Patrick comes out and at least ten for Abbie. They've got my number and yours. They'll ring as soon as there is any news."

"I don't want to impose..." She broke off. She had nowhere else to go. As far as she knew, she couldn't go home and she didn't have a key to Patrick's place. "I'll find a chair or something here and just wait."

"Sure you can impose. You're family now." A

smile just like Patrick's creased his father's eyes and lips. "Your wedding might have been unorthodox, but it makes you our daughter. So let's go home and wait for news."

"OK, Mr. Page."

"It's Dad. You're Patrick's wife, so it's Dad. Or Sean, if you'd find that easier for the time being."

Elle smiled. For the first time in a long time she felt accepted for who she was, faults and all, by someone other than God. "Dad sounds good."

****

Elle jerked awake as the phone rang. It was dark. Her heart pounded as she sat bolt upright. Where was she? How long had she been asleep? Then everything came crashing back down as Liam answered the phone.

"Page residence." He paused. "Which Mrs. Page? There are two. Sure. I'll get her for you." He held the phone out. "It's for you, Elle. It's the hospital."

Her hand trembled as she took the handset. Nausea rose in her throat. "H-hello."

"Hello, Mrs. Page. This is Sister Melrose from ITU. Just to let you know that Patrick is back with us."

Elle collapsed back into the sofa. "How...how is he?"

"He's critical. He'll be sedated for several hours yet. He's on a ventilator and several IV's. If you want to come in and see him, that's fine."

"What about Abbie?"

"There's no news yet. Probably won't be for another four or five hours."

"OK. Thanks." Elle hung up. She let the phone

drop into her lap, her whole body shaking.

Liam's hand covered hers. "Elle? What did they say?"

Glancing up, she saw everyone gathered around her. "Patrick's back in ITU. He's critical." The dam of emotion within her broke and she dissolved into floods of tears.

Over the next few hours, Liam, and Patrick's parents, or Mum and Dad as she was tentatively calling them, took it in turns to sit with her by Patrick's bed. His sister, Niamh, had left instructions to call as soon as he woke. She wanted to be there, but she was finding balancing her heavy work load and pregnancy hard and everyone agreed she'd be better off sitting at home, rather than in a hospital waiting room.

Elle held her husband's hand, talked to him, while the machines beeped and hissed and kept him alive.

It was almost midnight before they brought Abbie in and put her bed next to Patrick's. Elle watched, biting her nails, as the staff fussed around her daughter. "How is she?"

"It's too early to tell," the surgeon said. "We'll keep her sedated for at least twenty-four hours. Maybe more, depending how she responds. But she'll be in here for at least three days. Perhaps longer."

"All right, thank you."

Liam touched her arm. "Why don't we go home and get some sleep."

"I can't leave them."

"Sure you can, honey," Stacey, Patrick's nurse said. "I'm here, all night. And so is Patty. She'll be taking care of Abbie. If we need you, we'll call. Or if you want to call us at any time, you can do that."

Elle nodded slowly. She stood and leaned over

Patrick's bed. She kissed him gently. "Sleep well, my love. See you tomorrow."

Then she leant over Abbie's bed. "You too, squirt. We have a lot to talk about when you wake." She glanced down at the ring on her finger. "And most of it good."

****

Over breakfast, Elle looked up as Shay and the tall American came into the kitchen. "Morning."

Shay smiled. "Hey. Mind if we have a word?"

Her stomach twisted and she pushed the plate of food away. She knew what was coming and part of her wanted to run. She nodded slowly. "Have a seat."

Dad got up. "I'll be in the other room. Yell if you need anything."

"Don't go." Elle shook her head, her heart in her mouth as the two officers sat down. She didn't want to be alone. She couldn't take any more bad news. And if she was going to be arrested for her part in this mess, she wanted someone there.

Dad sat down again. "OK."

"What's happened?" Elle whispered. "Did he get away?"

Shay shook her head. "No. He's locked up. He isn't going anywhere this time. No plea bargain, no parole, no nothing."

"That's good," she whispered. Although no doubt he'd have told them how many packages she delivered, what was in them, and how involved she was.

Luke looked at her. "I'm DI Luke Nemec, originally from LA but now from Scotland. Agent

Page, Agent Williams, and I were working this case together. I've dealt with both RJ and PJ Foster in the past."

Elle frowned. "PJ said I was his sister. The letter Mum left me said the same thing."

Luke slid a file over the table to her. It contained official documents, and newspaper cuttings. "You're his half-sister."

She shuddered. "I'd rather not be."

"I can understand that." Luke nodded. "My wife, Sara, used to be married to Jamie or RJ—PJ's twin. Jamie faked his own death. Then he and PJ kidnapped her, trying to bring *her* into their drug business."

Elle shivered. "Like me…"

"Just like you." Luke smiled. "Sara was pregnant with Jamie's twins during all this."

She slowly looked up. "The niece and nephew…"

"Jennifer and Joshua. It's entirely up to you, but Sara and I are both in agreement here. If you want to stay in touch, see them, you can."

"Oh…" Tears filled her eyes.

"We don't need an answer yet. Just think about it."

She nodded and then studied her hands. "What about the drug trafficking? Aren't you going to arrest me? I honestly didn't know what the packages were. I mean, I had my suspicions, but he didn't give me any choice."

Even to her, that sounded like a feeble excuse.

"We've had instructions to arrest you, yes. Right now, we're going to treat it as helping with our inquiries. We'll interview you and you co-operate and it'll make things easier in the long run. You skip town, however, and you'll be hauled in faster than you can count to three and remanded in custody."

Her head shot up to look at him.

"But given the situation, we'll hold off on arresting you until Abbie is out of intensive care. But no longer."

She swallowed hard. Knowing it was coming didn't make it any easier. She felt sick, her hands shaking. There would never be an end to this.

28

Patrick ran around the track, endless circles with no end in sight. Wind and rain fought against him as he tried to reach the finish line. The old adage *just when I can make ends meet, someone moves the ends* ran through his mind as the finish line seemed ever further and further away. His feet pounded the track, squelching in the puddles, rain seeping into his clothes.

A scream echoed and he tripped over a root. He lay there, unable to get up. Water began to rise around him. He struggled to stay afloat. It hurt to breathe and he sank, drowning.

Voices echoed far above him. Hands reached out, but try as he might they were just out of range.

"He's fighting the vent. Let's take him off it."

"It's OK, Patrick. Just relax."

He sank below the water, then suddenly he was above it, gasping for breath. Bright lights on the ceiling blinded him, machines surrounded him, beeping and hissing, and pain such as he'd never imagined stapled him, through his stomach, to the bed.

He tried to sit up. Alarms blared, pain sliced, and hands pushed him back down.

"Don't try to move just yet."

"Abbie..." he gasped.

"Abbie's doing fine. You just need to lie still for me." A mask settled over his face. "We'll give you something for the pain."

"Elle…" His voice sounded like it was coming from a long way off. His throat hurt.

"I'll give her a call, just as soon as you've settled."

Cold ran up his arm, making him gasp and shiver uncontrollably.

The darkness rose and rushed full pelt to meet him, wrapping him in its shadowy embrace. He fell headlong into it.

The next time he fought to open his eyes, bright sunlight filled the room.

"Hey, you're awake." The voice sounded tired, but washed over him like a breath of fresh air.

"Elle…" He reached for her hand, gasping in pain.

Her hand took his. "Don't move. How are you doing?"

"Sore." He didn't want to worry her. "How's Abbie?"

"Still critical. They're not going to wake her for a while yet."

"What day is it?"

She smiled. "Sunday morning. I'm about ready to leave for church. I have something for you." She slid the scrunchie from her wrist onto his. "Your wedding scrunchie. They wouldn't let you wear it until you came around and said something sensible."

He struggled to focus on her face. There were two or three of her. Which one was really her? "I'm sorry…really tired again."

"It's OK, love. Sleep. I'll be here again later." Her lips pressed against his head, smoothing his way back into the darkness.

****

Three days later, Patrick gripped Elle's arm tightly

and shuffled the short distance from his bed on one side of the ward, to Abbie's bed on the other. He hated this. He hadn't had a day off sick in his career. He hadn't even taken leave in years and here he was, unable to even perform the simplest of tasks unaided. Unable to protect those he loved. Forced to stay in bed or shuffle like an old man.

"Slow down," he gasped, pressing an arm over his abdomen.

"Are you all right?"

"First time out of bed." Pain threatened to slice him in half and stars danced before his eyes. "At least we're on the same ward for now."

"Yeah. When do they move you?"

He sank gratefully into the chair by Abbie's bed. "I was hoping they wouldn't. But probably later today as I don't need an intensive care bed any longer. Or a nurse solely dedicated to my care." He closed his eyes.

"Oh, that's nice." Abbie's voice carried more than the normal amount of sarcasm. "You finally get your lazy butt out of bed to come visit and you fall asleep."

Patrick fought to open his eyes. "You can talk. You snore."

"Do not."

"Do too."

She giggled. "It's you that snores."

Elle looked confused. "Did I miss something?"

"Only him snoring," Abbie told her. "He keeps me awake."

"Nope, it's the bloke in the bed next to you."

"No, it's you."

Patrick raised an eyebrow. "Elle, is she always like this? Or did she hit her head when she fell and change into a monster?"

"Pretty much."

"Which one?"

Abbie laughed, then cried out in pain. "Don't make me laugh. It hurts."

The nurse winked from where she sat at the end of Patrick's bed. "Don't make me come over there and send him back to bed."

"I've only just got up," Patrick protested. "Give me at least five minutes."

Abbie scrunched her nose at him. "Before you go back to bed and snore?"

"Something like that."

Abbie took a deep breath. "I need to talk to you."

Elle looked at her. "We all need to talk," she said quietly. "But is here the place to do it?"

"I want to," Abbie said. "He said I should."

"Patrick?"

"No. The man with the sword and shiny shirt that spent the past few nights standing at the bottom of my bed...well alternating between mine and Patrick's beds. He said I needed to let you explain properly without getting cross."

"That's our guardian angel." Patrick reached over and touched her hand. "I saw him. So did Elle, but he didn't say anything to me like he did to you two."

"I was angry you kept something from me."

Elle took her other hand. "I couldn't tell you. Even though I wanted to. I made a promise and promises matter."

"Is that why you never had a boyfriend?"

"Yeah, because I gave my heart to your father and didn't want to lose what we had." Elle inclined her head slightly. "I have something to show you. Something you would have needed to see eventually anyway." She picked up her bag and pulled out an envelope. "Here, take a look."

"What is it?"

"Your birth certificate. Patrick hasn't seen it either."

Abbie read it, then gave it to Patrick. "You listed him as my father."

Patrick read the certificate, tears filling his eyes as he saw his name, place of birth and occupation on the document. A lump filled his throat and he swallowed hard, trying to shift it. He'd never told her where he was born, she must have found out somehow, because she was right. Belfast, Ireland.

"Why did you put him on it, too?" Abbie asked.

"Because it's a legal document and because it's the truth. Because I love him, and because I wanted you to have the choice as to whether you contacted him or not, once you learned the truth."

"Why?"

Elle reached across and slipped Abbie's mask back on. "Because, squirt, I love you. And I want you to have freedom to make your own choices."

"What's that?" Abbie caught Elle's left hand, pointing to the ring.

Elle turned to Patrick, a flustered look on her face, that he decided was downright cute.

He squeezed Abbie's hand. "Things happened really quickly on Thursday, the day you fell off the swing. The fall did more damage to your liver and they had to operate sooner than they planned. I asked Elle to marry me. I wanted her to know I loved her, and I needed to know she'd be looked after should anything go wrong. That you'd both be looked after if anything happened to me."

"You got married?" Her face dropped. "Without me?" She folded her arms across her chest, winced and pouted.

He nodded. "It was a spur of the moment thing, otherwise we would have talked to you first. We need to get a license and do it again, but yeah, Pastor Jack married us in the hospital chapel. Next time, we want you to be chief bridesmaid."

"I'd like that. What did you use for rings?"

Elle held out her hand. "It's Patrick's college ring."

"And I got a scrunchie," Patrick said showing her.

Abbie giggled. "With this scrunchie I thee wed?"

"That's more or less what she said. But you know what this means? Other than the fact I have to buy her a proper ring soon."

Abbie tilted her head. "I have a dad. And grandparents. And uncles and aunts…"

Patrick nodded. "Yeah and they are queuing up to come and visit." He closed his eyes, the pain building to a point where he couldn't hide it any longer. "But I need to go and lie down for a bit."

"OK." Abbie paused. "So do I call you Patrick, Agent P or Dad?"

"That's up to you. But Agent P is out. That's a cartoon character." He paused. He knew what his choice would be, but he wasn't going to insist on it. "And don't suggest Agent P to Liam…Uncle Liam either. Agent 3.14 is bad enough."

Abbie looked at Elle. "And what about you? Ellie? Mum? Oh, how about combining the two words and calling you Mellie?"

Elle poked out her tongue and flicked Abbie's ear. Patrick concluded that it must be a joke of some kind.

Elle shook her head. "I do not smell, thank you

very much."

Abbie giggled. "Isn't that what noses are for?"

"I think I'll leave you girls to it." He slowly pushed up, stifling a cry of pain.

Elle steadied him. "Easy."

The nurse came over. "Let me help. We're about ready to transfer you down to the main ward. They've found you a side room. Soon as Abbie is ready she'll join you. Should be a day or two."

"Yay, no more snoring spies keeping me awake," Abbie said, her eyes closing.

Patrick grunted. "Make the most of it, kiddo."

"That's squirt to you," she whispered.

Patrick lay back on his bed. "No need to come with me," he said to Elle.

"Abbie's fine for a few. I'll come see where they put you and pop back up here. And there is something I need to tell you."

He looked at her. "Luke Nemec already came in and brought me up to speed. I know they're going to arrest you, but it's routine. You'll be out on bail in no time."

"Are you sure about that?"

He squeezed her hand. "Yes. Talk to Niamh...she works for the CPS. She knows how it works."

"I don't want to go to prison."

He looked at her pale face. "It won't come to that."

"But if it does..."

"Then I'll take care of Abbie. You're my wife now and she's our daughter. She'll be safe come what may, and I'll be waiting right here for you." He paused. "Well hopefully not right here in this bed, but..."

She smiled slightly. "Thank you."

29

A week later, Patrick was home and bored. Even with the paperwork he'd persuaded Shay to bring him, the day dragged. Elle, out on bail for the next month, spent all day at the hospital with Abbie. His parents insisted he either lie on the couch or in bed. He sighed.

"What's up?" Liam sounded as amused as he looked.

"What's up is the fact that Elle and Abbie are in the hospital and I'm stuck here. I can't protect them. I can't work on the case. I can't do anything."

"Hey, you knew what was involved when you signed up for this. Four weeks doing nothing. And a further four weeks doing light stuff and working part time. And then you need to pass a medical before you can go running around, wielding your gun and fighting bad guys, again."

Patrick scowled.

"Anyway, even if you weren't on sick leave, you couldn't do anything until internal affairs clear you."

"I know how it works. With the charges against Elle and the drugs in my house and me not handing them over..." He sighed. The whole thing was a mess. The only plus was the fact that Shay knew about them and had at least written a report even if she hadn't handed it in before the kidnapping, which happened that same evening.

Surprise support had come from Luke Nemec,

who knew exactly how the system worked, from both sides. He'd also been kept in the loop and was still here, working the case with Shay and his boss, tying up all the loose ends and doing their best to clear both Patrick and Elle.

"Pi—you saved Abbie's life. Actually, you did more than that. You gave your daughter life twice. It's not every bloke gets the chance to do that."

"I guess."

"And you beat me in the marriage stakes, too. Jacqui reckons we should have eloped months ago."

"Mum would love that." Patrick looked at him. "Maybe we should talk the girls into a double wedding. Half the expense and double the fun."

"Sure. I'm game if you are. See what Jacqui and Elle want."

"OK. When I see Elle, I'll ask her. Is Jacqui coming over tonight?"

Liam nodded. "I'm going to pick her up around six."

The door opened, and Shay popped her head in and tapped on the wood. "Hey, you got a minute, Patrick? DI Nemec needs to talk to you."

"I have several very long, very boring minutes I will gladly give the both of you. Come on in."

Liam stood. "I might go put the kettle on. Keep up Pi's fluid intake."

Patrick scowled. "It's my liver they used, not my kidneys."

"Picky, picky."

Liam left and Shay stood over by the mantelpiece. She looked extremely ill at ease.

A rock settled in the pit of Patrick's stomach. Whatever was coming wasn't good.

DI Nemec sat down. He put a file on Patrick's lap. "This is everything. We found papers that prove Elle knew nothing about the drugs. Along with concrete proof that her father and adoptive mother were behind skimming money off the clubs. Although her mother wasn't the mastermind, she was definitely involved in a small way. She was trying to get Elle out of there."

"Hence the animosity towards Elle singing?"

"Exactly."

"Strange way to try to help someone."

"That's just the tip of the iceberg. PJ Foster knew about Abbie and he didn't get it from Mrs. Harrison either. She kept up the pretense of Abbie being hers right to her death. Foster found out from other sources. With that information and the fact Elle's father had been a criminal, he had enough leverage against Elle to keep her working for him."

Patrick looked up, shock and nausea running through him. "Where did he find out about Abbie?"

DI Nemec looked over at Shay and then back at Patrick. "Her birth certificate would be a matter of public record. From what I have been told by your agency, anyone can access it—it's as simple as putting in a request and waiting a couple of days or so. We checked with the records office as they keep tabs of what has accessed and who by. Zeke Whybrow pulled Abbie's birth certificate six months ago." He held his gaze. "He found out who Abbie's father was."

"Me."

"Yeah. Your boss and the Director of MI5 did some digging. Someone accessed your file about three months ago. About the same time the Harrison's moved to Headley Cross. They tapped your home phone, you've had a tail. Pretty much every place you've been and every single thing you've done for the past few weeks and months have been tracked."

A shiver ran down Patrick's spine. He leaned heavily back on the couch. He'd been compromised. He rubbed his temple. He knew the name Whybrow, but for the life of him couldn't think where from.

"It's a fairly good guess it was Whybrow. What we don't know yet is why. Chances are he did all this for Foster. But we can't find him."

Patrick looked up sharply. "What? You've lost Foster?"

"There's no chance of that. Foster's in custody and staying there. Zeke Whybrow has vanished. We have an APB out on him and Interpol's also been alerted."

"What are there ramifications of all this for me? Am I under arrest, too?"

"Fortunately you don't use your landline for work calls. As far as we can tell, and believe me we've run search after search and dug as deep as we would into a suspected terrorist cell, you haven't been compromised. As we speak, the Director has a team going through your house with a fine toothcomb. So, until we get this mess sorted, your boss wants you wired. Every single conversation, including private ones with Elle, I'm afraid."

Patrick slumped back in the chair. "I don't understand. They wanted me? They were using her to get to me?"

Shay spoke up for the first time since entering the room. "They knew your reputation. Who doesn't? Knew you'd do anything to keep her safe. But something isn't right here. Why dig so deep? I'm thinking it's more than just something Foster ordered. This feels like it's personal. My theory is for some reason Zeke Whybrow has a grudge against you and will stop at nothing to make you pay. Just like Foster was doing with Elle. Did you arrest him at some point...?"

"I don't know. I recognize the name, but can't place it. I need to go through all my old cases. Maybe I locked up a brother or shot his second cousin or pulled his grandmother over for speeding in a school zone or something."

"Already being done."

He looked down at the scrunchie on his wrist. "If this guy is after me, I have to send Elle and Abbie far away from me where they'll be safe."

"And that will prove what? That you care more about work than them?" Liam pushed himself away from the doorframe. He strode across the room and set the tea down on the table, spilling some of it. He braced his arms on the chair, shoving his face into Patrick's. "Just what are your priorities here?"

"I'm sorry?"

"Last week you married Elle for better or worse. In sickness and in health. Till death do you part. And now you're going to abandon them?"

Patrick sat upright, glaring at his brother. "I am not going to put her and Abbie in danger —"

"And why is it so different for you?"

"I'm sorry."

Liam's face grew red as he raised his voice. "You didn't hesitate to send Jacqui and I to Africa because it suited you. We both almost died out there. I got hit over the head, kidnapped, tortured, tied to a chair, doused in water and then had electric current run through me. Not to mention swimming with the crocodiles, before you finally turn up with the cavalry.

But I would do it again and again to keep Jacqui safe. And only a couple of weeks ago you were shot defending Elle and Abby. So what's changed?"

"Don't you yell at me."

"I'll yell until you get it through your thick head that it's not one rule for you and another for everyone else. You put your life on the line for people you don't know every single day. Yet, you would send your wife away without letting her make the same choice to protect you? What you need to do—"

Liam broke off and stood up straight. "No actually, I'm not going to tell you what to do. You need to pray and figure it out yourself. Neither of you chose this path, Pi, God did. And He wants you walking it together. Just grumble to Him and not to us."

Patrick sat there, stunned.

"He's right," Shay told him. "If someone got to me through Kevin, I know what I'd do. And it wouldn't be leave him."

DI Nemec chimed in. "I broke a few rules of my own where my wife is concerned, when she was kidnapped. But I'd do it again if it kept her safe. You have to let Elle make the choice. If she's anything like Sara, she'll be standing behind you with a rolling pin when you confront them."

Patrick closed his eyes. *Lord, I don't want Elle hurt, but I guess she married me knowing who I am and what I do and the risks involved. I have to track down Zeke and end this. But first she has to know and it should come from me.* He pushed up, grunting with effort. "Li…"

Liam glared at him. "What?"

"I need a lift to the hospital, please. My wife needs to be brought up to speed. Sir, I know you and Shay will keep trying to track Zeke down. I would do it myself, but I'm not meant to be working. When you find him, make sure he's brought in. He's not getting away with this."

DI Nemec nodded. "I'm on it. But first you're being wired."

****

Elle handed the book to Abbie. "Your turn to read."

"I'm too old for this," she complained.

"Rubbish. I like hearing you read and I'm enjoying the book as much as you are."

"Fine." She glanced down at the book and began to read. "Darren looked down at the figure sixty feet below. "Don't move," he shouted. "I'm going to abseil down the cliff to you." There was no response. He adjusted his harness and looked at Paula. "Find out where the backup is. I can't wait any longer." Before she had time to answer, Darren launched himself off the cliff, descending rapidly.""

"Sounds thrilling," Patrick said. "What are you reading?"

"*A Walk in the Park* by Louise Sutton. It's really good."

He slowly lowered himself into the chair. "They have cliffs in the park? Neat. What's it about?"

"No, they don't have cliffs in the park. It's about a bloke who works in cave rescue and stuff. Kind of a thriller, but without gunfights and really nasty bad guys. Darren is in love with Paula but can't do anything about it because he works with her. And there's a volcano in it too. I love things with volcanoes and earthquakes in. They always have really fit heroes, as well."

Patrick raised an eyebrow. "And how old are you again?"

Abbie grinned. "According to Mum, I'm thirteen going on twenty two."

He snorted. "Sounds about right. Might have to lock you up until you're thirty six. But isn't life currently exciting enough as it is?"

"No. My life is scary. So is almost dying several times. Not to mention being kidnapped and stuff. Mega scary."

He smiled. "Do me a favor and plug your headphones into that really loud, irritating music of yours for a few minutes while I talk to Elle."

Abbie nodded. "Sure." She immediately put her headphones in and whacked the volume up full blast.

Elle grimaced, hearing the music from where she was sat. She looked at her husband. "How are you doing, love?"

"Other than bored? I need to talk to you about something." He drew in a deep breath and shifted in his seat. If she didn't know any better, she'd say he was about to drop a bombshell on her.

"What is it?"

"Zeke Whybrow accessed Abbie's birth certificate. He knew about her and us." He paused. "And your mum—Jeanette—wanted you out of the club and away from PJ and the drug business. That's why she was so anti you singing."

Shock and horror resonated through her like a tsunami. Zeke's involvement didn't surprise her at all, but the other? Surely she'd misheard him. "Mum knew?"

"I'm sorry." He paused. "I wish we knew why

your mum was involved, but I guess we never will."

"I imagine that PJ forced her." She sucked in a deep breath. "But what about Zeke? What happens to him?"

"There's a team looking for him now. Once they find him, they'll charge him."

"So I won't need protecting any longer?"

"No."

She smiled. "Good. Means we can plan the wedding." She nudged Abbie and mimed taking out the headphones.

Abbie removed one. "What?"

"Tell him about your dress for the wedding."

"I decided what color dress I want," Abbie winked at him. "But I can't tell you 'cos it's a secret." She giggled. "But as you can keep secrets, I'll tell you. It's gonna be sky blue pink with yellow dots."

"You'll look lovely in it."

Abbie grinned and put the headphones back in.

Patrick shifted on his chair. He wouldn't meet her gaze. What was *he* hiding? Surely it couldn't be worse than what he'd already said? Could it? Didn't he want to go through with the formal wedding and doing it according to the law of the land? "What is it?"

"Thing is, it wasn't just you they were after."

She scrunched up her nose, confused. "I don't understand. What are you talking about? It wasn't only me they were after?"

"Abbie's birth certificate is a matter of public record, the same as everybody else's. Anyone can access it. About three months ago, just after you arrived in Headley Cross, someone accessed my file at work. And seemingly has been stalking me ever since. Some spook I am, I never noticed the phone tap or cameras."

"You admittedly live at work and sleep at your desk. You're hardly ever home." She reached over and took his hand. "So that's not your fault."

He ran his thumb over her hand sending tendrils of warmth through her. "It looks as if they were using Abbie and you to get to me. DI Nemec says I haven't been compromised that they know of yet, but it would only have been a matter of time. With the evidence we have, it looks as if Zeke is behind it. I just wish I knew why. I recognize his surname, but I don't know where from."

"You know too much."

The snarl from behind her sent shivers down Elle's spine. She turned around, her heart in her mouth. "Zeke."

The door slammed shut. Zeke stood, his gun trained unwaveringly on Patrick.

30

Abbie screamed. Her earphones and MP3 player fell to the bed as she reached for the call button.

"Don't even think it, little girl."

Elle gripped Abbie's hand tightly, swallowing her fear. She couldn't let on how scared she was. She had to be strong for Abbie.

Patrick pushed upright in the chair. "Why don't you put the gun down and we can talk about this. I'm not armed and if you fire that in here you could damage the equipment or hit Elle or Abbie."

"And why should that bother me? You're all as guilty as each other."

"But why?" Elle asked. "What did we do to you that was so terrible?"

Zeke kept his eyes and gun on Patrick as he spoke. "Remember the house party?"

She swallowed. "The one from university? You weren't there. I'd have remembered you."

"Garth was my older brother. He died because of you, Agent Page of MI5."

Patrick held his gaze. "Then you don't need the ladies in here. Why don't you and I go somewhere else and discuss this?"

"I don't think so."

"What happened to Garth?" Elle asked. She wrapped her arms around a whimpering Abbie to protect her. *Jesus, please protect us.*

"Because of you he wrapped his car around a tree."

"How is that my fault?" Patrick asked.

"Because if that fight between you hadn't happened, Dad wouldn't have noticed the black eye and asked questions." Anger spilled from Zeke, his face red, his voice loud and resonating. "Then Garth wouldn't have died." He shoved the gun into Patrick's face. "So because of you I lost the most important thing in the world to me, and now you are going to lose what matters most to you. PJ had traced Eleanor, and I couldn't believe my luck when it was the same Eleanor Harrison from college. I became her manager, figuring she'd have kept in touch with you. Finding she had an illegitimate daughter by you was the icing on the cake."

Patrick looked unswervingly at him. Elle glanced from him to the angry man in front of them. Why was Patrick so calm? Didn't he care what Zeke was saying?

"Put the gun down," Patrick said. He flicked his eyes to the window in the door.

Elle followed his gaze, seeing a uniformed officer in Kevlar standing there. She flicked her eyes back to Patrick. Had he expected this? Surely, he wouldn't willingly put Abbie in danger? Was he the man she thought he was?

Patrick held out his hands. "Look, you want to walk out of here, right? We all do. Put the gun down and we can do that."

Zeke shook his head. "No, I don't think so. Who do I start with? Her?" He pointed the gun at Abbie, ignoring her scream.

Elle pulled her close, shielding Abbie with her body. "I got you, baby," she whispered. Terror rose in her throat, she struggled to breathe, but at that moment she knew it didn't matter what happened to her, so long as Abbie was all right.

"Or her." Zeke pointed the gun at Elle.

She looked desperately at Patrick.

"How about neither?" Patrick slowly stood. "Just put the gun down."

"Don't move," Zeke yelled. He swung the gun back at Abbie.

Patrick lunged at him, grabbing his wrist and pointing the gun away from Abbie. The police officers burst in, pointing their weapons at the men. Patrick seemed to have the upper hand as he landed a swift punch on Zeke's chin.

Zeke fell back, the gun going off as he fell. The sound echoed in the small room.

Patrick fell to his knees, his hands clasped over his stomach. His eyes widened. "Elle..."

Abbie screamed. "Dad..."

Elle scrambled over to Patrick. He lay on the floor, a med team rushing in to surround him. Zeke started to come around, but the armed cops took charge, cuffing him and keeping him down.

"Patrick, stay with me..."

His eyes tried to focus, then closed, his head tilting to one side.

"Patrick..."

31

Patrick was flying so high he could see over the fence into next door's garden. Old Mr. Fawcett was planting more flowers. And they had a fish pond now. With a fountain. It was heaps bigger than their one. Wasn't his fault the fish didn't like stones in the water. And it wasn't just him throwing them in there either. But Niamh couldn't do anything wrong. Ever.

It was so unfair. Liam always stuck up for her and never him. And now he was in trouble because he got caught doing something they started. The angrier he got, the higher the swing went. He ignored his mother's voice. So what if the base was moving. Dad could fix it.

Then he really was flying and the ground was coming up fast to meet him. He landed with a jarring thud...

...Blue flowers nestled by his feet. Bluebells. Elle's hand in his. Her long hair flowed over her shoulders, her white shirt undone a couple of buttons. The short sleeves made her arms look more tanned than they were. The heady smell of her perfume filled his senses. "Stay with me," she said. "We need you. Stay with us."

"Don't make me come after you, Pi. I'll drag you back if I have to." Li sounded uncharacteristically gruff. Was he crying? Li never cried. Ever. Not even when Sally died.

"Dad..." a new voice. One that seemed familiar but who was she calling Dad? "Dad, please, it's Abbie. Don't die now I found you. Mum and I need you, so much."

Abbie? He knew an Abbie. He had to go back. He tried turning. Swimming against the tide that bore him toward the light. Then arms surrounded him, a breeze blew softly around him and he was aware of hissing and beeping and someone crying.

****

Patrick struggled to open his eyes. His whole body felt as if it were encased in lead. He couldn't move. Fear peaked, then eased as someone began singing quietly in the room. He smiled. The tune was *Danny Boy*. Abbie could play it on her flute. He gave up trying to open his eyes and lay there listening. The words washed over him comforting him.

> *"I take my refuge in the shadow of my God*
> *Under His wings, I have no need to fear.*
> *Though terrors of the night surround me in the dark*
> *And arrows fly, and men around me fall.*
> *He sends an angel to protect the ones He loves*
> *The darkness flees, it has nowhere to hide*
> *The Lord Himself is standing right beside me*
> *And with all of those who call upon His name."*

Patrick opened his eyes as they finished singing. "That is lovely."

"Dad! You're awake!" Abbie grinned, hugging him.

"I am and it was a wonderful way to wake up. The song was beautiful."

"Mum wrote it. She paraphrased Psalm ninety-one. There's going to be more when she's finished writing it." Abbie had a measure of pride in her voice and a huge smile on her face as she leaned over the bed. "Do you really like it?"

"Yes, I do. It was a really nice thing to wake up to. Second only to your smiling face. I just wish I could move and sit up a little."

Elle's face moved into his field of vision. "Hello, handsome."

He smiled. "Hey, love."

She kissed him gently. "How are you feeling?"

"I don't know. It'd be easier to say what doesn't hurt. What happened?"

"Zeke shot you as you took him down. You've been in a coma for a week."

"A *week*?"

"The doctor said it was for the best. Since you can't follow orders and rest..."

Patrick's laugh turned into a groan as pain speared him in two. "Figures..."

"It's no laughing matter." She broke off. "You almost died...you did die. They had to resuscitate you for ages. Then they put you in a medically induced coma to give your body time to heal. You scared me. Scared us."

"I'm sorry." He longed to take her hand, but was still unable to move. "Am I tied down or something?"

"Yes," Abbie interjected. "Even in a coma you couldn't lie still. The nurse said she'd untie you when you woke. But you have to promise to behave."

"I promise." He sucked in a deep, painful breath. "Did I imagine you calling me Dad?"

She shook her head. "No. I'd like to, if that's all right. I mean, you are my real Dad. Just like Ellie's my mum and now you're married and stuff...Where are we going to live? You only have one bedroom."

"We'll get a bigger house. For now, you get to camp out in the lounge."

"Cool. I get the TV all night."

Elle chuckled. "Think again, squirt. Keep Dad company while I go find the nurse."

Patrick looked at her. "Elle…a week…Wait what's happening?"

"They dropped the charges against me in exchange for my testimony. I'll let Shay and Luke fill you in about work, but everything is going to be fine."

32

Two months later...

Patrick and Liam stood at the top of the aisle, just before three o'clock. Patrick wasn't sure who was the most nervous, even though he'd technically done this before. They were doubling up as groom and best man to each other. Organizing a double wedding in less than eight weeks hadn't been as hard as he'd thought. Both Elle and Jacqui loved the idea.

The only fly in the ointment was Niamh. She'd gone into labor the day before, two weeks before her due date, and it looked like she and Jared would miss the service.

Her last words to them had been on the phone on the way to the hospital. "Don't you dare call the wedding off now. I want pictures."

"Hope she's OK," Patrick said.

"Jacqui, Elle or Niamh?" Liam said wryly.

"Niamh. I've got my phone in my pocket on vibrate, but nothing. Did Jared call and I missed it? How's the pain?" It was a standing joke that Liam had also been in labor for most of the previous thirty-six hours.

"The pain stopped a while ago. Maybe she's sleeping now. No, there's been nothing yet from either of them."

Patrick nodded and glanced over his shoulder. "I

can see Abbie. They must be here."

Liam nodded. "Have you got the rings?"

"Yes. Have you?"

Liam patted his pockets as if he'd forgotten, then winked. "Yes I have, but I don't have the scrunchie."

"Elle's got it. A gold one she's wearing around her wrist to start with. The original pink one is here." He pulled his jacket sleeve up slightly to show him.

"Are you two really going to do that? Did you warn Pastor Jack?"

Patrick chuckled. "Nope, we didn't. And yes, Elle is going to say with this ring and scrunchie I thee wed. Or whatever it is she has to say at that point."

He glanced behind him and smiled at Luke and Sara Nemec sat on Elle's side of the church. Their twins sat on their laps, playing with the order of service. Elle and Sara looked to becoming firm friends as both were glad to have found each other. Some good had come out of PJ—

He brought himself up short. *Thank you, Lord, for taking a bad situation and working it for good.*

Pastor Jack came up to them. "Elle and Jacqui are here. Shall we make a start?"

Patrick nodded and he and Liam moved to the front of the church. The music began and he risked a glance over his shoulder.

Abbie, dressed in a full length emerald dress, walked slowly up the aisle, a huge grin on her face. She carried a white Bible with a spray of yellow and purple freesias over the top.

Behind her came the two brides, escorted on each arm by their future father-in-law. Elle wore a long ivory silk gown, which swirled around her figure, trailing behind her. Jacqui had gone for white, with layers of lace and tulle. Both had matching veils, tiaras and bouquets. Each wore an identical beaming smile and, in Patrick's somewhat biased opinion, looked like princesses.

The wedding began. Pastor Jack started speaking. Once the introduction was over, he began the legal declarations. Then he looked at the congregation. "If anyone here knows of any legal reason why these people may not be joined in matrimony, they must speak now or forever hold their peace."

Silence. Patrick looked at Elle and smiled faintly.

The door at the back of the church opened and footsteps echoed. Clothes rustled as heads turned.

His heart sank.

A baby's cry resounded and he, Liam, Elle and Jacqui spun around in unison.

Niamh and Jared slid into the front pew, a tiny bundle in Niamh's arms. "Sorry," she mouthed.

Pastor Jack smiled. "Don't be," he said. "I'm assuming the baby doesn't really object?"

She smiled. "No."

Patrick looked at her. "Well, am I an aunt or an uncle?"

Abbie burst out laughing. "You can't be an aunt, Dad. You're a man. That makes you an uncle by default."

"Girl or boy," he said wrinkling his nose at her. He turned back to his sister. "Well?"

"It's a girl," Niamh said. "Siobhan Caitlin. Born at eight ten this morning, weighing in at eight pounds ten ounces. We wanted it to be a surprise."

Patrick's grin matched Liam's as applause broke out around the church.

When things calmed down, they resumed the

wedding, exchanged vows and had the congregation in fits of laughter with the scrunchie line. Not a moment too soon, Patrick lifted Elle's veil and kissed her. "I love you so much, Mrs. Page."

"I love you too, Mr. Page."

Liam grinned at him as he broke an equally passionate kiss with Jacqui. "This could get confusing. Two Mrs. Page's at the reception. Three if you include Mum."

Elle laughed. "Well, we won't get you confused." She looked at Patrick. "Let's go sign the register. I don't know about you, but I want a cuddle with my new niece."

Patrick laughed. "Looks like our daughter got there before you."

Abbie grinned at him, the baby in her arms.

"Means she'll want a baby for Christmas," Elle sighed. "Still, at least it'll be a change from the puppy and the rabbit she's been asking for the past few years."

Patrick took her arm and followed Liam and Jacqui into the vestry. "No reason we can't have all three, is there?"

She blushed. "I guess not."

Jacqui nudged Liam. "Now there's an idea."

"Just don't go getting any ideas about double births and double infant thanksgiving services." Patrick pulled Elle close. "I want to spend a few months with my current family before we expand any." He wrapped his arms around Elle and kissed her.

Clare Revell

I take my refuge in the shadow of my God
Tune: Londonderry Air 12.10.12.10

I take my refuge in the shadow of my God
Under His wings, I have no need to fear.
Though terrors of the night surround me in the dark
And arrows fly, and men around me fall.
He sends an angel to protect the ones He loves
The darkness flees, it has nowhere to hide
The Lord Himself is standing right beside me
And with all of those who call upon His name.

The Lord will save you from infection and the snare
His faithfulness will be your shield and tower
And when you make the Lord Your God your dwelling
place
The wicked fall, but you alone will stand
He sends an angel to protect the ones He loves
The darkness flees, it has nowhere to hide
The Lord Himself is standing right beside me
And with all of those who call upon His name.

"Because he loves Me, therefore I will save him
He calls on Me and I will answer him.
I will be one with him in all his troubles
Deliver him, and show him salvation."
He sends an angel to protect the ones He loves
The darkness flees, it has nowhere to hide
The Lord Himself is standing right beside me
And with all of those who call upon His name.

Thank you for purchasing this White Rose Publishing title. For other inspirational stories, please visit our on-line bookstore at www.pelicanbookgroup.com.

For questions or more information, contact us at customer@pelicanbookgroup.com.

White Rose Publishing
Where Faith is the Cornerstone of Love™
an imprint of Pelican Ventures Book Group
www.PelicanBookGroup.com

May God's glory shine through
this inspirational work of fiction.

AMDG

www.ingramcontent.com/pod-product-compliance
Lightning Source LLC
Chambersburg PA
CBHW020222260626
47156CB00002B/490